THE CROWN ROSE	*Fiona Avery*
THE HEALER	*Michael Blumlein, MD*
GENETOPIA	*Keith Brooke*
GALILEO'S CHILDREN: **TALES OF SCIENCE VS. SUPERSTITION**	*edited by Gardner Dozois*
THE PRODIGAL TROLL	*Charles Coleman Finlay*
PARADOX: **BOOK ONE OF THE NULAPEIRON SEQUENCE**	*John Meaney*
CONTEXT: **BOOK TWO OF THE NULAPEIRON SEQUENCE**	*John Meaney*
TIDES	*Scott Mackay*
SILVERHEART	*Michael Moorcock* *& Storm Constantine*
STARSHIP: MUTINY	*Mike Resnick*
HERE, THERE & EVERYWHERE	*Chris Roberson*
SILVER SCREEN	*Justina Robson*
STAR OF GYPSIES	*Robert Silverberg*
THE AFFINITY TRAP	*Martin Sketchley*
THE RESURRECTED MAN	*Sean Williams*
MACROLIFE	*George Zebrowski*

MIKE RESNICK

STARSHIP:
MUTINY

BOOK ONE

an imprint of **Prometheus Books**
Amherst, NY

Published 2005 by Pyr™, an imprint of Prometheus Books

Inquiries should be addressed to
Pyr
59 John Glenn Drive
Amherst, New York 14228–2197
VOICE: 716–691–0133, ext. 207
FAX: 716–564–2711
WWW.PYRSF.COM

09 08 07 06 05   5 4 3 2 1

Library of Congress Cataloging-in-Publication Data

Resnick, Michael D.
    Starship—mutiny : book one / by Mike Resnick.
        p. cm.
    ISBN 1–59102–337–8 (hardcover : alk. paper)
    1. Space ships—Fiction. 2. Mutiny—Fiction. I. Title: Mutiny. II. Title.

PS3568.E698S735 2005
813'.54—dc22

2005023835

Printed in the United States on acid-free paper

To Carol, as always,

and to Lou and Xin Anders

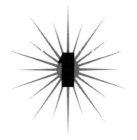

The ship hung in space, all but motionless, a dull gray in color. There was no rust on it, of course, but it looked like there should have been.

"Not a very impressive sight, sir," said the shuttle pilot as the tiny vessel approached the ship.

"I've seen worse," said the officer.

"Really?" said the pilot, curious. "When?"

"Give me an hour to think about it."

"I wonder if it's seen a lot of action?"

"Out here?" said the officer with a grimace. "I think its primary function is to *avoid* action."

"So you're going to sit out the war out here?" said the pilot with a smile.

"Looks like."

"I'll believe it when I see it, sir."

"I've done my bit. I can use the rest."

The shuttle approached the ship's hatch, and when it was close enough a section extended and bonded to it. Then the hatch irised and the officer boarded the ship. He offered the uniformed woman who greeted him a lazy salute. She snapped off a smart salute in return.

"Welcome aboard the *Theodore Roosevelt*, sir!" she said as he surveyed his surroundings unenthusiastically. Finally he realized that she was staring at him.

"Is something wrong, Ensign?" asked the man.

"You're supposed to request permission to come aboard, sir," was the answer.

"But I already *am* aboard."

"I know, sir. But—"

"My shuttle's five hundred miles from here and getting farther away every second. What am I expected to do if you refuse me permission?"

"I would never refuse you permission, sir," she said, flustered.

"Then it wasn't necessary for me to request it, was it?" he said.

"I'm just following regulations, sir. I'm sorry if I have offended you in some way."

"We'll kiss and make up later, Ensign," said the man. "Now suppose you take me to your leader."

"I beg your pardon?"

"The captain of this vessel, Ensign. My orders are to report to him. Or her. Or it."

"Yes, sir," she said, saluting again. "Follow me, sir."

She turned and began walking down a corridor that, like the exterior of the ship, had seen better days and better decades, then stopped at an airlift and waited for him. He joined her, and they ascended three levels on an invisible cushion of air. Then she stepped off, he followed her again, and she soon stopped before a door.

"In there, sir."

"Thank you, Ensign."

"Before I leave, sir," she said, clearly nervous but determined, "may I shake your hand?"

He shrugged and extended his hand. She took it and shook it vigorously.

"Thank you, sir," she said. "*That*'ll be something to tell my children when I finally have them. Go right in."

He waited for the door to read his retina, facial features, weight, and skeletal structure and match them against his records in the ship's computer, then stepped forward as it dilated. He found himself in a small, unimpressive office. Seated behind a desk was an exceptionally tall man of Oriental descent, almost seven feet in height, wearing the insignia of captain.

The new officer took a step forward. "Wilson Cole reporting for duty."

The captain looked at him impassively without speaking.

"Wilson Cole reporting for duty," repeated Cole.

Again there was no response, and Cole began to grow noticeably irritated. "I apologize, sir," he said. "They should have told me that my new captain was a deaf-mute."

"Shut up, Mr. Cole."

It was Cole's turn to stare in silence.

"I am Captain Makeo Fujiama," said the tall man. "I am still waiting for you to salute and present yourself properly."

Cole saluted. "Commander Wilson Cole reporting for duty, sir."

"That's better," said Fujiama. "I've read your record, Mr. Cole. It is, to say the least, unusual."

"I found myself in unusual circumstances, sir."

"I'd be more inclined to say that you put yourself in unusual circumstances, Mr. Cole," replied Fujiama. "However, there is no arguing with three Medals of Courage and two Citations for Exceptional Valor. That is truly remarkable, quite possibly unmatched in the annals of the Service."

"Thank you, sir."

"On the other hand, you have also been given command of your own ship twice, and have been demoted twice. That is shameful, Mr. Cole."

"That is bureaucracy, Captain Fujiama," said Cole.

"In point of fact, that was insubordination. You disobeyed your orders in time of war."

"We've been at war with the Teroni Federation for eleven years," said Cole. "As I see it, my job is to win the damned war and go home, so when I was given stupid orders, I ignored them."

"And put your ship and every man under your command at risk," said Fujiama.

Cole looked directly into his new captain's eyes. "War is hell, sir," he said at last.

"Made more so by your contribution, I suspect."

"My tactics were successful on both occasions," said Cole. "They only took my command and my ship away. If I'd failed, I'd be rotting in a brig somewhere and we both know it."

"You're in a brig right now, Mr. Cole," said Fujiama. "We all are."

"Sir?"

"The *Theodore Roosevelt* may not look like a brig, but for all practical purposes that's precisely what it is," answered Fujiama. "This ship is more than a century old. By rights it should have been decommissioned fifty years ago, but we keep getting into wars and we need every ship that's still functional and spaceworthy. Most of the crew should have been decommissioned one way or another as well, but the Republic isn't about to reward bad actors by returning them to their civilian lives. The *Theodore Roosevelt* is operating out here in the least populated section of the Rim. We rarely touch down on any planet, we're unlikely to see any action, and in short we are the ideal holding pen for all those crew members who, like yourself, seem incapable of taking orders and becoming smoothly functioning cogs in the vast military machine. Discipline is in short supply, and most of the crew holds the Navy in no higher esteem than the Teroni Federation." The captain paused. "I believe that describes the situation, Mr. Cole."

Cole considered what he had been told for a moment. "What was your particular sin, sir?" he asked at last.

"I killed seven naval officers."

"Ours or theirs?"

"Ours."

"By accident, I presume?"

"No," answered Fujiama in a tone that said the subject was closed.

There was an uneasy silence, which Cole finally broke. "I am happy to operate on the assumption that they deserved killing, sir. I want to make it clear that I'm not here to cause any trouble."

"I hope not, Mr. Cole," said Fujiama. "I think both sides can testify that it's one of the things you do with exceptional skill and elan. I'll be perfectly frank: whether I like it or not, and whether *you* like it or not, your exploits have made you a hero to most of the crew. You could make my job a lot easier if you took it upon yourself to lead by example."

"I'll do my best, sir," said Cole. "Will there be anything else?"

"Your duties will be posted on every computer in the ship. Any private message or orders from myself or Commander Podok will show up only on your personal machines."

"Commander Podok?"

"Our First Officer."

"It doesn't sound like a human name," said Cole.

"She's a Polonoi," replied Fujiama, studying him carefully. "Is that a problem?"

"It makes no difference to me, sir," said Cole. "I was just curious."

"Good. If there was any chance of our coming into contact with a Teroni warship, I'd have you serve with me or with Podok for a few days until you got your feet wet. But we're in the back of beyond, and you've commanded bigger ships than this one. You'll take over the blue shift."

"The blue shift, sir?"

"That's the way we label them here," said Fujiama. "The red shift is from 0 hour to 800 hours, ship's time. The white shift is from 800 hours to 1600 hours, and the blue shift is from 1600 hours to 2400 hours. Commander Podok is currently in charge of the white shift, and you'll be replacing Third Office Forrice, who has been temporarily in charge of the blue shift."

"Forrice?" repeated Cole. "I knew a Molarian named Forrice a few years back. We used to call him Four Eyes. It sounded like his name, and besides, he *did* have four eyes."

"Our Forrice is a Molarian."

"There can't be two Molarians with that name serving out on the Rim," said Cole. "It'll be nice to be working alongside an old friend." Then: "Who did *he* kill?"

"In point of fact, he's here because he refused to kill someone," said Fujiama. Cole seemed about to ask a question, and Fujiama held up his hand. "I do not discuss the details of my crew members' falls from grace."

"Ever?"

"Not until such time as Sector Command feels one of them might endanger the safety of the ship."

"I wonder how many ship endangerers Sector Command thinks you've got on the *Roosevelt*," said Cole, curious.

Fujiama sighed deeply. "Now that you're here, one."

"I suppose I should be flattered."

"Don't be," said Fujiama seriously. "I'll be honest, Mr. Cole—I am second to none in my admiration for your courage and your accomplishments. But I will not hesitate to deal with you in the harshest terms if you disobey an order or have a deleterious effect on the crew's already lax discipline."

"I already told you, Captain Fujiama—I know which side is the enemy."

"Good," said Fujiama shortly. "Follow proper Service procedures and obey regulations and we won't have any problems. You're dismissed."

Cole left the office, and found his ensign still standing in the corridor, obviously waiting for him.

"I'm glad to see you survived, sir," she said with a smile.

"Was there some doubt?" he asked.

"Mount Fuji has killed officers before."

"Not for reporting for duty, I hope," answered Cole, returning her smile. "Is that what you call him—Mount Fuji?"

"Not to his face, no, sir."

"Well, he's as big as a mountain," said Cole. "And what do I call you?"

"Ensign Rachel Marcos, sir."

"How's about I pull rank and just call you Rachel?"

"Whatever you wish, sir."

"Right now what I wish is to see my quarters," said Cole. "I assume someone has already moved my luggage there?"

"Your cabin is being thoroughly cleaned right now by the service mechs, sir," said Rachel. "Your luggage is aboard ship and will be moved there once the room has been sterilized."

"Sterilized?" repeated Cole, frowning. "Just what the hell did my predecessor die of?"

"Nothing, sir. He was transferred."

"Then why—?"

"He was a Morovite."

"So?"

"The Morovites are insectivores, sir. He kept a number of snacks in his room. As near as we can tell, they got loose almost four months ago. They didn't bother him, of course, but some of them are inimical to Men. We're just making sure that there weren't any larvae or eggs left behind."

"I promise that anything I eat in bed was dead a long time before I ever got my hands on it," said Cole.

"The galley never closes," she replied seriously. "There's no reason for any crew member of any race to bring food to his room."

"Sometimes it's just fun."

"Fun, sir?" she asked, furrowing her brow.

"Rachel, you've been in the Service too long."

"My thoughts precisely, sir."

"Ah, so you do have a sense of humor after all." He paused, hands on hips, and looked around. "Okay, I'm not on duty yet, and I have no quarters to go to. You want to give me the guided tour?"

"Most of the ship won't concern you, sir—they're the crew's quarters, the crew's mess hall, and the like."

"It all concerns me," replied Cole. "I'm going to be in command of this vessel one-third of every day. I ought to know what it looks like."

Rachel frowned again. "I thought you were the Second Officer, sir."

"I am."

"Then you *won't* be in charge of the *Teddy R.*"

"Is that what the crew calls her—the *Teddy R?*"

"That's one of the nicer things, yes, sir."

"As for being in command, it would be ridiculous to have all the ranking officers on duty at the same time and sleeping at the same time. Unless we're under attack, I'll be commanding during my duty shift."

"All right, I see what you mean, sir. It just sounded like . . ." She let the words hang in the air.

"Like I was usurping command?" said Cole. "No. I can't recite the regulation word for word, but if an attack seems imminent, my first duty is to alert the Captain of that fact." He smiled. "He looks like he can be pretty formidable if he's awakened in the middle of his night. I think if the situation arises, I'll send you to do it for me."

"Yes, sir," she said, and Cole decided that his original assessment—that humor was not her long and strong suit—was correct.

"Well, now that that's settled, shall we proceed with the tour?"

"Yes, sir."

"Just a minute," said Cole, staring at the creature that was ambling down the corridor toward him. "What the hell kind of critter is that?" he continued, raising his voice.

"I love you, too, you ugly malcontent," rumbled the creature. It stood perhaps five feet tall, locomoted on its three legs by spinning rather than walking straight ahead, and had three boneless arms to match. Its boxlike, angular head boasted four eyes, two trained straight ahead, one each at right angles on the side of the head. Its nostrils were two vertical slits, its mouth round and protruding, its ears hidden beneath the blue down that covered its body top to bottom. It wore a metallic red garment, on which were bonded the insignia of its rank and an impressive number of medals.

"How've you been, Four Eyes?" asked Cole.

"Keeping out of trouble." The equivalent of a smile crossed the creature's face. "Trust me, it doesn't take much effort out here."

"You know Commander Forrice, sir?" asked Rachel.

"Yes, Ensign," said Cole. "I'd give him a hug, but I hate to get close to anything that ugly."

"Just for that, I'm never asking you to help me hunt for Molarian females in season," said Forrice.

"Thank God for small favors." Cole laughed, and Forrice emitted a pair of high-pitched hoots. "You know what I like about these Molarian bastards, Ensign? They're the only beings in the galaxy besides Men who laugh, the only other ones with a sense of humor. It makes a hell of a big difference when you're stuck on a ship with them." Then, to Forrice: "It's good to see you again. Are you on duty right now?"

"No. I was just going to the mess hall. Why don't you come along and I'll fill you in?"

"Sounds good to me." He turned to Rachel. "I won't require a guide at this time after all. If you can tell me where my quarters are, you can be on your way."

"He's got the Morovite's cabin?" asked Forrice.

"Yes, sir."

Forrice hooted again. "Now, *that's* a proper introduction to the *Teddy R.*" He turned to Cole. "I'll be happy to take you there after we leave the mess hall. I hope you don't mind sleeping in your space suit for the first couple of months."

"Spare me your humor and let's get something to drink."

"Drink?" repeated Forrice. "You're not hungry after your trip here?"

"One look at you would take away anyone's appetite," said Cole. He turned to Rachel and saluted. "That'll be all for now, Ensign."

She returned his salute and began walking down the corridor in the direction they'd been going.

"So how have you been—really?" asked Cole as the Molarian led him to an airlift.

"Very well. They let me keep my rank." He looked at Cole's insignia. "I see they took yours away."

"Twice." They stepped out of the airlift and found themselves facing the officers' mess. There were two human officers and a Molarian, all sitting at separate tables. Cole and Forrice found a table in the corner, seated themselves, and spoke their orders into the table's computer.

"You still drink coffee," noted Forrice.

"And you still drink the blood of Englishmen."

"I beg your pardon?"

"Forget it," said Cole. "How's the food here?"

"For me, fine. For you, who knows?"

"Okay, let's get down to business. Has the *Teddy R* seen any action?"

"Maybe seventy or eighty years ago," replied Forrice. "You've seen it. If it had knees and it was attacked, it'd get down on them and beg for mercy."

"Seriously, *can* it defend itself if it's attacked?"

"Let's hope we never have to find out."

"What about the crew?"

"They're like us."

"Like us?" asked Cole.

"Most of them have . . . *histories*." Forrice lowered his voice. "They're so bored or bitter that a third of them are on drugs at any given moment—and since it was authority that got them busted and sent to the *Teddy R*, they're resentful of just about every form of authority."

"That sounds like a lot of drugs. Where are they getting them?"

"I suppose a lot were smuggled onboard over the last two years," answered Forrice. "Also, on most ships people want to get out of the infirmary. On the *Teddy R*, they make a habit of breaking into it."

"So we're patrolling an area that nobody wants with a crew nobody wants in a ship nobody *should* want," said Cole. "There seems to be a certain mathematical purity to that."

"Optimist," said Forrice.

"Damn, I've missed you, Four Eyes!" said Cole. "Molarians may be the ugliest things God made, but you're the only race that thinks like we do."

"He created us after He'd gotten all His mistakes out of His system on Men."

"What other races have we got onboard? The captain mentioned a Polonoi."

"Yes, we've got a handful of Polonoi, plus a few Mollutei, some Bedalians, and we've even got a Tolobite."

"A Tolobite?" repeated Cole. "What the hell is it? I never heard of it."

"We didn't know they existed until fifty years ago. Wait'll you see it. It lives in symbiosis with a nonsentient little creature."

"I've seen symbiotes before," said Cole, unimpressed.

"Not like this one," Forrice assured him. "And we've got a Bdxeni, though of course we almost never see him."

"Every damned Republic ship's got a Bdxeni these days. They never sleep, so they make ideal pilots. I assume that's what our Bdxeni's doing?"

"Yes," answered Forrice. "They've got him wired into the navigational computer. I mean that literally—there are cables going from his head to the computer, or maybe it's the other way around. I don't know if he reads its mind or it reads his, but the ship goes wherever he wants it to go, so I guess it all works out."

"Tell me about the Captain," said Cole. "What's he like?"

"Mount Fuji?" said Forrice. "Very competent, very proper. And very unhappy."

"Unhappy?"

"Terminally depressed is a more accurate way of putting it."

"Why?" asked Cole. "He's still got a ship to command."

"He's lost three sons and a daughter in the war. And his youngest just enlisted last month."

"He told me he killed a bunch of officers. Can you tell me anything about it?"

"Just rumors. As far as I'm concerned, most officers probably deserve killing. Present company excepted, of course. Why are you smiling?"

"I know you guys think like humans," said Cole. "But I'm still impressed at how fast you pick up human speech patterns."

"What do you expect? Terran is the official language of the Republic. If we're going to serve with you, we have to learn the language."

"Everyone learns it, or at least uses a T-pack to translate. But only the Molarians seem to have appropriated it."

"Just clever, I guess," said Forrice.

The top of the table slid to a side, revealing their drinks. Cole picked his up and held it forward.

"Here's to a long, dull, peaceful tour of duty."

But of course, he was just an officer, not a prognosticator.

Forrice showed Cole the four armored shuttles that were bonded to the hull, then took him up to Security, where a small wiry woman was seated at a desk, studying a series of holographic screens that floated in the air just above it. The moment she saw them she uttered a low command and the screens vanished.

"Wilson Cole, meet Sharon Blacksmith," said Forrice. "Colonel Blacksmith is our Chief of Security."

"And I know who you are," she said, getting to her feet. "Your reputation precedes you, Commander Cole."

"Just Wilson will do," said Cole.

"Fine. And unless Mount Fuji or Podok are around, I'm Sharon."

"Colonel Blacksmith is atypical of the *Teddy R* in that she actually knows what she's doing and is damned good at it," said Forrice.

She stared at Cole. "You're a little smaller than I expected."

"Bullshit," he responded.

"Wilson!" said Forrice, surprised.

"You've run a couple of background checks on me, and you were almost certainly the one who programmed my statistics into the security system. If I was half an inch taller or shorter than you expected, five pounds heavier or lighter, every fucking alarm in the ship would have gone off." He paused and smiled at her. "Did I pass the test?"

"With flying colors," she said, returning his smile. "I hope you're not offended."

"Not at all. It's nice to know we have a competent Security Chief onboard. Now let me ask you a question."

"Go ahead."

"As far as I can tell, the *Teddy R* hasn't touched down on any planet in more than half a year. I'm only the fifth replacement to come aboard since then. So my question is: What do you do with your time?"

"It's a reasonable question," replied Sharon. "I monitor all transmissions, I keep all sensitive areas under surveillance, I try to cut down on the intraship drug trafficking, I make sure that the crew isn't killing each other—they've tried, from time to time—and I make sure that the Officer on Deck performs hourly scans of our immediate vicinity."

"I thought there wasn't supposed to be a Teroni ship within parsecs of us," said Cole.

"We hope not, but their fleet isn't the only danger. Seventeen ships have been sabotaged in the past year. Six had entirely human crews, three more were close to eighty percent nonhuman, and one had no humans at all. That means someone has gotten to both human and nonhuman members of the Navy. I don't know what kind of inducement it would take to get someone to blow himself up with his ship, but there's no question that it's been done—and it's my job to see to it that it's not done here."

"Seventeen? I'd heard about two or three, but I hadn't realized that there were that many."

"It's not something the Navy brags about."

"So they keep it quiet, thereby guaranteeing that people who might see something suspicious don't recognize it as such."

"I *like* you, Commander Cole," she said.

"Wilson," he corrected her.

She reached into a desk drawer and pulled out a silver flask. "Want a drink?" she said.

"What's the penalty for drinking on duty?"

"It depends whether Security knows about it or not."

"Then I'll have one," he said, accepting the flask, opening it, and taking a swallow. He turned to Forrice. "I'd offer some to you, but you'd probably bathe in the booze and eat the container."

"The next time a Teroni offers a reward for your head, I'm going to have to seriously consider it," said Forrice.

"I really shouldn't tell you this," said Sharon, "but Forrice has practically been jumping out of his skin since we learned you were being transferred here. He'll probably never say anything nice about you while you're listening, but he's filled me in on your various exploits."

"I think the Navy would label them misadventures," said Cole wryly.

"The crew of the *Teddy R* knows better," she said. "You've become a kind of legend."

"Don't embarrass me during my first day on the job," said Cole uncomfortably.

"All right, then," said Sharon, taking the flask back. "Is there anything I can do for you?"

"Yeah, as a matter of fact there is. What's the total complement of the crew?"

"Thirty-seven Men, five Polonoi, four Molarians, a Tolobite, a Morovite, a Bedalian, and a Bdxeni."

He shook his head. "Stupid."

"What is?"

"If they're worried about unhappy crewmen, why the hell did they give us lone members of four races? They've got no one to talk to, no shared worldview or experiences."

"Well, that's not quite true. The Tolobite's got its symbiote, and the Bdxeni is working every minute of every day and doesn't need any distractions."

"Nevertheless."

"We're not responsible for who or what the Navy assigns us," replied Sharon.

"I didn't mean to imply that *you* were stupid," said Cole. "A policy this dumb has to come from the very top."

"You were right, Forrice," she said to the Molarian. "He has qualities. Commander Cole—Wilson—I think we're going to become great friends."

"Good," said Cole. "I can use all the friends I can get."

"Do you require anything else?"

"I haven't made my request yet."

"I thought you wanted to know the crew's racial breakdown," she said.

"That was preamble. I want to be able to access everything you have on each crew member. I might as well learn what I can about the Men and aliens I'll be dealing with."

"What's your security clearance?"

He shrugged. "Probably a level or two below where it used to be," he said.

"I'll find out, and let you access up to that level," she said.

"Thanks," said Cole. "I've enjoyed meeting you, but I suppose I should continue with the chef's tour before I go to work."

"We'll be seeing a lot of each other," said Sharon.

"If I can ask, what's a competent officer like you doing on a ship like this?"

"That's such a flattering way of putting it that I won't disappoint you by answering it."

"What would you like to see next?" asked Forrice. "The bridge?"

"One bridge looks pretty much like another," replied Cole. "Let's look at something else."

"But you're going to be spending most of your time there," said the Molarian.

"The hell I am." Forrice looked at him curiously. "You've got a pilot, you've got a gunnery officer, you've got an Officer On Deck. I can access whatever they're seeing or hearing from anywhere on the ship, and issue orders from anywhere. Why should I waste my time looking at viewscreens or at the backs of their heads for hours on end?"

"No wonder you can't keep a command," said Sharon. "You make too much sense."

"All right," said Forrice. "What would you like me to show you next?"

"What kind of exercise facility has the *Teddy R* got?"

"A small one, about half for Men and half for the rest of us."

"Let's at least pass by it so I'll know where to find it. Then I'll want to see the infirmary."

"Come along, then," said Forrice.

He walked out into the corridor, led Cole to a different airlift, and ascended a level. They looked in at the exercise room—it was far too small and cramped to be called a gymnasium—and then went to the infirmary.

"Nice," said Cole, looking at the small operating theater. "More up-to-date than I'd have expected." He walked through the even smaller recovery room to a room with four beds for humans, a near-invisible partition, and three beds of wildly varying shapes for non-humans. "Optimistic."

"Optimistic?" repeated Forrice.

"What if ten crew members get wounded—or if we get a bad batch of food?"

"The *Teddy R* hasn't seen enough action for ten crew members to get wounded," replied the Molarian. "And we've never had a *good* batch of food. I think we're probably immune by now."

"How many medics?"

"It's going to sound like a bad joke," said Forrice.

"Why am I not surprised?" said Cole. "How many?"

"One—a Bedalian named Tzinto."

"No human doctor?"

"There was one."

"And?" prompted Cole.

"He had an attack of . . . of some useless organ only humans have."

"A burst appendix?"

"That's it!" said Forrice. "An appendix. He died on the operating table."

"Thanks. I can't tell you how much confidence that gives me in this Tzinto."

"It wasn't really his fault. His specialty is nonhuman physiology."

"Have we requested a replacement for the human doctor?" asked Cole.

"Yes, but there's a war going on," replied Forrice. "A *real* war, not a meaningless patrol like we're on out here. And they can't spare any more doctors."

"Fujiama was wrong," said Cole. "You get decent medical care in a brig."

"I don't know what you're talking about."

"Nothing," said Cole. "Okay, I've seen enough. Let's continue the tour."

"It's a pretty ordinary ship," said Forrice. "All that's left are the weapons sections, a couple of science labs that get almost no use, the crew's quarters, and the bridge."

"Take me up and down every corridor of every level," said Cole. "Even the galley, the storerooms, the public bathrooms, everything. If I'm going to spend a few years aboard this ship, I'd better learn every inch of it."

"On the first day?"

"You never know. There might be a surprise test." Cole could see that Forrice didn't understand his humor, so he shrugged and started off toward the nearest airlift. The Molarian caught and passed him, then indicated that they wanted a different airlift farther down the corridor.

"How the hell many decks can there be?" said Cole. "Don't all the airlifts lead to the same levels?"

"Yes," answered Forrice. "But this one is large enough to accommodate a stretcher or an airsled, and we've been asked not to use it except in emergencies."

"How many times has a stretcher or airsled been brought to the infirmary since you've been onboard?"

"Four, I think. Possibly five."

"Out of how many months?" said Cole. "We'll take this lift."

"I can't argue with an officer who outranks me," said the Molarian pleasantly as he followed Cole into the airlift.

They ascended to the gunnery section, where Cole met the three sergeants—a Man, a Polonoi, and a Molarian—who were in charge of keeping the weapons in working order. He wondered how anyone kept the ranks straight before the services combined and there were five varieties of yeoman, eight of seaman (though it was likely that none of them had ever been to sea), and six of lieutenant. It made much more sense to appropriate sergeants, majors, colonels, and the like.

A brief inspection confirmed his suspicions that the *Teddy R* would probably be outgunned by just about any Teroni ship it went up against. He actually signed an autograph (to his surprise, it was the Molarian who requested it, not the Man), and then stopped by the science labs. They seemed up-to-date, but they were deserted, both scientists being on their sleep breaks while a bored-looking ensign stood guard.

Forrice then took Cole on a tour of the crew's quarters, which resembled nothing more than a run-down hotel. He practically expected to encounter the scent of urine in the corridors. The rooms covered three levels, and it was clear that the cubicles on the lowest level had been modified to fit the needs of the nonhuman members of the crew.

"Is your room near here?" asked Cole when he'd finished inspecting the alien level.

"Just down the hall," answered Forrice.

"Let's go there for a minute."

Forrice seemed about to ask him why, then thought better of it and simply led the way. The room boasted a bed built for the Molarian's body contours, chairs to match, nightmarish holographs on the walls that seemed to delight their owner, and a desk with a pair of computers, one with a Steinmetz/Norton bubble memory, the other a model Cole had never seen before.

"All right, we're here," said Forrice. "Now what?"

"Close the door."

Forrice uttered a command and the door snapped shut.

Cole pulled out his pocket computer and ordered it to make contact with Sharon Blacksmith. Suddenly her image appeared a few inches above the computer, hovering there and staring curiously at him.

"Yes, Commander?" she said.

"There's an ensign guarding the science labs," said Cole.

"That's correct."

"Why? You're probably monitoring them round the clock. Has there been a threat against them?"

"No, there has not."

"Then why isn't the ensign being put to better use?"

"Commander Cole, we're four hundred and eighty-three days out of Port Royale in the Quinellus Cluster. It's been a hundred and thirty-two days since there's been any sign of enemy activity. We're in the emptiest sector of the galaxy, we're carrying a full complement of fifty officers and crew, and it is essential that we maintain discipline. What would *you* suggest?"

"All right," said Cole. "I *thought* it was just a make-work assignment, but I didn't want it confirmed in public."

"Thank you for your tact," she replied. "Of course, if I didn't know you and Commander Forrice were alone in his quarters, I wouldn't have answered you."

"Just how much of a problem *is* discipline with so little to do?" continued Cole.

"I'm just in charge of Security, and I keep busy," replied Sharon. "I'd suggest you discuss the matter with the Captain or Commander Podok."

"I suppose I'll get around to it," said Cole, breaking the connection. He turned to Forrice. "What's going on beside the drug use? Any same-species or even interspecies fraternization?"

"No."

"There will be," said Cole. "If *I* know that it's a meaningless job and I've been onboard for maybe three hours, don't you think the crew knows it? They probably feel safer here than in their own home-towns—and these aren't earnest and idealistic young warriors. Fujiama tells me that most of them have caused problems wherever they came from. That implies a certain disregard of discipline under far more dangerous conditions than we're facing here."

"It makes sense," agreed Forrice.

"You don't seem too concerned."

"Out here on the Rim it really doesn't make a bit of difference. The only person who has to stay sane and sober is the pilot, and he's locked into so many computer circuits I don't think he could go crazy even if he tried."

"I can't tell you how comforting I find that," said Cole.

"Were you always this cynical?"

"Only since I was old enough to talk. Let's go see the bridge."

Forrice ordered the door to open. Then his computer started gently calling his name.

"There's a message coming in," he said apologetically.

"No problem," said Cole. "I'll find my way."

"Top level, any airlift. All the corridors lead to it."

Cole stepped out into the hall, found the nearest airlift, ordered it to ascend, stepped off at the top level, and found himself in a wide corridor. There were a number of closed doors, and he began walking past them until he came to a large open area filled with impressive viewscreens. In a transparent pod attached high on the wall was the Bdxeni pilot, a bullet-shaped being with insectoid features, curled into a fetal position, multifaceted eyes wide open and unblinking, with six shining cables connecting his head to a navigational computer hidden inside the bulkhead.

A human gunnery officer sat at her station, idly watching a series of alien paintings that passed across her computer screen. The Officer on Deck, a tall young man with a shock of black hair, immediately confronted Cole.

"Name and rank, sir?" he said.

"Commander Wilson Cole. I'm the *Teddy R*'s new Second Officer."

The man saluted. "Lieutenant Vladimir Sokolov, sir. I'm pleased to meet you, sir."

"Then relax and stop calling me 'sir,'" said Cole.

"That would be unwise, sir," said Sokolov.

"I suppose there's a reason?"

"The reason will be returning to the bridge any second, sir."

As Sokolov spoke, a Polonoi female entered the bridge, and Cole was forced to admire, as he had on previous occasions, the engineering that went into her.

The Polonoi were humanoid and bipedal, averaging about five feet in height. Males and females alike were burly and muscular, and were covered with a soft down, top to bottom.

But those were normal Polonoi, like the gunnery sergeant he'd met earlier. Many of the Polonoi in the military, such as Podok, were members of a genetically engineered warrior caste. They boasted orange and purple stripes, not unlike a miscolored tiger, and were more muscular than their normal brethren, able to respond faster physically to any dangerous situation.

What made the warrior caste really unique, observed Cole, was that their eating and breathing orifices, their sexual organs, and all their soft vulnerable surfaces had been engineered onto their backs. They were created to triumph or die; for a warrior Polonoi to turn his back on an enemy was to present that enemy with all his vulnerable spots. The warrior Polonoi's face possessed large eyes that could see exceptionally well at night and far into the infrared, a speaking orifice, and large ears that were cupped forward and could hear very little that happened behind them.

"Who is this?" said the Polonoi in heavily accented Terran.

"Our new Second Officer, Commanded Podok," answered Sokolov.

"His name?"

"Commander Wilson Cole," said Cole.

Podok stared at Cole expressionlessly for a long moment. "I have heard of you, Commander Cole."

"Nothing too terrible, I hope?"

"You were in the process of being relieved of your command when I heard it."

"The fortunes of war," said Cole with what he hoped was a friendly smile.

Podok made no reply.

"Well, Commander Podok," continued Cole at last, "I look forward to working with you."

"Do you?" replied Podok.

It was Cole's turn to stare silently at the Polonoi.

"Have you any business here on the bridge?" asked Podok after almost a minute had passed.

"I'm just acquainting myself with the ship before I take charge during blue shift," said Cole.

"I file a duty report at the end of white shift," said Podok. "I will remove Forrice's clearance and add yours, so that you may access it."

"I gather nothing's happened for the past hundred or more days," said Cole. "Why don't you just tell me if something changes?"

Podok stared coldly at him. "I file a duty report at the end of white shift," she repeated. "I will add your clearance so that you may access it."

"I'm incredibly grateful," said Cole sardonically.

"Good," said Podok seriously. "You should be."

She walked over to a computer console and began to work.

"Come on, sir," said Sokolov. "I'll escort you to the airlift."

Cole nodded and fell into step.

"What do you think of our Commander Podok, sir?" asked Sokolov with a grin when they were out of earshot.

"I think there are worse things than a shooting war," replied Cole.

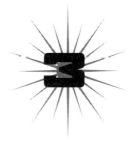

After word came that his cabin was once again fit for habitation, Cole entered it, found his single piece of luggage sitting on the floor next to his bed, and opened it. There were five uniforms and a civilian outfit, not much to show for eight years in the military. He owned three pairs of shoes, one pair of boots, a week's worth of socks and shorts, and some toilet items. He was surprised to see that he possessed more hand weapons than uniforms.

After he'd put his gear away, he decided to take a nap and instructed the computer to awaken him ten minutes before white shift ended. He was asleep almost as soon as his head hit the pillow, and he felt more stiff than rested when the computer woke him an hour later.

He made his way to the bridge, decided to wait in the corridor until it was exactly 1600 hours, then walked forward, traded silent salutes with Podok, and watched the Polonoi make her way to the nearest airlift.

"May I have your attention, please?" he said in a loud voice, and the three other occupants of the bridge turned to him. "I'm Wilson Cole, the new Second Officer. I'll be in charge during blue shift from now on. I'm not much for formality; you can call me Commander, sir, Wilson, or Cole—whatever makes you happy." He paused for a moment, then continued. "Since we're going to be working together, I'd like to know your names and duties."

Before anyone could speak, Rachel Marcos walked onto the bridge, and the Molarian sitting at the gunnery station got up, saluted, and left. Rachel immediately went over and took his place. "I'm sorry, sir," she said. "But—"

"No explanations are necessary—*today*," said Cole. "If it happens again tomorrow, you'd better have a good one. I know your name. Would you please define your duties for me?"

"All of them?"

"No. Just when you're stationed on the bridge."

"I'm the weapons officer, sir," she replied.

"What does that involve?"

She smiled. "For the past four months, just about nothing, sir."

"So I gathered." He turned to the Officer on Deck. "Your name?"

"Lieutenant Christine Mboya, sir."

"Your duties?"

"They've never been clearly defined, sir. I am at the disposal of yourself, the pilot, and the weapons officer, and in the event of undefined disturbances my job is to keep order on the bridge."

"That's probably as good a definition as I've heard." Cole looked up at the transparent pod that was attached to the bulkhead. "Pilot, what's your name?"

"You couldn't pronounce it," replied the Bdxeni.

"Doubtless you're right, but I'd like to know it anyway."

"Wxakgini, sir."

"I can come close," said Cole, "but I think I'll just call you Pilot." He turned back to the two human officers. "According to our standing orders, which were given to me before I came aboard, we are in charge of protecting some seventy-three populated Republic worlds on this section of the Rim. Does anyone understand otherwise?"

"No, sir," they both answered.

"Well, I guess that's everything. It looks like a long, dull shift. Still, we might as well keep busy."

The two women looked at him suspiciously. "How, sir?"

"Don't worry," he said. "I don't believe in meaningless assignments just to create the illusion that we're all working. Lieutenant Mboya, to the best of your knowledge are we under radio silence at this time?"

"No, sir, we are not."

"Then, barring an attack on the bridge that requires your attention, I'd like you to contact headquarters on Deluros VIII and get a list of every world that has joined the Teroni Federation since our last update."

"The captain ordered that about seven weeks ago, sir."

"Do it anyway."

"Is there any particular reason why, sir?"

"Since the sides in this conflict are in constant fluctuation, I think we need a weekly information update. Last week's friend could be this week's enemy and vice versa. Have the computer remind you to update the list every week."

"Yes, sir."

"Rachel?"

"Yes, sir?"

"Program your weapons to fire a random shot into deep space every twenty to forty hours. Make it a different weapon each time, and a different duration between each shot. If there are any Teroni out there, let's let them know that we're here and we're armed, and maybe they'll think twice about whatever they're doing. If not, at least this should encourage them to come after us before they attack any of the planets, which should buy a little time for the populaces to erect whatever defenses they've got."

"Yes, sir," said Rachel. "It'll take me about two minutes. Will there be anything else?"

"If there is, I'll assume Captain Fujiama or First Officer Podok have already thought of it," said Cole. "I'm going to grab some breakfast. I'll be back in half an hour."

"We can have it brought to you here, sir," said Christine Mboya.

"Why bother?" asked Cole. "Unless you feel the ship is due to malfunction or come under attack in the next few minutes?"

"I'd almost welcome it, sir," she replied. "It gets so boring here. I would love to see some action."

"I've seen some action, Lieutenant," said Cole. "Take my word for it: boredom is better."

"Can you tell us about your experiences, sir?" she asked. "After you get back from the mess hall, that is?"

"There's not much to tell."

"Come on, sir," she urged him. "You're a hero; everyone onboard knows that."

"I'm an officer who has twice been relieved of his command. Do they know that, too?"

"I think we'd all like to hear your side of it, sir."

"Maybe someday," Cole said vaguely, and left for the mess hall.

As he sat down at an empty table, Forrice, who had been passing by the mess hall, stopped to join him.

"How was your first day at work?" he asked.

"It hasn't started yet," answered Cole.

"What's your impression of the *Teddy R?*"

"It's undermanned by at least a third, its weapons are inadequate, the hydroponic gardens need tending, and the crew has fallen into slovenly habits. Other than that, it's fine."

"And your opinion of your superiors?"

"Ask me after we've been in battle."

"*This* ship?" said Forrice. "There won't be enough of you left to bury, let alone question."

"You'd be surprised what a competent officer can do with even this ship."

"Find me a competent officer and we'll talk," replied Forrice. "As far as I can tell, every time one gets a command, he's demoted or tossed in the brig."

"I ignored a command and you refused one," said Cole. "We're each here for a reason."

"We're here because the Navy doesn't like to be proven wrong. You ignored orders and accomplished missions that proved to be of enormous value to the Republic. I refused to kill three spies who I knew to be deep-cover covert agents for the Republic. The Navy's happy we did what we did, but they certainly don't want to encourage anyone else to disobey orders."

"Stop talking about the Navy," said Cole between mouthfuls of artificial eggs and soya products. "You're ruining my digestion."

"I'd tell you dirty jokes, but you wouldn't understand them."

"You could just stare at me in worshipful silence, or maybe go find something to do."

"I'm doing it—helping you get acclimated."

"My gratitude is boundless."

"It should be. Everyone else wants to shake your hand or get your autograph. I just want to talk."

"I'd rather talk to them and give you an autograph."

"I know when I'm not wanted," said Forrice.

"Does that mean you're going to leave and let me finish my meal in peace and silence?" said Cole.

"Of course not," said the Molarian. "It would make you too happy."

"Okay—but no dirty Molarian jokes until I'm done with my coffee." Just then his communicator came to life and told him that the bridge was trying to contact him. "If it's Podok, demanding that I spend my entire shift up there . . ." He activated the mechanism and Christine Mboya's image instantly materialized in front of him. "What is it?" he asked irritably.

"I thought I should inform you that a Bortellite ship just touched down on Rapunzel."

"Rapunzel—the fourth planet of the Bastoigne system? That's about thirty light-years from here, isn't it?"

"Yes, sir."

"You don't have to tell me about every ship that comes and goes on the Rim, Lieutenant."

"I'm just following your orders, sir. You told me to update the list of member worlds of the Teroni Federation. Bortel II formally joined them eleven days ago."

"All right," said Cole. "Let's get over to Rapunzel and take a look."

"That's out of the question, sir. We're under orders to maintain our patrol orbit between the McDevitt and the Silverblue systems."

"I'll be right there, Lieutenant," said Cole, breaking the connection. He took a final swallow of his coffee, wiped his mouth on his sleeve, and got to his feet.

"Want me to come along?" asked Forrice.

Cole shook his head. "No, this is nothing special. And if leaving our patrol route turns out to *be* something special after all, why should we both get in trouble?"

He got up, carried his tray and dishes to an atomizer, tossed them in, and walked to an airlift. A moment later he was on the bridge.

"Pilot!" he said in a loud voice.

"Yes, sir?" replied Wxakgini from within his plastic enclosure.

"Break out of your patrol orbit and take us to Rapunzel."

"Right now, sir?"

"Right now."

The Bdxeni's face came as close as it could to a disapproving frown. "That contradicts my standing orders, Mr. Cole."

"Take a look around and tell me who is the highest-ranking officer on the bridge?"

"You are, sir."

"Then I suggest that you obey me."

"Perhaps we should awaken the captain, sir."

"Are you going to suggest we wake him up every time I give you an order you don't like, Pilot?"

"No, sir."

"Then don't start now."

There was a brief pause. "Yes, sir."

Cole turned to Rachel Marcos. "The odds are hundreds to one that there is a reasonable explanation for the Bortellite ship's presence on a Republic world." He paused. "Until they're millions to one, make sure your weapons are activated and ready to fire on my command. When we get within range, lock any five of them onto the ship and await the command of the ranking officer, either me or whoever's in charge if blue shift is over."

"Five, sir?"

"I know it's overkill," said Cole, "but even these weapons have been known to miss, and you can be sure the Bortellite ship won't be without its defenses."

"What I meant, sir, was that I have eighteen long-range weapons at my disposal. Why only five?"

"Because we're in a state of war, and ships of the Teroni Federation don't tend to travel alone in enemy territory. In the event of a confrontation, I don't want either you or the *Teddy R*'s weapons computer to have to decide which ones to keep trained on the Bortellite ship and which ones to bring to bear on whatever else we're facing. It's better to sort these things out now, before there's a crisis."

"Yes, sir."

"Is there anything I can do, sir?" asked Christine Mboya.

"You're on the bridge until the end of blue shift?" asked Cole.

"Yes, sir."

"Start scanning this section of the Rim and see if the sensors can pick up any other ships that don't belong to Republic worlds. And Lieutenant . . . ?"

"Yes, sir."

"Thorough is more important than fast. We already know there's one ship that doesn't belong here."

"Yes, sir."

"Is there a bathroom up here? Human or alien, it makes no difference."

She gave him an odd look, but pointed toward a door at the end of a short corridor. He thanked her, approached it, entered the small human lavatory, ordered the door to close and lock, and activated his pocket computer, instructing it to contact Sharon Blacksmith.

"You heard every word, I presume?" he said when her image appeared.

"Most of them. I can go back and view the videos and holo recordings if there's any question."

"There's not. We have a ship out there that doesn't belong in this sector. I know my reputation. As soon as Fujiama or Podok hears we've altered course to approach it, they're going to think I'm some half-baked glory hound and order me to return to the ship's scheduled route. Until we learn why a Bortellite ship is on a Republic planet, that would be foolhardy in the extreme."

"I agree," said Sharon. "But what do you expect *me* to do about it?"

"Nothing too proactive," answered Cole. "People who stick their necks out for me tend to find out they're on a chopping block. All I want you to do is notify me when Fujiama gets out of bed, or if Podok approaches the bridge for any reason."

"And what are you going to do when I report such activities to you?" asked Sharon. "Take over the ship?"

"Spare me your humor. I'm a Republic officer, subject to their authority."

"Then I don't understand."

"Once you give me the word, I might take a small crew to the shuttle *before* anyone can order me not to. And if we're in a shuttle approaching an enemy ship, I don't think it's unreasonable to order my crew not to break radio silence."

"It sounds good, Wilson, but just what the hell do you think a shuttle can do against a fully armed Bortellite ship?"

"Talk to it. Find out why it's here, if it's alone, what its plans are. Bluff it if I have to."

"I hear a lot of ifs."

"Would you prefer maybes?"

"Do you *have* to do this your very first day on the job?"

"I'm not the one who ordered the Bortellite ship to go to Rapunzel, and I'm not the one who spotted it," said Cole. His voice hardened. "But I'm the one who ordered a computer update on our friends and foes, or we wouldn't know it *was* an enemy ship. Fujiama should do that every week."

Sharon sighed. "Okay, Wilson. I'll let you know when he wakes up."

Cole broke the connection, then left the bathroom and walked onto the bridge again.

"Pilot, how long before the Bortellite ship is within range of our weaponry?"

"Five hours and seven minutes at maximum speed, sir," said the Pilot.

"Rachel, will you need any help with the weapons?"

"I don't know, sir. I don't think so."

"Lieutenant Mboya?"

"Yes, sir?"

"If Ensign Marcos requests the presence of any gunnery personnel, they are permitted to come onto the bridge. Beyond that, this bridge is now closed to all personnel below the rank of commander. Is that understood?"

"Yes, sir."

He raised Security on the ship's computer.

"Hi, Sharon. It's me again. The three gunnery sergeants I met earlier when I was inspecting the ship—are they just the white-shift sergeants, or are they all we've got?"

"Since the last rotation, they're three of the four that we've got," replied Sharon Blacksmith.

"Is the fourth on red or blue shift?"

"Let me check. . . . He's on red."

"So there's no one there now?"

"That's right."

"Check on the four. If any two are awake, have them report for duty. If three or four are asleep, wake them at random. I want two of them down there in an hour's time, and I want two on the red shift. One of the blue shifters will take white shift. Do we have a personnel officer?"

"Not at the moment."

"Then I'm appointing you temporary Personnel Officer," said Cole. "Find two qualified crew members and transfer them to gunnery duties."

"From where?"

"From any duty that won't be vital if that Bortellite ship has entered the Rim with what we call bad intentions."

"You understand that either Mount Fuji or Podok is going to cancel your orders the moment they're made aware of them, don't you?"

"Then let's see if we can find out just how bad its intentions are before the end of blue shift," said Cole. "It's always possible they were headed there before Bortel II joined the Teroni Federation. It's possible that it's simply an unarmed merchant ship. But it's also possible that it's here to cause trouble—and if it is, let's encourage it to take a shot at us before my orders can be countermanded."

"I still like you, Wilson," said Sharon, "but I wouldn't want to bet the family jewels that you'll still have your commission tomorrow."

"Maybe I'll get lucky and they'll bust me all the way down to civilian," said Cole with a smile. "But in the meantime, though it's easy to forget it out here, we're at war, and these guys have just joined the other side."

He broke the connection, then walked over and stood beneath the Bdxeni's pod.

"Pilot," he said, "if this Bortellite ship should prove hostile, how quickly can our ship respond to your orders for evasive maneuvers?"

"With the speed of thought, sir," replied the Bdxeni.

"You're sure?" persisted Cole. "If there's any lag time at all, I can contact them from a safe distance, maybe try a bluff or two."

"There will be no lag time," Wxakgini assured him. "Newer ships may be more responsive, but the problem will not be with the transmission and reception of commands."

"All right," said Cole. "If I order you to take evasive action, I want that order carried out instantly—but under no circumstance, even if we are fired upon, do I want you to anticipate my order. Is that clear?"

"My first duty is not to any officer, but to the ship," responded Wxakgini.

"This ship has screens and shields and half a dozen other defenses against attack," said Cole. "They may not be as efficient as those the newer ships possess, but we're not looking at an enemy fleet here. We can handle anything the Bortellite ship can throw at us for at least ninety seconds, probably longer."

"Agreed. I will not respond without orders until I feel my defenses weakening."

"*Your* defenses?"

"When I am connected to the computer, it is very difficult to separate the ship from myself," said the Bdxeni. "I am sorry if my answer was confusing."

They raced across the edge of the Rim for the next few hours, quietly preparing for whatever awaited them. Cole checked every hour to make sure Fujiama and Podok were still asleep, made a trip to the gunnery area to confirm that the weapons were operative, stopped by the mess hall for more coffee, and spent the rest of his time studying computer simulations of the various merchant, passenger, and military ships of Bortel II.

Finally the pilot informed Cole that they were within firing range.

Cole walked over to Rachel. "Get ready, just in case," he said. Then, to Wxakgini: "Is the ship still on the ground?"

"Yes."

"Can you get me an image of it?"

"From this distance? No, sir, I can't."

"How soon can you?"

"Another six or seven minutes, sir."

"Will it be light enough?"

"The planet has a twenty-two-hour rotation period, sir. The ship will be in daylight for six more hours."

"Throw it up on every screen on the bridge as soon as you can."

"Yes, sir."

Five minutes later Cole's pocket computer informed him that he had a written message waiting for him.

"Written?" repeated Cole, frowning.

"That is correct," responded the computer.

"Let me see it."

Small lines of type appeared in the air and vanished as quickly as Cole read them:

> I figure you don't want to share this little tidbit until you have to, so I'm writing it. Fujiama is awake. He's in the bathroom now, taking a shower. It'll probably be five minutes before he finishes, dries himself, and comes back into his room. Give him another minute or two to dress, and then he's going to request his daily briefing. I'm going to have to tell him that we're twenty-eight light-years from where we're supposed to be, and closing in on a potential enemy. He's got enough other sources so that even if I lied, he'd know the truth half a minute later. So unless you think he's going to back you up, you've got maybe six or seven minutes to do whatever you're going to do.
>
> Sharon

Cole deactivated his pocket computer and turned back to the pilot. "How about that image?" he demanded.

"It's coming through now, sir," replied the Bdxeni.

Suddenly the image of a sleek golden ship appeared on every screen.

"That's no merchant ship," said Cole. "It's one of their newer warships, with a crew of three hundred and weaponry that makes ours look like so many slingshots." He checked the chronometer on one of the screens. He had at most five minutes before Fujiama learned what had happened and where they were, and probably another thirty seconds before the captain took over command. Fujiama would take one look at the golden ship, realize that the *Teddy R* was no match for it, and retreat to his original position while sending a message to headquarters requesting help that would never come, because the Republic's military was stretched too thin already. There was only one way to ascertain the intentions of the Bortellite ship and crew without endangering the *Teddy R*, and Cole, aware of his constricting time frame, acted promptly.

"Pilot, shear away as gently as you can and take up a holding pattern. Ensign Marcos, remain at your station until relieved. Lieutenant Mboya, come with me on the double."

He walked swiftly to the airlift. Even before he reached it he was in contact with Forrice.

"What is it?" asked the Molarian.

"Is there protective gear on the shuttles? And weapons?"

"Yes."

"Meet us down there," said Cole. "You've got ninety seconds."

Cole and Mboya got off at the shuttle level and ran to the closest one. Forrice, coming from a different airlift, arrived a few seconds later.

"What's going on?" demanded the Molarian.

"Later," said Cole, entering the craft. "Break the bond holding us to the ship and get us the hell away from here." He turned to Mboya. "Lieutenant, deactivate the radio. Pull a chip or a bubble, snip a wire, do something that we can repair later but that will let me truthfully say that I could neither send nor receive prior to reaching Rapunzel."

She fell to work instantly, and seconds later the shuttle pulled away from the *Teddy R*.

"Head toward Rapunzel," Cole ordered the Molarian.

"Do you want me to land the *Kermit* in any particular place?" asked Forrice.

"What the hell's the *Kermit*?" asked Cole.

"We're in it," interjected Christine, triumphantly holding up a fuse from the subspace radio. "The shuttles are named after four of Theodore Roosevelt's children—Kermit, Archie, Quentin, and Alice."

"Fine," said Cole distractedly. "Locate the Bortellite ship and request permission to land at the same location. They're a Republic world, we're a military vessel, there shouldn't be any problem."

"He can't request anything," said Christine, holding up the fuse. "Remember?"

"Shit!" said Cole. "We can't land without coordinates. All right, Lieutenant—put the fuse back when we're ready to enter the Bastoigne system."

"Then what?" said Forrice.

"Then hope the *Teddy R* doesn't blow us out of the ether before we land, and that the Bortellites don't kill us before we take off again."

"Sir, we're going to have to break radio silence," said Christine, who was seated at the communications station. "The spaceport is asking us to identify ourselves."

"Don't answer yet," said Cole.

"But sir—"

"It would be nice if Rapunzel controls its own spaceport—but our sole reason for coming here is the possibility that the Bortellites are in charge. There's no sense letting them know we're a Republic shuttle." He lowered his head in thought for a moment, then looked up. "Four Eyes, how do you say 'Kermit' in Molarian?"

"We don't."

"But *if* you did . . ."

Forrice considered the word, then uttered something that seemed halfway between a cough and a grunt.

"That'll do. Lieutenant, insert the fuse and get the radio working. Then turn it over to Four Eyes, who will tell them we're the *Kermit*— but he'll tell them in his own language."

"They probably won't have anyone there who can speak it," said Forrice, inserting a tiny receiver into his left ear.

"I'm counting on it," said Cole. "The *Teddy R* will almost certainly be monitoring our transmission, so explain why we're here. There are three more Molarians aboard; Fujiama may not speak your lingo, but he'll know what it is and call in one of the Molarians while you're buying us time with the spaceport."

"What if the spaceport fires on us anyway?" asked Christine.

"If the locals are still in charge, they're only going to fire on an enemy. This is a Republic world; we're a Republic ship."

"But what if the locals *aren't* in charge?" she persisted. "What if the Bortellites have taken over?"

"That's why we're here, isn't it?" responded Cole. "To find out what's going on. One way is to have them try to blow us apart."

"If it's all the same to you, sir, I hope they don't," said Christine.

"I hope so, too. I know it's going to come as a surprise to you, Lieutenant, or perhaps a disappointment, but I really don't like being shot at."

Forrice, who had been speaking softly on the radio, looked up. "Well, it's going to take them a few hours to figure out what I said— but nobody's shooting. Yet."

"And you explained our situation to the *Teddy R*?"

"Yes. Of course, I've no idea if they heard it."

"They heard it, all right," said Cole. "And they've already translated it."

"How can you be so sure?" asked Forrice.

"Because now that they know our radio's functional, they'd be ordering us to get the hell out of here if they *hadn't* gotten the message."

"Makes sense, at that," agreed Forrice.

"No it doesn't," said Christine. "Are you saying that Captain Fujiama *wants* us to land on Rapunzel?"

"Of course not," responded Cole. "But he doesn't want us blown to bits either, and he's afraid that if he contacts us or identifies us in any way, that's what will happen."

"I know Wilson Cole better than you do, Lieutenant," said Forrice. "I wouldn't put it past him to get us in a situation where our lives depend on Mount Fuji doing the right thing whether he wants to or not."

"Is this the way you did it before?" asked Christine.

"I've never landed on Rapunzel before," replied Cole noncommittally.

"You know what I mean, sir."

"I have absolutely no idea what you mean, Lieutenant," said Cole.

"I hate to interrupt all these earnest denials," said Forrice, "but they're requesting more information."

"Give it to them—in Molarian."

Forrice uttered two sentences in his native tongue, waited for a response, then turned to Cole.

"They won't let us land until we get someone who speaks or can transmit in Terran."

"What a shame," said Cole. "I guess we'll just have to land elsewhere."

"On Rapunzel?"

"Do you see any other oxygen world around here?"

"You never intended to land at the spaceport, did you?" demanded Christine.

"Well, if they'd had a Molarian handy, I wouldn't have had much choice, would I?" said Cole. "Four Eyes, what's the biggest city on the nightside?"

Forrice checked his computer, then looked up. "There's a city of about two hundred thousand." He paused. "It's called Pinocchio. Does that mean anything to you?"

"Yeah," said Cole. "It means whoever mapped this planet read too many fairy tales as a kid."

"May I ask why we aren't landing at the spaceport, sir?" asked Christine.

"Just adapting to the situation," answered Cole. "The Bortellites may have parked that warship at the spaceport, but they didn't leave it empty—not something that valuable and powerful. They'll be feeling vulnerable on the ground, so they'll have all its scanners and sensors activated. That means they know we're here."

"All right, they know we're here," she said, wondering what he was getting at.

"We're at war," continued Cole. "And they've landed on Republic territory."

Christine frowned in puzzlement. "So?"

"So they're not firing at us. What does that imply to you, Lieutenant?"

"They don't want to get into a shooting war?" she asked, confused.

"We've been in a shooting war for years."

"Then I don't see what you're getting at, sir."

"The fact that they didn't try to shoot us down means they don't mind if we land at the spaceport. I can't think of a better reason *not* to land there. Let's orbit the planet and see if we can spot whatever it is they *don't* want us to see."

"What makes you think there *is* something, sir?"

"They're here, and their ship is intact. You don't put down on an enemy planet for supplies or repairs. You do it with a military objective in mind. Right now, the only thing we know is that the military objective isn't in the vicinity of the spaceport, so let's go looking for it."

"And you think it might be in Pinocchio?" asked Forrice.

"I doubt it like all hell," replied Cole. "This is a Republic world. You've got to figure *someone* in Pinocchio would find some way to let us know about it. You can buy off or intimidate a lot of people, but not all of them."

"Just what is it that we're looking for, sir?" asked Christine.

"Beats the hell out of me, Lieutenant," admitted Cole. "But whatever it is, we'll find it. Half the trick in finding clues is knowing that they're there—and we know that an enemy warship is sitting on Rapunzel and that it's practically inviting us to land at the spaceport."

"They didn't land that many hours ahead of us," said Forrice. "Maybe they haven't set anything up yet."

"This isn't their first trip there," said Cole with certainty. "Or at least they're not the first Teroni Federation ship to land on Rapunzel."

"That's an awfully far-fetched conclusion," said Forrice.

"It's an obvious conclusion," said Cole. "At the risk of being repetitious, they didn't fire on us. If they hadn't dispersed their men and equipment yet, if everything was still at the spaceport and vulnerable to an attack, we'd be dodging laser and pulse fire right now."

"Well, at least we're free to go where we want. The Bortellites aren't going to say 'Don't look there' and the *Teddy R*'s not going to say a thing." Forrice displayed the Molarian equivalent of a grin. "You'd almost think someone planned it that way."

"Do you think you might pay a little attention to your navigation?" said Cole.

"What should *I* be doing, sir?" asked Christine.

"Rapunzel isn't worth conquering. The Teroni couldn't defend it, not out here on the Rim with Republic worlds all around it—and they obviously haven't destroyed it. What does that imply to you?"

"That Rapunzel has something they want, something they think they can take with the crew of a single ship."

"Very good, Lieutenant," said Cole. "What do you suppose that is?"

"A man, perhaps? A political leader or a scientist?"

Cole shook his head. "If they wanted a man, they'd have killed him and left, or captured him and left."

"They're only a few hours ahead of us," noted Forrice.

"If they came here for a man, they knew where he was before they touched down," said Cole. "They've got shuttles that are probably faster than this one. Believe me, they'd have found him by now."

"So that leaves . . . I don't know, something native to the planet," said Christine.

"We can do better than that, Lieutenant. Have the computer run a check and see just what's on or in Rapunzel that would be valuable to a military machine. It could be anything from diamonds to fissionable materials to other elements they use in their weapons systems. Then, when you've found a few things that seem to be worth the trip and the risk, match them against what's available in the Bortellite system. There's no sense coming here for plutonium, for example, if they've got it at home or right next door. Once you narrow it down, we'll know what they're here for and where to find them."

"And then what, sir?"

"Then we'll decide what to do," answered Cole. "There's not much sense having a plan before you know what you're facing."

"You're facing the bad guys," said Forrice. "What else do you have to know?"

"Do they have hostages? Can the *Teddy R* get here before they find what they're after? Are the people their willing accomplices or their enemies? What kind of firepower did they bring with them from the ship?" Cole paused. "There have to be a dozen more considerations. You want me to enumerate them?"

"I'll let you off the hook this one time," said Forrice, flashing another alien grin.

"Thanks for small favors," said Cole. "Now do me a large favor and tell me how long it'll be before we're over Pinocchio."

"We're sublight, but we're still above the stratosphere. I can get us there in thirty seconds."

"Once we've over it, match velocities with the planet and enter the atmosphere."

"The atmosphere, not just the stratosphere?"

"Right," said Cole. "It's night, and they'll see our heat shields glowing. Stay over the city until we're dark again, and then get the hell away from it, any direction you choose."

"I assume there's a reason for this?" asked Forrice.

"The warship knows we're here, so it's doubtless alerted that portion of the crew that's left it," explained Cole. "But since it can't see through or around the planet, it doesn't know exactly where we are now that we're on the nightside. Once we're seen over Pinocchio, someone there is going to report it, the ship will monitor the transmission and pass the word that we're interested in Pinocchio, and the crew, wherever they are, will be just a little more secure and a little less alert."

"You hope," said Forrice as the *Kermit* plunged through the stratosphere and into the atmosphere.

"I hope," agreed Cole.

They could see the lights of Pinocchio on their viewscreens. It didn't look that impressive, but two hundred thousand was actually a big city for a colony world, especially one out on the Galactic Rim.

"The heat shields are back to normal," announced Forrice. "Which way?"

"Indulge yourself," said Cole. "It doesn't make any difference until Lieutenant Mboya comes up with the information we need."

"I'm working on it," said Christine. "So far I haven't found anything worth coming here for—no fissionable materials, nothing worth mining, no rare earths. Hell, I can't even find much iron on the planet."

"They didn't come here so they could load a very expensive warship down with iron ore to take home and smelt. Keep searching."

"What direction are we heading?" she asked without looking up from the computer.

"Southwest," answered Forrice. "Do you want degrees, minutes, and seconds?"

"Southwest?" she repeated. "Just altitude."

"About fifteen thousand feet."

"Not enough," she said. "Get up above thirty thousand."

"What's up ahead?" asked Forrice, adjusting their altitude.

"A mountain range."

"Anything else to the southwest?" asked Cole.

"Not according to the computer," she answered. "It looks unpopulated, rather than underpopulated."

"That makes sense," said Forrice. "You can't grow anything in the mountains."

"We're over them right now," said Christine. "We're not picking up anything—no rare metals, no fissionable materials, nothing. Just as well. It's a young range with a lot of volcanoes; quite a few of them are due to blow their tops any day now. I'd hate to be a miner stationed there."

They continued for another half hour. Then Forrice spoke up. "We haven't seen a thing. You want me to stay on this course?"

Cole didn't answer.

"Hey, Hero," said the Molarian. "Are you awake?"

"I'm awake."

"You want me to change course?"

No answer.

"Are you all right?" asked Forrice.

"Be quiet for a minute. I'm thinking."

Forrice immediately fell silent and concentrated on his navigation, while Christine continued studying her computer, looking for something—*anything*—that could have drawn the Bortellites to Rapunzel.

Cole sat perfectly still, his chin on his fist, staring at some fixed point only he could see. He remained motionless for almost two minutes, then suddenly looked up.

"Lieutenant, I need some information," he said.

"I haven't found anything useful yet, sir."

"Not about Rapunzel—about Bortel II."

"Sir?"

"Find out what kind of power they're using. Not just the military, but the whole damned planet."

She queried the computer, gave it a few seconds to come up with the data, and turned to Cole. "Bortel II has no fissionable materials at all, sir."

"I didn't think so."

"But their ship has to be using fissionable fuel, sir," she continued. "It's certainly not running on wood or coal."

"I know," said Cole. "What about their planetary fuel reserves—gas, coal, oil, whatever?"

Christine looked at the computer. "About ninety percent depleted, sir."

"And let me guess that their planetary economy is in a depression, and that it's probably been pretty bad for at least a couple of years, maybe longer."

She checked, then looked up at him with a puzzled expression. "Yes, sir. They're in the fourth year of a major economic depression."

"Four Eyes, bank a hundred and eighty degrees and take us back the way we came," said Cole.

"You've figured it out!" said Christine. "You know why they're here and where they are, don't you?"

Cole nodded an affirmative. "Yeah, I think so."

"Well?" demanded the Molarian.

"It was a number of things," he replied. "Individually, they didn't mean anything. Put them together and they give a pretty clear picture."

"Whatever they are, we all saw the same things and only you seem to make sense of them," said Forrice. "Why is that?"

Cole allowed himself the luxury of a smile. "Do you want a frank answer or a friendly one?"

"Just tell us what you've figured out."

"The first hint was that Lieutenant Mboya couldn't find a damned thing worth coming to Rapunzel for—no treasure, no fissionable material, no one worth holding for ransom, no gold or diamonds buried beneath the surface. Then there was the fact that Bortel II has stayed neutral for years and then suddenly joined the Teroni Federation. And of course there was the mountain range."

"And from that you think you've figured out what's going on?" said Forrice. "How did you make all those guesses about conditions on Bortel II?"

"They weren't guesses," answered Cole. "There's only one thing this planet has in abundance, if you know how to utilize it, and that's energy."

"Energy?" scoffed Forrice. "Lieutenant Mboya already told you there's no plutonium, no uranium, no—"

"You weren't listening," interrupted Cole. "We passed over a thousand-mile stretch of active volcanic mountains. With the right technology, you could power a planet for centuries with the energy that's trying to burst out of that range. That's why I asked about the power reserves on Bortel; if they were as low as I thought, then I knew why the Bortellites were here. And since they're clearly not here on a mission of conquest, they probably brought everything they need in one ship: scientists with the know-how and technology to siphon off a lot of that energy and store it, and just enough military personnel to safeguard them. They desperately need that energy, which is also why they joined the Teroni Federation. The Republic will never admit it, of course, but I'll bet Bortel II held an unofficial little auction, and the winner was the side that was willing to fuel their warships. Think of the power that baby at the spaceport consumes, and then consider what Lieutenant Mboya told us: they have no fissionable materials on their home planet. They didn't develop the technology to power that ship overnight. They've been buying their fuel, probably from both sides, but if their economy went south they had to take other measures. Joining the Federation was one measure; coming here was another."

"It makes sense when you explain it like that," said Christine.

"He's right," agreed Forrice. "I just hate it when he's right. It usually means big trouble for everyone who's anywhere near him."

"But the sensors didn't pick up any activity or even any large life-forms when we flew over the mountains before," she said.

"We flew *across* them," said Cole. "This time we're going to fly the whole thousand-mile length of them, up one side and down the other. Before we're done, we'll find what—and who—we're looking for." He turned to Forrice. "How long before we reach the foothills?"

"Not long," answered the Molarian. "Maybe two or three minutes."

"I wish to hell I knew what kind of technology is required to pull and store all that energy," said Christine. "Then I could program the sensors to look for it."

"Since we can't do that, find out what lives on the mountains," said Cole. "If it's four- or six-legged, just tell the sensors to look for groups of bipeds."

"Yes, sir. I'll get right to work on it."

Cole got to his feet. "Well," he announced, "if you're doing that and Four Eyes is driving the ship, I guess I'm free to grab something to eat."

"At a time like this?" demanded Forrice.

"I'm hungry," replied Cole. "That's usually the best time to eat." He looked around. "Where the hell do we store food on the shuttle?"

"Last cabinet on the lower left."

Cole walked to the back of the shuttle, found the cabinet, opened it, couldn't find anything that appealed to him, and finally pulled out a cookie. He stared at it distastefully for a moment, then shrugged and took a bite. He chewed it thoughtfully, decided he liked it after all, and took another bite. He was just about to look for some coffee or tea to wash it down with when Forrice called back to him.

"I hate to disturb you," said the Molarian. "But we just found the bad guys." The small ship shuddered and began losing altitude. "More to the point, they've found us."

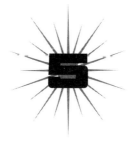

The ship shuddered again.

"I think we'd better set the *Kermit* down," said Cole. "Pretty soon they're going to get tired of firing warning shots."

"You don't want me to fire back?" asked Forrice.

"Hell, no. We don't know what kind of weaponry they've got down there, but we know we can't match fire with the warship, and if we managed to blow these guys away, it can reach us a hell of a lot quicker than the *Teddy R* can."

"Pardon a question, sir, but what makes you think they'll let us land?" asked Christine.

"We're flying at cruising speed, and their weapons are almost certainly under computer control," answered Cole as the turbulence became worse. "Just how many times do you figure they'd miss the *Kermit* unless they wanted to? They're just inviting us to land and showing us what they've got in case we decide to fight or flee."

"Are you sure about this?" asked Forrice. "We're a shuttle against a ground position. We can go to light speeds if we want—but if we land there are an awful lot of them and only three of us."

"You're not thinking clearly," answered Cole. "If you try to go to light speeds while we're still in the atmosphere, the friction will incinerate us. And you can bet your alien ass that they'll shoot a lot straighter if we start climbing. Now, take us down nice and slow, and don't activate any weapons. Lieutenant, leave the radio open. They're almost certainly going to give us some orders; there's no reason why Fujiama and Podok shouldn't hear them."

"I have another question, sir," said Christine.

"This would be a good time to ask it," said Cole. "We might be a bit occupied once we touch down."

"Why are we even in this position?" she said. "Surely you must have known they would have weapons with them, and could force us down."

"They certainly figured to have some," he agreed. "They're pretty exposed out here."

"Then why have you purposely endangered us?" she continued. "I don't mean to sound insubordinate, sir, but if I'm going to die I'd like to think it was for a good reason."

"I don't know who indoctrinated you, Lieutenant," responded Cole, "but there aren't any good reasons for dying. We're in this position because I have a feeling that the Bortellite commander shares *my* sentiments rather than yours."

"I don't follow you, sir."

"There's only one Bortellite warship at the spaceport, and our sensors didn't spot any when we passed over Pinocchio. We know the ship carries a crew of three hundred. We know Rapunzel is a Republic world. What does that imply to you?"

She stared at him, a puzzled frown on her face.

"All right," he continued, "let me add one more fact to consider: Bortel II didn't officially join the Teroni Federation until a week ago."

A look of dawning comprehension spread across her face. "Of course!" she said. "You think they've been infiltrating Rapunzel, landing hundreds, maybe thousands, of their agents here while Bortel II was officially neutral."

"It helps explain how they could land their ship without being challenged, and why no one's out here trying to stop them. If I'm right, they'll leave when they've gotten what they came for. This world is militarily indefensible against the Republic. There's no way they can establish supply lines, and it's not worth losing any ships over. They probably wanted to get in and out fast."

"It makes sense up to this point," put in Forrice. "But we're going to be on the ground in another ninety seconds. What do we do then?"

"Assess the situation," said Cole.

"I'll assess it right now," said Forrice. "We're going to be prisoners of the Teroni Federation. They don't know Lieutenant Mboya, and they couldn't care less about me, but they've got good reason to remember you. Wilson Cole would be quite a prize to bring home."

"I know you're going to have a difficult time believing this, but we're safer now than if we'd gone covertly into Pinocchio or one of the other cities and tried to find out how thoroughly they've been infiltrated."

Forrice snorted his disagreement. It sounded like a tuba playing a B-flat.

"Think it through," continued Cole. "If you're found out in the streets or the back alleys on Pinocchio, you're just a spy who asked too many questions, and the obvious course is to slit your throat. Maybe they'd try to make it look like a robbery and maybe they wouldn't, but it wouldn't make any difference to you, because you'd be dead and whatever you'd learned would have died with you. At least this way we're officers who are in a military shuttle, so they know if they kill us they've got the mother ship to contend with—and since they're new to the Rim, they probably don't know that the *Teddy R* belongs in a geriatric ward. Also, they have to know we're here because we spotted their ship; if we don't mention the conclusions we've reached, there's every chance they won't credit us with the intelligence to figure out that they're here to plunder some energy. After all, we're officers—and if theirs are as dumb and hidebound as ours, they're not going to think much of our collective brainpower."

"If you hold officers in such contempt, why did you become one?" asked Forrice.

"The food's better, and I don't have to share my cabin," replied Cole, and neither of his companions could tell if he was kidding.

"We touch down in twenty seconds," announced the Molarian.

"Do we have any kind of an escort?" asked Cole.

"No."

"So whatever brought them here is so unimpressive that they don't want us to see it."

"Our sensors don't see any sign of a ship at all, or even any ground transport, sir," said Christine. "I think they were dropped off, and they'll probably signal whatever brought them when they want to be picked up."

Cole removed his laser and sonic pistols. "Leave your burners and screechers here," he said. "If we take them with us when we leave the shuttle they'll just disarm us. Why give them any more weapons?"

Forrice and Christine followed suit, and Cole locked them in a cabinet. "Just in case they inspect the ship," he explained.

"Do you plan to let them come aboard?" asked Christine.

"Of course not," he replied. "But you know what they say about the best-laid plans."

The ship jarred them slightly as it landed on the uneven ground.

"I think it would be best if you'd defer all questions to me," said Cole. "If we start contradicting each other, we'll almost certainly be separated and interrogated rather painfully."

The hatch opened and a ramp emerged, allowing them to descend comfortably to the ground.

They found themselves and the shuttle surrounded by some fifty Bortellite soldiers. They were humanoid in appearance, taller than Men, very slender, with six-fingered hands that possessed a pair of opposable thumbs. Their feet were quite small, as if they had evolved from hooves. Their heads were almost circular, with two exceptionally large eyes, a pair of very wide-set nostrils and no discernible nose at all, and wide mouths that revealed flat teeth and no canines when they spoke. The most interesting thing about them was that they all wore helmets and oxygen packs.

"I thought Bortel II was an oxygen world, Lieutenant," said Cole under his breath.

"It is, sir."

So you need a much higher or lower oxygen content than you can get on Rapunzel, thought Cole. *There's a little tidbit that might come in handy.*

"Why did you fire on my ship?" asked Cole aloud.

"Why are you here?" demanded a Bortellite who seemed to be the leader. He uttered his words into a T-pack, which translated them into Terran in a mechanical monotone.

"Rapunzel is a Republic world, and we are officers in the Republic's Navy," said Cole. "We have every right to be here. Let me ask you the same question: Why are members of the Teroni Federation here and why did you fire on my craft?"

The leader stared at Cole for a long moment. "Rapunzel is a neutral planet, and is no longer affiliated with the Republic. We have as much right here as you have."

"Since when did Rapunzel withdraw from the Republic?" asked Cole.

"It will be announced soon."

"Has Rapunzel held a planetary plebiscite?" asked Cole. "Where were the vote totals posted, and by what percentage did the populace choose to leave the Republic?"

"I have no knowledge of such things," said the leader noncommittally. "I am an officer, not a politician."

"Then let me ask another question," said Cole. "Who are you guarding these uninhabited mountains from?"

"That is none of your business."

"I beg to differ. It becomes my business when you fire on a Republic shuttle."

"Your business on this world is at an end," said the Bortellite. "Surely you realize that we could have shot you down. We elected not to, because you obviously did not know of Rapunzel's neutrality."

Son of a bitch! You're weaker here than I thought. Any minute you're going to offer us safe passage out of here.

As if on cue, the Bortellite said: "If you will give me your pledge that you will honor Rapunzel's neutrality, I will let you leave in peace."

Forrice and Christine looked questioningly at Cole. He nodded his head almost imperceptibly.

"You have my pledge," said Forrice.

"And mine," added Christine.

"And you?" said the leader, facing Cole.

"You go to hell," said Cole. "I'll make no such pledge. My crew may be traitors, but I'm not."

"*What?*" bellowed Forrice.

"You heard me," said Cole. "You're a disgrace to your uniform."

He reached out and pushed the Molarian in the chest, while mouthing the words *Grab me.*

Forrice stared at him as if in shock, but made no attempt to reach out for him.

Shit! thought Cole. *You can speak Terran, but you form the words differently. You can't read my lips.*

"And you," he said, turning on Christine. "You're no better than he is!"

Hit me! he mouthed.

Christine stepped forward. "You almost got us all killed!" she yelled. "Don't you call me a traitor!"

She took a swing at Cole. He ducked, slipped around behind her, and wrapped his arms around her. Lowering his head, he whispered: "As soon as you're out of here, tell—"

"Mount Fuji, I know," she whispered back.

"*No!*"

They were pulled apart by the Bortellites before he could say anything further.

I've got to get the message to you somehow. "It's going to make headlines when they court-martial you," he said bitterly. *Do you understand? Did you spot the key word? If you didn't, I'm in* big *trouble.*

"I hope they cut you into pieces!" she snarled. She turned to the Bortellite leader. "Am I free to go?"

I hope to hell that means you've figured it out.

"Yes," he replied. "But if you return, we will destroy your vessel."

"I thought Rapunzel was supposed to be a neutral planet," said Forrice.

"It is," said the Bortellite. "But we will view your reappearance as an act of aggression and will respond in kind."

"What if we consider *your* presence an act of aggression?" the Molarian shot back.

Shut up and get out of here before he changes his mind!

"We are not under the command of an officer who refuses to acknowledge Rapunzel's neutrality, or our right to be here," was the reply.

Cole was sure that Forrice was about to argue the point, so he decided he had to put an end to it. "Get out of my sight, you spineless coward!" he snarled. *Please,* he added mentally.

Forrice finally realized what Cole wanted. "Don't kill him too quickly," he said to the Bortellite. He began walking toward the hatch, followed by Christine. Cole could tell by their body language that they were leaving reluctantly, almost under protest.

The *Kermit* took off a moment later, and the Bortellite leader studied Cole carefully. "Your features seem familiar," he said at last. He continued staring. "*Very* familiar." Pause. "But I couldn't be that lucky. Why would they send you to this nothing in the middle of nowhere?"

"I have no idea what you're talking about," replied Cole.

The Bortellite kept studying Cole. "Probably I'm wrong. Men all tend to look alike. But just in case, I think we'll run a scan on your implanted ID chip."

"I'll save you the trouble. I am Commander Wilson Cole, Second Officer of the *Theodore Roosevelt*."

"I *knew* it!" exclaimed the Bortellite. "We have captured the notorious Wilson Cole!"

Cole shrugged. "These things happen."

The leader turned to a subordinate. "Notify the ship, and have them prepare a cell with the proper oxygen content for our prisoner." Then, to Cole: "What is a warrior of your credentials doing out here on the Rim?"

"Wondering what you feed your prisoners."

"You do not seem very concerned about your situation."

"I'm a reasonable man," said Cole. "I'm willing to negotiate."

"For your freedom?" said the Bortellite with what passed for a harsh laugh.

"For yours."

"Bold words for a prisoner whose ship and crew have deserted him."

"I'm an optimist," said Cole.

"Somehow you do not seem like the legendary warrior we have heard so much about."

Cole smiled at him. "The day is young yet," he said.

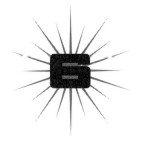

The day got older quickly. Cole was kept under heavy guard, given some foul-smelling food that his captors seemed to relish, and questioned interminably. He answered every question freely and willingly, never once telling the truth, but creating such a cohesive fabric of lies that it would take the Bortellites a few days to check them all out.

By midafternoon he had pretty much decided that Christine Mboya had either misunderstood his hint or—more likely—had totally missed it. If there had been no attack by now, there probably wasn't going to be one, and that meant if he was to escape and get back to the *Teddy R* he was going to have to do it on his own.

He knew Pinocchio would be home to hundreds, probably thousands, of men and women who would help him if he could make it that far. The trick was getting from here to there; getting all the way back to the ship was something he couldn't even bother considering yet.

All right, he told himself. *Think it through. They haven't laid a finger on me. That could mean they're waiting for a master inquisitor, but more likely it means they're afraid of harming the goods before they deliver me to their superiors; after all, I'm a hell of a trophy. Still, I can't just make a break for it; they may want me alive, but they'll shoot me down before they'll let me get away.*

He looked around. *Okay, then—can I get my hands on a weapon? That means disarming a guard. Which one—the closest, the smallest, or the best-armed? The closest, I suppose. I can do it fastest. But there's a couple of hundred of them. One weapon won't do me much good. All right, so a weapon is out. What about their helmets? Is there a single oxygen source on the ship I can disable? No, I can't see any—but that means they've got a limited supply of breathable air. I don't care how much they compress it, those packs their helmets are tied into can't hold more than a day's worth—and they've been here more than two-thirds of a day already. That means a ship or a shuttle, something with an air supply, is due to land here in the next few hours.*

And that gives me a time frame. Whatever I do, I have to do in the next two or three hours, tops—and I probably have to do it without getting my hands on a weapon.

He stood up and stretched. The sun was starting to get lower in the sky. It had to be soon. The mountain terrain was so rocky and uneven that he could break a leg—or his neck—racing across it in the darkness.

And then it dawned on him: as hard a time as he would have racing down the mountain, the Bortellites would be considerably more at risk. If he fell, he'd get a bruise. If he fell the wrong way, he might break something—but if a Bortellite fell, he could crack his helmet, and that would be fatal, for if the Bortellites could breathe Rapunzel's air, they wouldn't be wearing helmets in the first place.

So all he needed was a head start. They didn't dare negotiate the landscape as recklessly as he could. The trick was getting that start.

There *had* to be a way. If there was a problem that was incapable of solution, he hadn't come across it yet. Sometimes it just required a new perspective, a different way of looking at things.

And suddenly he knew.

It wasn't a matter of looking at things, but rather of things they *couldn't* look at. The key was the Bortellites' huge eyes. That implied a world with a small or distant sun, a world where they needed those enormous pupils to function. That was why they were working at night. He'd assumed they felt a need for secrecy, but he realized he was wrong. They'd already infiltrated Rapunzel, and they had the best weapons. There was no need for secrecy. They were working at night because they were more comfortable in the darkness.

So he'd been looking at it all wrong. They could negotiate the mountains in the darkness. But what they *couldn't* do was fire with any accuracy at a moving target that was running toward the setting sun!

Cole figured that he had about half an hour before the sun was at exactly the right position. He decided to make use of the time, studying each Bortellite as he came or went, trying to see what surfaces and angles they avoided, which ones they were most comfortable on. Steep slopes didn't seem to bother them. They dug those hooflike feet into the ground and leaned forward as they walked. But if there was any rubble on the paths, any loose rocks, anything that could cause them to stumble, they avoided it. If they came to a sharp turn, they looked first before they took a step. They didn't seem to be aware they were doing it, but it helped Cole plan his escape route. Steep didn't matter; twists and turns and obstructions did.

Let me check one last thing, just to make sure I'm not committing suicide here. He slowly adjusted his position until there was a guard between him and the setting sun. He looked at the star through the glass of the Bortellite's helmet. It wasn't polarized, which meant they would be every bit as blind looking into the low-hanging sun as he hoped.

He had about three minutes left. *Is there anything I've overlooked, any way to distract them during the first ten or twenty seconds?*

I wonder . . . , he thought. *Your shoulders are rigid, and your arms are joined very differently from mine. I'll bet you couldn't scratch an itch on your back if your life depended on it.*

His hand snaked down to his pocket. They'd taken his weapons, of course. He felt around. Had they left him anything? Then his fingers came into contact with three coins. He closed his hand around them, withdrew it carefully, then stood still, waiting for the sun to drop just the tiniest bit lower.

When it did, he whipped his hand around his back and threw the coins. One of them clicked off a helmet forty feet away. Another bounced off a Bortellite's wrist. Both Bortellites emitted little exclamations of surprise. Cole didn't turn to look, but his guards did. Since their bodies weren't capable of allowing them to throw something behind their backs, they never considered that Cole might have been the cause of the exclamations. They turned to see what had happened, and as they did so Cole took off, straight toward the sun.

The maneuver only bought him about three seconds, but that was better than nothing. Pulse fire tore up the ground around him, but their eyes hadn't adjusted yet. At this angle the sun bothered his eyes; it had to be excruciating to them. He dove over a slight rise as a laser beam barely missed him, then began racing down the rockiest slope in a zigzag pattern.

The element of surprise had given him a fifteen-second head start, but now they were chasing him down the slope. He couldn't continue running straight into the setting sun; the terrain wouldn't allow it. He saw a rocky outcropping about thirty yards ahead. If he could make it there, he could change direction before they saw him do it; that might help him extend his lead by another few seconds.

He heard the thud of a body falling and chanced a quick look back. The Bortellite closest to him had slipped on a patch of gravel, and the one immediately behind him had fallen over him. The terrain was such that no Bortellite was going to risk jumping over both bodies, so they began altering course and running around them, and that bought him still more time to add to his margin.

He reached the outcropping, took a hard left, and ran past a number of caves. The rocky ground was too hard to show any footprints; that meant some of his pursuers were going to have to inspect each cave, just to make sure he hadn't ducked into one of them.

There was a forest coming up on his right, and his first urge was to head for it and hide among the trees, but he realized that all they would have to do would be to train their laser pistols on the trees and both he and the forest would go up in smoke.

He knew he had to do something soon. When the sun dipped just a little lower, he'd lose his advantage. He'd still be able to negotiate the rocky surface better than they would, but their eyes would adjust to the dark far better than his, and their fire would become that much more accurate.

He couldn't just keep running. No matter how fast and surefooted he was, he couldn't outrace an energy pulse or a laser beam. He glanced up the mountain. Could a good loud yell start a landslide? He doubted it—and if it could, he'd be caught in it, too.

He looked at the forest again. *What's the point? They'll just set it on fire.*

And then: *Wait a minute! I've been looking at it all wrong! It won't be a furnace—it'll be the biggest damned lightbulb on the planet!*

He veered for the trees and was less than ten yards into them when the first laser beam hit a huge old tree, which erupted into flame. He kept going, never slowing his pace. *They can't shoot around or over me, not with laser pistols. They've got to burn 'em one at a time until the fire spreads and takes on a life of its own. All I have to do is keep ahead of them and hope the forest doesn't go on for miles.*

The ground leveled out and he increased his speed. He could hear the wood and leaves crackling behind him, could smell the acrid scent of burning wood, but he didn't look back. After he'd gone a quarter of a mile the heat became oppressive, and he sensed that the fire would soon surround him.

He thought he saw a clearing a little way ahead, and he forced his legs to carry him across that final stretch of ground. When he arrived he saw that it wasn't a clearing but rather a mountain stream wending its way through the forest. With burning branches falling all around him he didn't have time to see if it was more than a few inches deep; he simply plunged into it and hoped the current was strong enough to carry him down the mountain before falling trees blocked his way.

The water was cold, but not icy. It was about four feet deep, and he tried to stay beneath the surface except when he needed to take breaths of air. Rocks tore gouges in his legs and belly, but he didn't dare to swim on the surface until he felt he'd put almost a mile between himself and his pursuers. They weren't going to swim in a stream that had hidden rocks, not with those helmets, and they weren't going to make any progress through the blazing inferno they'd created. They'd have to walk around it, and they had no way of knowing that he hadn't been caught in the conflagration. They'd keep looking, of course, but with a decreasing sense of urgency. He was out of visual range by now; unless one of them lucked out and spotted him with a sensor, he was probably safe for the time being—and the chase had begun so suddenly that he didn't think any of them had had the presence of mind to grab a sensor before racing after him.

Which didn't mean he could stop or even slow down. He rode the stream another mile, then climbed onto the shore and began walking alongside it. When the area became more open, he turned away from the stream and began descending along rockier ground.

The sun finally set, and he had to proceed more carefully, fully aware that the advantage was now all with the Bortellites. His legs began cramping. He ignored the pain as long as he could, but finally he had to stop. He counted to two hundred, then got up and began walking, a bit more slowly this time.

He looked up the mountain, hoping for a sign that would let him know how close they were and how vigorously they were pursuing him, but they used no lights and there was simply no way to know. He was reasonably sure that they'd circle the forest and, finding no sign that he had emerged on the far side, would assume he'd been caught in the fire. Then one of them would spot the stream and suggest he'd used it to escape the blaze. They'd send a few soldiers down the stream to be on the safe side, but if he could keep going for two more hours he was in the clear, because they weren't going to get too far away from where their shuttle would land. He may have been running low on energy, but they were running low on their oxygen mixture.

Suddenly he heard a shuffling sound on the path below him.

How the hell did they get past me? I thought I had at least a mile on them.

The sound repeated, and then he saw the silhouette of a large four-legged animal. It sniffed the air, caught his scent, and bolted in the opposite direction while Cole breathed a sign of relief.

He continued walking for another fifteen minutes, and then he saw a shuttle of alien design approaching the mountain. It hovered near the spot where he'd been held all day, then began descending, and he lost sight of it.

He felt pretty confident that any Bortellites that were still following him would be returning to the mountaintop now to replenish their air supply. They'd tell the shuttle about him, and he could expect the ship to start searching the mountainside. He considered altering his course, staying at this altitude for a few miles, and then descending again, but he rejected the notion; the shuttle could cover much more ground than he could. He'd be better off trying to get off the mountain than elude the craft while still on it.

He saw another stream in the distance and approached it. This one was broader than the last one and flowing more rapidly. When he got there he took a step into the water, then another, and realized that this stream was almost six feet deep down the middle of the groove it had worn into the mountain. He stretched out and let it begin carrying him down the mountain, hoping he didn't hit too many submerged rocks. He rode the stream almost to the foot of the mountain and stopped only when it reached a huge mud-and-wood dam that had been constructed by some local animal.

Cole climbed back onto solid ground, and in another five minutes he was finally off the mountain, or at least onto the vegetation-covered foothills. He knew that Pinocchio was to the northeast, probably two hundred miles or more, and he also knew he was a marked man. He couldn't simply walk two hundred miles in the open, not if the Bortellites had made as many inroads as he suspected. Besides, he was exhausted, and except for the stuff they'd tried to feed him in the afternoon, he hadn't eaten in more than twenty-four hours. His first needs were food and shelter; Pinocchio could wait.

This was an empty quarter, but Rapunzel wasn't an unpopulated or undeveloped world. There had to be roads. The problem was that they might be twenty or thirty or fifty miles away—and even if they weren't, even if there was one within a mile, he wouldn't be able to spot it for hours, until the sun rose again.

There also had to be rivers flowing out of the mountains. A range this size would doubtless give birth to a major one, perhaps two or three. But the range was almost a thousand miles long, and he didn't know where the rivers were.

He decided that his best bet was to walk to where the dammed-up stream came out—after all, *some* of it had to get through, or he'd have found himself in a lake when he reached the blockage. Then he'd follow it on the assumption that if any humans lived out this way, prospectors, fishermen, whatever, they'd want to be near a source of water.

It took him about eight minutes to find the stream, and then he began walking alongside it. Suddenly his surroundings became a bit brighter, and he realized that Rapunzel's two moons were now overhead and reflecting off the water. The moons were moving rapidly through the sky. He decided to make the most of the minimal light they provided, and he broke into a trot. He felt he'd covered about four miles when the moons disappeared over the horizon, one right after the other, and he slowed his pace, fearful of twisting or breaking an ankle in the darkness.

After another mile the stream was joined by a bigger, broader stream, and became a small river. Cole realized that he was near the limit of his physical endurance, so he looked around for a log, found one, and carried it into the river. He had hoped to straddle it and ride it like a long-extinct horse, but he couldn't adjust his weight properly and it kept shooting out from under him. Finally he settled for stretching out behind it and letting it pull him downstream.

He rode the river until sunrise. Every now and then he'd fall asleep. Then his face would hit the water and he'd wake up, coughing and choking, and desperately trying not to lose his hold on the log. He had no idea exactly how far he'd come. The mountain seemed to be about twenty miles behind him, but the river wasn't running a straight course, so he might have traveled much farther.

He now faced another decision: Was he less likely to be spotted *on* the water or walking beside it? He was still considering his options when he nodded off yet again, and this time he breathed in so much water that he had to go ashore to clear his lungs. He decided he didn't want to plunge back into the cold water and realized that he couldn't go much farther, that he had to get some sleep. He looked around, saw a stand of shoulder-high shrubbery about fifty yards away, trudged over to it, lay down with the shrubbery shielding him from the river, and was asleep almost before his head hit the ground.

He didn't know how long he slept, but when he awoke he didn't feel especially well rested. For a moment he couldn't figure out why he woke up with the sun still high in the sky; he had assumed after his experiences of the past thirty-six hours that he'd probably sleep until nightfall.

Then he realized what had awakened him. He was being prodded with the barrel of a sonic rifle.

"Who the hell are you?" said a gruff voice.

Cole sat up and tried to focus his eyes. "Where am I?" he asked groggily.

"I'm asking the questions here. Who are you and what are you doing here?"

"Just give me a second to get my bearings," said Cole.

"You look pretty torn up. Where's your outfit?"

"My outfit?" repeated Cole.

"You're wearing a military uniform. Well, what's left of one, anyway."

"My ship's light-years from here," answered Cole.

"You're a one-man invasion party, are you?"

Cole finally looked up at the man who was speaking. He was middle-aged, on the slim side, his clothes expensive but well-worn, his face in need of a shave.

"I'm a one-man escape party," said Cole at last.

"From the mountain? I saw a bunch of Bug-Eyes working up there."

"Bug-Eyes?"

"Bortellites."

"Yeah, that's where I came from."

The man reached down and helped him to his feet. "Some of those cuts and gouges look pretty deep," he said. "Come on back to my cabin and we'll get you patched up."

"You live out here?"

The man shook his head. "No. I just get away whenever I can for some serious fishing."

"Do you deafen them first?" said Cole, indicating the sonic rifle.

"You never know what you'll run into up here," replied the man. "Devilcats, Bug-Eyes"—suddenly he smiled—"even escapees. You got a name?"

"Wilson Cole."

"Very funny," said the man without smiling. "Now how about your real one?"

"I just gave it to you."

"You expect me to believe that someone like Wilson Cole would come to a little backwater world like Rapunzel? Let's see some ID."

"The Bortellites took it from me."

"Well, whoever the hell you are, if you're running from them, I'll help you all I can. My name's Carson Potter. Pleased to meet you." He extended his hand, and Cole shook it.

"Where's this cabin of yours?"

"About a mile."

"I don't suppose you have a subspace radio there?"

"Now, what the hell would I be doing with a subspace radio in a fishing cabin?"

"I've got to get to Pinocchio," said Cole. "Can you take me there?"

"Once we get you patched up," said Potter. "Going to contact your ship?"

Cole shook his head. "My ship wouldn't go an inch out of its way for me. I've got a captain who won't bend a regulation and a first officer who makes the captain look like a flaming radical."

"Hit the dirt!" said Potter urgently. "Here comes one of their shuttles."

"Keep walking," said Cole, waving his hand at the shuttle.

"You got a death wish?" retorted Potter. "I have to think they're not after *me*."

"We can't hide from their sensors, so we might as well not try. If we keep walking and give them a friendly wave, we're a couple of hunters or fishermen. If we try to hide, we're insurgents."

"You sound like you've had some experience at this sort of thing."

"A little."

"Are you *really* Wilson Cole?"

"I told you I am."

"Then what the hell are you doing out here on the Rim? All the big battles are being fought halfway to the Core."

"I go where I'm ordered," answered Cole.

"Well, damn it, if they order someone like Wilson Cole to go out to the Rim, I don't have a lot of confidence in the brainpower of whoever's running this goddamned war."

"Welcome to the club," said Cole.

They reached the top of a ridge, and suddenly a small cabin came into view.

"There it is," said Potter. "It doesn't look like much on the outside, but it's livable—and I've got a medical kit." He glanced at Cole. "When was the last time you ate?"

"It's been a while."

"I hope you like fish."

"I hate fish."

Potter shrugged. "Have it your way. I hope you like starving."

"How do we get to Pinocchio from here?"

"I've got a small aircar out behind the cabin. I can have us there in two hours."

"Good."

"That's two hours after I start, not two hours from now. First I'm going to patch you up as best I can and give you a chance to develop a taste for God's finny creatures."

"My wounds and my appetites can wait till we get to Pinocchio," said Cole.

"You don't want to get an infection on this world," said Potter. "Your body doesn't produce the right antibodies to fight it off until you've had some specialized vaccinations, and I'd be willing to bet you haven't had 'em."

"Two hours won't make that much difference."

"It won't take that long to patch you up, and I ain't going down in the history books as the man who let Wilson Cole die," said Potter adamantly. "Even if you're just *a* Wilson Cole and not *the* Wilson Cole."

"All right," said Cole as they reached the cabin. "Let's get it over with and get the hell out of here."

"Take off your tunic while I get out the kit," said Potter, opening the door and entering the cabin.

Cole followed him in. There was a large state-of-the-art holoscreen, an airsled that doubled as a bed, two leather chairs and one made of some alien hardwood, and a kitchen with unique appliances that could gut, scale, and cook a fish without any human ever having to touch it. He decided that what made it rustic was its size and location, not its conveniences.

"The exterior is a little misleading," remarked Cole. "This place must have cost you a bundle."

"I had a bundle to spend," replied Potter. "My wife died five years ago, and both my daughters were killed in the Battle of Diablo III."

"In the service, or civilians?"

"One of each."

"From everything I've heard, that was a disaster."

"It sure as hell was for my bloodline," said Potter. "Anyway, now I've got no one to spend it on except me." He opened the kit. "Sit down and let me assess the damage."

Potter began spraying and patching various wounds, some of which Cole hadn't even known he possessed. After about ten minutes he told Cole to put his tunic back on.

"How about your legs and hips?" asked Potter. "Any serious wounds?"

"A couple of cuts."

"I hate strong silent types. Pull your pants off and let me take a look." Cole hesitated. "Take 'em off. I'm going to medicate you, not grab you."

Cole pulled his pants off.

"That's one hell of a wound on your hip," said Potter. "How'd you get it?"

"Sliding down the mountain in a stream."

"Didn't anyone ever tell you mountain streams are full of rocks?"

"Yeah, but mountain paths are full of armed Bortellites. At least, *this* mountain's paths."

"What the hell are they doing on Rapunzel anyway? One day we'd never seen a Bug-Eye, and suddenly we turn around and there are hundreds of 'em, maybe thousands. Damned arrogant bastards, too. I sure as hell don't remember anyone inviting them."

"They've got an energy-poor planet. I think they're here to swipe some from yours."

"Swipe? You mean buy?"

"I meant what I said."

"That sounds like an act of war to me."

"We *are* at war."

"Not with them," said Potter. "They're neutral."

"Not anymore," replied Cole. "They joined the Teroni Federation a week ago."

"And you're here to throw 'em off the planet?"

"You see anyone with me?" asked Cole with an ironic smile.

"We'll pass the word and throw 'em off ourselves," said Potter.

Cole shook his head. "They've got a warship parked on the other side of the planet that could destroy Rapunzel in seconds."

"Then what are we supposed to do?" demanded Potter. "Just sit around and let them run roughshod over us?"

"I'm working on it."

"Looks like *they've* been working on *you*," said Potter. He finished working on the hip and turned his attention to Cole's left shin, then the right knee and ankle. Finally he stood up. "Okay, you won't die before you get to Pinocchio. Not from *these* wounds, anyway."

"Let's go."

"You're sure you don't want something to eat?"

"I don't like fish." Pause. "You got a beer?"

"I don't drink."

"Then, like I said, let's go. Take the rifle with you. Have you got a second gun?"

"Got a burner, but it's in the shop," answered Potter. "It was draining power from the battery pack, and I couldn't figure out why."

"All right. We'll make do with what we've got." Cole walked out the door and circled the cabin, then came to a stop in front of a small aircar. "You think *that* can carry both of us?" he asked dubiously.

"It carried me and a five-hundred-pound horndevil to the taxidermist in Pinocchio."

"I'm sure it did," said Cole. "I'm also sure you tied the horndevil to the hood."

"You've been spending too much time in space," said Potter, getting into the vehicle. "Watch."

He uttered a command, and the left side of the vehicle suddenly transformed itself into a sidecar. "Hop in and we'll be on our way."

"I never saw one of these before," admitted Cole.

"I'm surprised your military vehicles don't all have 'em."

"We don't do much fighting on the ground."

"You also don't do much fighting on the Rim. Do you plan to change that?"

"It's not up to me," answered Cole as the aircar began skimming two feet above the ground. "I just go where they send me."

"Then what's all this crap about you don't fight on the ground and you only go where they send you? You're *here*, aren't you?"

"Let me qualify that," said Cole. "I just go where they *should* send me."

"Now, *that* sounds more like the Wilson Cole I've heard about," said Potter. "What are you going to do when you get to Pinocchio? Lead a revolt?"

"And get fifty thousand Men killed? Don't be silly."

"Well, then, what *do* you plan to do?"

"Hide."

"You could have hidden at my cabin."

"Yeah, I suppose so."

"But you didn't want to," continued Potter. "There's something in Pinocchio you want. You're joining up with some secret force, right?"

Cole shook his head. "You've been reading too much cheap fiction. I told you: all I'm going to do is hide."

"There's a huge cache of weapons in Pinocchio," guessed Potter.

"If there is, I don't know anything about it."

"If you're not going to fight," said Potter, "what the hell are you doing here?"

"Running away from the enemy."

"Okay, it's a secret plan and you don't trust me," said Potter in hurt tones. "I can accept that."

"Look," said Cole. "I don't have any secrets from anyone. When we get to Pinocchio I'm going to send one radio message—"

"To the Fleet?"

"No, it'll be to someone on the planet. Then I'm going to make a vidphone call, and then I'm going to find some place to hide."

"For how long?"

"Not very."

"Then what?"

"Then, if things go the way they should, I'll rejoin the *Theodore Roosevelt* and go back on patrol."

"You're on the *Roosevelt?*" said Potter. "You must have got someone pretty high up really mad at you."

"A lot of someones," replied Cole wryly.

"I'll start pointing out the sights to you as soon as there are some," offered Potter. "But the landscape stays like this for another forty miles or so."

"That being the case," said Cole, "I think I'll shut my eyes and take a little nap. Wake me when there's anything interesting to see."

"You got it."

It seemed to Cole that he had only closed his eyes for a few seconds when he felt Potter gently shaking him by the one section of his right arm that wasn't covered with cuts and bruises.

"We're there."

"Where?" asked Cole, blinking his eyes rapidly. "Is there something to see?"

"We're in Pinocchio," said Potter. "You look like you needed the sleep."

Cole looked around and found that they were in the center of town, surrounded by office buildings for two or three blocks in each direction.

"Where's the nearest subspace sending station?" he asked.

"Almost all these big buildings have one," said Potter. "Take your choice."

They got out of the aircar, and Cole walked into the closest building.

A robotic doorman directed him to the subspace station, where a white-haired woman looked up from her desk as he approached.

"Good afternoon," said Cole. "I want to send a message."

"Booth Three is empty. Just walk into it, wait until it matches your thumbprint and retina against your credit account, and then tell it where you want your message to go."

"This is military business," said Cole.

"Fine. Show me your ID and we'll charge the government."

"I don't have any ID with me."

"Then you'll have to pay."

"I'm in uniform."

"I can buy a much better uniform down the street, and I've never been in the military."

Suddenly Potter spoke up. "It's all right," he said. "You can bill my account."

"Then you'll have to go into the booth with him," said the woman.

"I understand."

"There's another problem," said Cole.

She gave him an annoyed look. "What now?"

"I want this to go on the broadest possible wavelength, and I want it aimed not into space but at the mountain range that's to the southwest of here, and also at the spaceport on the other side of the planet."

"Then you don't want to make a subspace transmission at all," she said irritably.

"Yes, I do," replied Cole. "It will be received by a starship and a shuttlecraft of alien design. I know they can receive a subspace transmission; I don't know if they can receive anything else."

She frowned, pulled a manual up on a holoscreen, scanned through it, and finally froze a page. She took a small slip of paper and wrote a four-digit number on it, then pushed it across her desk toward Cole.

"That's the subspace bandwidth you want," she said coldly. "Now, is there anything else you need, or can I get back to work?"

"Now that you mention it, there's one more thing," said Cole. "Can I route this message through a series of stations on nearby planets and then have it beamed back to Rapunzel so that the recipients can't trace it to its source?"

"Given enough time every message is traceable, but I'll program Booth Three to bounce it back and forth between some nearby Republic worlds before sending it back."

"Thank you."

"You're sure that's all?"

"I'm sorry to have taken up so much of your time."

"We're here to serve," she said in automatic, bored tones, already concentrating on her computer again.

Cole and Potter went to Booth Three, where Potter immediately got his credit certified.

"It's just as well you're here," said Cole. "I probably need a witness. But it means you're going to have to go into hiding, too. I don't want them killing you for an act of friendship."

"Just do whatever it is you have to do and don't worry about me. Not only is this the most fun I've had in years, but I have the feeling that if I stick near you, I may get the chance to avenge my daughters."

Cole followed the instructions he found in the booth, then sent his message through a T-pack so that it came out in an unidentifiable mechanical monotone: "We understand that Wilson Cole is your prisoner. Will you allow him safe passage off the planet to return to his ship?" Cole deactivated the T-pack and leaned back on his chair. "It'll take a couple of minutes to reach them, and probably just as long to get the message back to me."

"Waste of time," said Potter. "You know what they're going to say—that you're an escaped prisoner and they refuse to give you safe passage to leave Rapunzel."

"I know. I just want to make it a matter of record."

And five minutes later it became a matter of record, when the Bortellites, demanding to know who was making the transmission, unequivocally stated that Wilson Cole was a military spy and under no circumstances would he be allowed to leave the planet.

"Very good," said Cole after breaking the connection. "Now let's find a vidphone."

"Right down the hall," said Potter, pointing them out.

Cole walked up to the closest one, then turned to Potter again.

"I know," said Potter. "No money or ID, right?"

"Right. But before you pay for it, tell me the name of the biggest news organization on the planet—video, disk, holocube, I don't care which."

"The biggest is probably the Francesco Organization. But we've also got a division of New Sumatra News here. It's not very big on Rapunzel, but if you add all their outlets together they reach a couple of hundred planets."

"That's the one I want. Get them on the vidphone for me."

Potter went through the same verification procedure again, then contacted the New Sumatra News offices and stepped aside so that Cole could sit in front of the camera and speak to them.

"I want the news desk," he said.

"City, planetary, or interstellar?"

"I don't care. Just put me in touch with a competent reporter. I've got a breaking story here."

A moment later a young woman's face appeared. "This is Cynthia Duvall. How can I help you."

"Cynthia, I don't have any ID with me, but I want you to take a good look at my face. I can also transmit a fingerprint if you want."

"Why would I want that?"

"To verify my identity."

"I thought you were calling in a news story. At least, that's what I was told."

"You were told correctly. I *am* the story. My name is Wilson Cole."

Her eyes widened. "Stay right there!" she said excitedly. A moment later a man and another woman were standing beside her, staring into the screen at their end of the connection.

"It's him, all right," said the second woman.

"Yeah, I'll vouch for it," said the man. "I've done half a dozen stories on him over the years. What are you doing here, Captain Cole?"

"*Commander* Cole," Cole corrected him. "I must ask you to please not attempt to trace this transmission to its source. I am currently in hiding from the Bortellites, who captured me early yesterday. I managed to escape, but they have stated that they have no intention of allowing me to leave Rapunzel."

"What were you doing here?"

"That's classified information."

"Why are you in contact with *us*?"

"This is a Republic world, and I'm a Republic naval officer being hunted by enemies of the Republic. That's news, and you're newspeople. I've got to run. Please don't try to find me. My life depends on it."

He broke the transmission.

"All right," he said to Potter. "Now we get the hell out of the building, because of course they'll trace the transmission and they'll have someone here in five minutes."

"Where do you want to go?"

"Out to the suburbs somewhere. You'll need to get some cash along the way; we don't want them tracing credit transactions. We'll rent a place for a few days, maybe a week at most."

"Why not just go to my place?"

"By now they know you paid for the transmission. That's the first place they'll look."

"All right, the suburbs it is," said Potter. "Then maybe you'll tell me what the hell this was all about."

"I serve under a couple of rigid, by-the-book officers," said Cole. "They're going to believe that I exceeded my orders when I took a shuttle-craft to Rapunzel after I saw enemy activity here, and they're never going to risk a military engagement with the Bortellites on their own authority, even though Bortel II has just joined the Teroni Federation. If we wait for decisions to come down through channels, the Bortellites will finish plundering that mountain range and leave the planet. And since we're at war, they might very well poison the air or the water when they're done. So we're going to put a little pressure on the Navy to do the right thing."

"Just by speaking to the press?"

"Right now almost no one knows that Bortel II is no longer neutral, or that they've got military personnel on Rapunzel. But by tomorrow hundreds of worlds will know that they're here, that they captured me when I landed, that I escaped and I'm hiding somewhere on the planet, and that they've stated that they will not let me leave Rapunzel. By tomorrow night quite a few million people are going to want to know why the Navy is not doing everything within its power to rescue the most decorated officer in the Fleet. The Navy, being the Navy, will ignore the pressure for a day or two, but that will just make it build until, against their will and their better judgment, they are forced to do the right thing."

"You really think it'll work?"

Cole smiled. "I *know* it'll work. They don't give a damn about saving me, they may not even care with happens to a strategically unimportant little world like Rapunzel—but believe me, they'll do whatever they have to do to save their image."

They found a nice, nondescript house for rent in the middle of an unmemorable residential area. Potter paid for a month's rent with cash, they bought enough food to hold them for seven days, Cole bought some civilian clothes, and then they left the aircar in a private underground garage and took public transportation to their new living quarters.

"Ugly as sin," remarked Potter as they began filling the kitchen cabinets with food and disposable dishes and utensils. "And small."

"You ought to try living on a starship someday," said Cole with a smile.

"I don't know how you keep from going crazy, being cooped up on one of those ships for months, maybe years."

"You work long hours," answered Cole as he changed clothes. "You do everything you can to keep occupied and not dwell upon the fact that while you may be flying all over the galaxy, your personal universe is two hundred and sixty-three feet long, forty-four feet wide, and from five to seven levels deep." He tossed his tattered uniform into the kitchen atomizer, eliminating all trace of it.

"I thought they were bigger than that."

"They are—much bigger. But the rest of it is taken up by the FTL drive and the weaponry." Cole smiled wistfully. "You don't know how we envy those luxury liners with their pools and gymnasiums and dance floors."

"They cost an arm and a leg, and probably an eyeball or two," noted Potter.

"Serve even one month on a military ship and then tell me you wouldn't pay it."

They put the last of their packages away. "We should have rented one with a robot butler," said Potter. "One that could cook and clean up after us."

Cole shook his head. "Robots are expensive."

"I told you: I've got nothing to spend it on."

"You're not following me," said Cole. "We took this dump because it *is* a dump. The rental agency knew it: they took cash and didn't ask for any ID. You rent a place with a robot, you're going to have to put at least a thousand credits in escrow, and they won't return it until they check the robot out at the end of your stay."

"So?"

"Do you have a thousand credits in your pocket?" asked Cole.

"All right, I see your point. If I give them anything but cash, it can be traced." He paused. "But do the Bug-Eyes know enough to trace it?"

"They won't have to," said Cole. "The media will trace it and camp outside, waiting for a statement or a holo, and the Bortellites will just follow them."

"I hadn't thought of that."

"No reason why you should have. You've never run for your life before."

"What's it like?"

"It's not as exciting as bad books and worse entertainments would lead you to believe. If it works, it's boring as hell, and if it doesn't work, you *wish* it was boring as hell."

Potter looked around the house again. "I guess we're in the boring part," he said.

"Just hope it stays that way."

"Well," said Potter, "there's one way to find out."

He activated the holoscreen, which formed one entire wall of the parlor. A documentary about the rare life-forms on the planet Peponi seemed to fill the room.

"News," he ordered.

"Headlines or in-depth?" replied the holo.

"Headlines."

"Cole in hiding on Rapunzel!" blared the voice. "Parliament takes up tax bill. Blasters defeat Ramparts in overtime."

"Stop."

The voice was silent.

"Give me more coverage of the Cole story."

"Condensed or in-depth?"

"Condensed to begin with."

"Wilson Cole, the most decorated officer in the Republic's military, is known to be on Rapunzel. In an exclusive interview with the New Sumatra News Agency, Cole claimed that he is being hunted by soldiers from Bortel II, which he claims has recently declared its allegiance to the Teroni Federation. He further claims that these same Bortellites have threatened to kill him if he tries to leave the planet. Attempts to locate Commander Cole or authenticate his claims are ongoing . . ."

"Claims, claims, claims!" snapped Potter. "They make you sound like a liar!"

"*They* don't know that Bortellites aren't here as a neutral power; *you* do. More to the point, the *Navy* does. This is local news now, but within a few hours someone on some other planet's newsdesk is going to notice my name, and then all hell is going to break loose." He allowed himself the luxury of a smile. "Poor Mount Fuji. I've been on the *Teddy R* less than one day, and suddenly he's going to find himself in a shooting war."

"Mount Fuji?"

"Captain Makeo Fujiama," said Cole. "He's the captain of the *Theodore Roosevelt*."

"Will you now require in-depth coverage of the story?" inquired the holo.

"No," said Cole. He turned to Potter. "They're just going to say the same thing with a lot more adverbs and adjectives."

"Probably," agreed Potter. "Get back to Mount Fuji. Why is he the captain of a starship if he's afraid to fight the enemy?"

"He's not afraid," answered Cole. "You don't get command of a starship if you're a coward. But he won't see any reason to risk his ship just because I exceeded my orders."

"Did you?"

"I don't think so—but I'll give plenty of twenty-to-one that *he* thinks I did."

"What if he's not interested in public opinion?"

"I'm sure he couldn't care less about it—but somebody higher up has got to have political ambitions. Give it a day or two to build and—*shit!*"

"What is it?" asked Potter.

"Look at the screen."

A large aircar, with all kinds of transmitting equipment attached to the roof, was shown traveling through the suburbs of Pinocchio. It came to a stop in front of a plain-looking house.

"They're here!" exclaimed Potter. "That's *this* house!"

"Let's go out the back," said Cole, already heading to the back door.

They ran across the small yard and raced between two neighboring houses. They hadn't quite made it to the street when they heard the explosion.

"What the hell was that?" asked Potter, stopping.

"Don't slow down. I'll tell you what it was once we're out of here."

He reached the street and flagged down a passing aircar.

"We need a ride," he said as the car came to a stop and hovered above the pavement. "There's two hundred credits in it for you if you'll take us back into the city."

"I won't take money to help Wilson Cole," said the driver. "Get in fast!"

"You know me?" asked Cole as he and Potter piled into the back of the aircar.

"Your holo is plastered everywhere," said the driver. "Did that explosion over on the next block have something to do with you?"

"Yeah," said Cole. "They found us sooner than I figured they would."

"How?" asked Potter.

"The newspeople must have traced your vehicle, then checked to see if anyone had rented a place in the last few hours. The Bortellites just followed the media." Cole grimaced. "I thought they'd have to spend a couple of days finding the damned aircar. I guess they put out a reward for information. I'd be a lot more annoyed at those reporters if they hadn't died for their trouble."

"Where am I taking you to, Captain Cole?"

"I'm not a captain," answered Cole. "Has Pinocchio got a slum?"

"Afraid not," replied the driver. "It's not all upscale, but it's all clean and safe." He paused. "There's a military outpost south of town. Do you want me to take you there?"

"No. Just drive us through the city. I'll tell you where to stop."

"What's wrong with getting dropped off at a Republic outpost?" asked Potter.

"I don't want to put myself in a position where they can give me orders just yet. I've got to remain flexible as long as I'm on Rapunzel."

"If you want to organize a militia, I'll volunteer," said the driver. "So will almost everyone I know."

"Here I am, doing my damnedest to stay alive, and you're lining up to get killed," said Cole. "I appreciate your courage and your patriotism, but there's a Bortellite warship on the planet that can destroy anything you throw against it in seconds."

"Why are they after you?"

"Initially to keep me quiet," answered Cole. "Now it's just retaliation because I've alerted the planet to their new status as members of the Teroni Federation."

"I heard the newscasts," said the driver. "There were all kinds of qualifications and a lot of hedging about that."

"That's probably because someone in your government made a sweetheart deal with them, and doesn't want to end it just because they've joined the enemy."

"Do you know that for a fact?" asked the driver sharply.

"No, but it figures. Probably most of your leaders are good, moral, God-fearing men and woman—but it only takes one to sell you out to the enemy."

"Well, it seems to me if the Bortellites heard it, they'll be out of here before any Navy ships arrive."

"I don't think so," said Cole.

"Why not?"

"Rapunzel has something they desperately need," explained Cole. "They know if they leave without it they're never going to be allowed back."

"So they're just going to sit around and wait for the Fleet to show up?"

"I don't know what they're going to do," admitted Cole. "They're just dumb enough to think I'd make a good hostage—my life for what they want." He chuckled ironically. "As if the Navy cares."

"I'm still trying to figure out how they found us so fast," said Potter.

"Once the press found out that you paid for my subspace message, everything followed logically," said Cole. "That was *our* mistake. *Theirs* was not figuring that the Bortellites would be watching them."

"The war hasn't reached Rapunzel," said Potter. "None of us are used to thinking like that."

"As long as you're on the run from a common enemy, why don't the two of you stay at my place?" offered the driver.

"You got any family?" asked Cole.

"A wife and three kids."

"Thanks for the offer, but there's no sense endangering five of you."

"It's no trouble."

"Forget it."

"It's my duty," said the man stubbornly.

"I'll tell you what," said Cole. "Contact your wife and tell her you plan to harbor a man that every Bortellite on the planet is hunting. Ask her if she's willing to trade the lives of your three children for mine. If she says yes, we'll take you up on your offer."

"She'll probably turn the security system up to lethal before we get there," answered the driver. "But I've got to do *something*. We're at war. I can't just turn my back on a man the enemy is hunting."

"You can do something," said Cole. "What's the closest city to Pinocchio? Not a suburb, but a city?"

"Cinnamon, about forty miles north."

"God, who named these places?" said Cole. "All right. Once you drop us off, wait twenty minutes, long enough for us to get off the street and out of sight. Then contact all the major news organizations and tell them you spotted us heading toward Cinnamon." He paused. "No! Wait a minute. It's going to take them an hour or more to determine that we weren't in the explosion. Let's get them off my back for as long as possible. Wait until you hear a report on any of the newscasts that there was no trace of us and they don't know what happened to us. Then pass the word to the press."

"Can't I do anything more?"

"Believe me, if you do that, that'll be plenty," Cole assured him.

They rode in silence for a few more minutes.

"Say when and where," offered the driver as they approached the center of Pinocchio.

"Here and now," said Cole.

The vehicle came to a stop and gently lowered itself to the pavement. Cole reached forward and shook the driver's hand.

"It's been a privilege meeting you," said the driver. "If you need any help in the future, just ask for—"

"*NO!*" shouted Cole so sharply that the driver and Potter both jumped.

"What is it?"

"If I don't know your name, no one can force it out of me," explained Cole. He turned to Potter. "By the same token, don't look back at the vehicle. We don't want to know its ID or any identifying marks." Then, to the driver: "Thanks for your help. Try to make that call in a way that can't be traced. Then forget you ever met us."

He got out of the vehicle and began walking. Potter fell into step behind him.

"Where to?" asked Potter.

"Off the street," answered Cole. "I may have dumped the uniform, but like he said, my face is plastered all the hell over."

They ducked into an office building, and Cole called up the directory on a holoscreen.

"There's an office for rent on the fifteenth floor," said Cole, "and there have to be janitor's quarters somewhere, probably in the basement. That'll do until it's dark, but it won't work on a permanent basis. We're going to need food, and there doesn't seem to be anything resembling a cafeteria or a restaurant in the building."

"I know they went after you out in the suburbs," said Potter, "but would they really attack you in the heart of the city?"

"They just wiped out a news crew, probably while it was broad-casting," answered Cole. "Just how secret do you think they're keeping their allegiance to the Teroni Federation now?"

They took an airlift to the fifteenth floor. The door to the empty office was unlocked. They entered, closed the door, and sat down.

"What now?" asked Potter.

"Now we wait long enough for them to find out we're still alive and for our saviour to feed them that phony story about Cinnamon."

"Damn!" said Potter suddenly. "We left in such a hurry I forgot to grab my sonic rifle. I never thought of it until just now."

"If you're going to regret leaving something behind, regret the food."

"I'm not hungry."

"Neither am I—but we're going to be, and we're going to have to show our faces to get anything to eat."

"I could get it and bring it to you."

"You're not used to being on the run, are you?" said Cole. "They didn't trace *me* to the rental unit. They traced *you*. They know what you look like by now."

"But that's the media, not the Bug-Eyes."

"Do you really think the media isn't getting all the mileage they can out of this?" responded Cole. "By now your image will be on every newsdisk and holo channel on the planet."

"But they're Men!" protested Potter. "They wouldn't help the enemy!"

"When did a little thing like giving aid and comfort to the enemy ever stop the media?" answered Cole. "We'll stay up here until it's closing time, then go downstairs before we bump into the robot cleaning crew. Who knows what kind of alarm they're programmed to sound if they find someone in an office that's supposed to be for rent?"

An hour later the offices on the floor began emptying out. They waited until the last of them was closed and locked so that no one would see them leaving and report them, then took an airlift back down to the ground floor. Cole began looking for another airlift or even a staircase to the basement. The lobby was crowded, and he found himself the recipient of quite a few curious stares.

Then, suddenly, an alien voice filtered through a T-pack broke the silence.

"Don't move, Wilson Cole!" said the mechanical monotone. "Keep your hands in plain view."

The crowd parted, and a single Bortellite, armed with a Teroni pulse rifle, strode forward from the building's entrance.

"The others thought you were on your way to Cinnamon," he said, "but you've already escaped us once and tricked us again. I knew you would be in the least likely place of all—the middle of Pinocchio." He waved the rifle at the crowd. "I will kill anyone who tries to hinder me. This man is an escaped prisoner, and I am taking him away with me."

"The hell you are!" shouted a voice, and Cole heard the hum of a burner. He couldn't spot who had the laser pistol, but the Bortellite's rifle turned red-hot and he had to drop it. The second he did so he vanished beneath an outraged crowd of men and women who pummeled him mercilessly until what was left was hardly recognizable.

"I never did like Bug-Eyes," said a woman, dusting herself off. "Ugly creatures."

"If Bortel II wants a war, we'll give them one!" said another.

Then a tall man, the butt of his laser pistol visible where he had tucked it into his belt, walked up to Cole.

"I'm sorry, sir," he said. "I don't know why the hell he thought you were Wilson Cole. Everyone knows Cole is stationed near the Core."

"I heard he'd taken a desk job on Deluros VIII," volunteered a woman.

"Well, wherever he is, he's sure as hell not on Rapunzel," said another woman. "I don't know where the Bortellite got that crazy idea."

"Someone get the cleanup crew here and get rid of this mess," said a middle-aged man, dabbing at his bloody knuckles with a white handkerchief. "We wouldn't want the police closing the building down for a sanitation violation."

"Let's break this up and go home before we attract any more undesirables," said a third woman. She turned to Cole. "You look like a stranger in town, sir. I'd be happy to give you a sample of Rapunzel hospitality and take you and your friend home for dinner."

"So would I," echoed a man, and soon almost everyone in the lobby was inviting Cole and Potter to their homes.

"I appreciate all your offers," said Cole at last. "But you've done enough already. I wouldn't want to get any of you in trouble—with your spouses," he added with a sardonic smile.

"Then come with me," said the first woman. "I haven't got a spouse."

"It could be very dangerous," Cole said seriously.

"What's a little danger compared to what a military officer, for example, faces every day?" she replied.

Cole shrugged. "Then I thank you, and we accept your invitation."

"I live in the city and take public transportation," she said. "You never know what kind of nasty passengers you might run into, and we want to make a good impression on our guest. Perhaps someone will volunteer to convey us to my place?"

She was overwhelmed with offers, chose one, and a moment later a small balding man pulled up and hovered right outside the entrance to the building. Cole, Potter, and the woman got in, and he raced off instantly.

It took them about five minutes to get to her building—she lived on the seventh floor—and a few minutes later Cole was enjoying his first meal since Potter's cabin.

"You two go to sleep," said the woman when they'd finished eating and adjourned to the parlor. She sat down by a window that overlooked the street. "I'll keep watch."

"You'll wake me the instant you see anything unusual—Bortellites or anything else?"

"I promise."

He turned to Potter. "You take the guest room. I'm sleeping here on the couch."

"There's room for both of you in there," said the woman.

"If anything happens, I can be ready a few seconds sooner if I sleep right here."

She shrugged. "Have it your way, Mr. Smith."

Cole looked at her for a long minute. "You're good people here on Rapunzel. If I were an officer in the Navy, I'd be goddamned proud to serve folks like you."

Potter went off to the bedroom. Cole was going to stay up and talk to the woman, but the accumulated weariness suddenly hit him. *I'll just close my eyes for minute, just to rest them*, he told himself. *Then we'll visit for a bit. It's the least I can do for a woman who's risking her life for me.*

The next thing he knew she was gently shaking him awake. He glanced out the window. It was still dark.

He jumped to his feet. "Where are they?" he said. "Are they on this floor yet? How many did you see?"

She smiled. "Relax, Captain Cole. It's all over. In fact, I can even tell you my name now. It's Samantha."

"What's going on?" he asked, confused.

"It's all over the holos," she said. "The Navy attacked while you were asleep. They destroyed the Bortellites' warship, killed about a hundred of them on the mountain, and the rest have surrendered, both the ones on the mountain and those here in the city." She paused. "The only reason I woke you is that the Navy has announced that this entire operation has been for the sole purpose of rescuing you, so I contacted the authorities and told them to inform the Navy they can find you here." She smiled at him. "I thought it might make a better impression if you were awake when they arrived."

"Thank you."

"I suppose they'll be sending an honor guard for you," said Samantha.

"I'll just bet," muttered Cole.

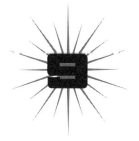

Cole sat in the outer office, cooling his heels, for almost an hour. It was designed, he was sure, to make him nervous, but it served only to make him irritated.

He was aboard the *Xerxes*, the flagship of the Fleet, which had just arrived on the Rim fifteen hours ago. It was a hell of a vessel, he decided. It could easily have swallowed up half a dozen *Theodore Roosevelt*s, and it was immaculate. The weaponry was state-of-the-art, the appointments and furnishings were top-of-the-line, and somehow he knew that not a single speck of dirt would dare to take up residence on the *Xerxes*.

He glanced at the wall. There was a holo of John Ramsey, considered the greatest Secretary of the Republic, plus smaller holos of the last five Admirals of the Fleet, the predecessors to the woman sitting in the office behind the closed door. He looked at the lieutenant sitting at the desk opposite him; the young man smiled.

"You got anything to read?" asked Cole.

"I am afraid not, Commander."

"Coffee?"

"You can get some in the mess hall after your meeting," he replied.

"I may be too weak from hunger and thirst to make it to the mess hall by then."

"Relax, Commander," said the lieutenant. "She'll see you soon." A light flashed on his desk. "In fact, she'll see you right now."

Cole stood up, waited for the door to iris, then stepped through into Fleet Admiral Susan Garcia's office. It would have been small by planetary standards, but for a spaceship it was immense, almost fifteen feet on a side, with a ceiling a full eight feet high. Seated behind a large desk made of alien hardwoods that floated just above the floor was the Admiral, a striking woman in her midforties, with coal black hair, piercing dark eyes, a firm mouth, and a rather pointed chin.

She stared at him coldly for a moment. "Have you injured your hand, Mr. Cole," she said, "or have you merely forgotten how to salute?"

He snapped off a salute.

"Well, Mr. Cole," said the Fleet Admiral, "you seem to have done it again."

"Ma'am?"

"Who told you that you could take a shuttlecraft and two officers from the *Theodore Roosevelt* and go to Rapunzel on your own authority?"

"I was the officer in command at the time, ma'am," answered Cole. "The Officer on Deck spotted a Bortellite warship approaching Rapunzel. Rapunzel is a Republic world, and Bortel II declaired its allegiance to the Teroni Federation within the past month. Under those circumstances, I felt it was my duty to find out what the Bortellites were doing on the planet."

"Did that include leaving the shuttle once you had landed, and confronting a force of two hundred of the enemy?"

"Aren't officers supposed to use their initiative?" asked Cole.

"Not really," she replied. "Somebody else usually has to pay for it."

"I'll keep that in mind in the future, ma'am."

"Oh, shut up, Mr. Cole!" she said irritably.

He stood at attention and waited for her to continue.

"Why did you alert the local press to your situation?" she said at last.

"There were enemy soldiers on their world. I thought they had the right to know."

"They knew there were Bortellites on Rapunzel long before you did, Mr. Cole." She glared at him, barely able to contain her anger. "You did it because you knew word would get out and that public pressure would become so great that the Navy would have to respond, didn't you?"

"Certainly not, ma'am," he said. "In wartime every man is expendable, and no man is irreplaceable."

"You lie with grace and style, Mr. Cole," she said. "Please don't insult my intelligence by continuing to do so."

"Ma'am, I assure you—"

"Stop it, Mr. Cole," she said. "You really and truly do not want me as an enemy. Now cut the crap and tell me, briefly and succinctly, why you did what you did."

"Yes, ma'am," said Cole. "I saw a potentially dangerous situation and I responded to it."

"Why didn't you alert Captain Fujiama?"

"He was asleep, ma'am."

"And you didn't think an enemy warship approaching a Republic planet was important enough to wake him?"

Cole stared at her for a moment, as if making up his mind how frank to be. Finally he spoke. "Ma'am, you and I both know that neither Captain Fujiama nor Commander Podok would have approved of risking the *Theodore Roosevelt* in such a situation. They would have pointed out that there could be ten more warships on the planet, just waiting for us. I knew what they'd say, so I took the shuttlecraft instead."

"And risked getting blown out of the ether by an infinitely more powerful ship."

"It wasn't much of a risk, ma'am," answered Cole. "The shuttle presented no threat to them, and they are far outnumbered here on the Rim. If they'd destroyed us, they could have counted on instant retaliation." She stared at him, an inscrutable expression on her face. "Well, *they* would have thought so, anyway," he amended.

"Go on, Mr. Cole."

"Once we touched down, I arranged safe passage away from the planet for Commander Forrice and Lieutenant Mboya, so no one was at risk except myself."

"They have been thoroughly debriefed, Mr. Cole, so I know exactly how you arranged their safe passage."

"Officers are taught to improvise in unique situations, ma'am."

"That's even more dangerous than using their initiative," she replied dryly. "Continue."

"After I escaped and made it to Pinocchio, I realized that the Bortellites had to be stopped before they accomplished their mission, so I arranged to let you know they were there."

"More to the point, you arranged to let tens of billions of Republic citizens know *you* were there and at risk, counting on the fact that they would insist we come to your rescue."

"I'm deeply moved that so many people care about me," said Cole. "But of course the Navy is not influenced by the emotional whims of the citizenry. I am certain that you attacked Rapunzel to prevent an enemy power from replenishing its vastly diminished energy resources."

She stared at him for another long moment. "Don't ever go into politics, Mr. Cole. I don't think the galaxy is ready for it."

"I have no interest in politics, ma'am," replied Cole. "My sole concern is doing whatever I can to help us defeat the Teroni Federation."

"That's probably true," said the Fleet Admiral. "And you know what? It still sounds like bullshit."

"I'm sorry you should think so, ma'am."

"Spare me your protests, Mr. Cole," she said. "You've managed to put the Navy on the spot, and not for the first time. It is my own belief that you were responsible, in large part, for my predecessor's early retirement." He was about to reply, but she held up a hand. "Don't say it, Mr. Cole." She signed deeply, opened a desk drawer, and pulled out a small box. "Have you any idea what's in this box?"

"No, ma'am, I haven't."

"I'll just bet," she said. "It's a Medal of Courage. Your fourth, I believe."

"Thank you, ma'am," said Cole. "I'm deepily honored."

"Personally, I'd much rather be demoting you than honoring you. But the press has got hold of this story, and the people need their heroes. So here I am, half a galaxy away from the *real* war, to give you a medal for what amounts to blatant insubordination. Whoever said war is hell lacked an appreciation of the ridiculous. War is lunacy." She put the box back in her drawer. "You will receive the medal at a public ceremony this afternoon. Try not to look *too* smug for the press."

"Where is the ceremony to be held?"

"On Rapunzel, of course. Captain Fujiama is also receiving a medal, and the entire crew of the *Theodore Roosevelt* will receive commendations." She paused. "Of course, neither the medal nor the commendations will mention the fact that they were forced into their heroic actions against their will, nor will it be noted that three warships were pulled away from strategically important positions to serve as backups to the *Roosevelt*. As for you, Commander, you'll remain on the *Xerxes* until it's time to land, and then you will go down on my personal shuttle."

"Under guard?" he asked wryly.

"In essence," she said seriously. "You will speak to no one, you will not mingle with the crowd before or after the ceremony, and you will memorize the acceptance speech that my staff has written for you. If you cause the Navy any embarrassment at all, I won't hesitate not only to demote you, but to put you in the brig. Look at my face and tell me if you think I'm kidding."

"I'm sure you're not, ma'am."

"You bet your troublemaking ass I'm not. Now get into your dress uniform and remember that as long as the press is around we're great friends."

"Easily done, ma'am."

"Oh, shut up, Mr. Cole," she said. "Neither of us has to pretend until this afternoon. You are dismissed."

He turned and left the Fleet Admiral's office. Only as he was taking the airlift to his temporary quarters did he remember that he had forgotten to salute.

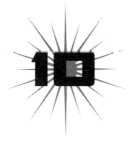

"Well, Ensign Marcos?" said Cole.

"You're supposed to ask permission to come aboard, sir," replied Rachel Marcos.

"I think we've been through this once before. The shuttlecraft is already a thousand miles away. Where else am I going to go?"

She shrugged. "Welcome aboard, sir." She shook his hand. "And thank you for my commendation."

"I believe we've done the hand-shaking as well," he said. "I assume I'm in the same quarters as before?"

"Certainly, sir. Where else would you be?"

"Oh, I don't know. The brig, maybe."

She laughed. "You have an interesting sense of humor, sir."

Let's hope Mount Fuji does, too, thought Cole. Aloud he said, "That's me—a barrel of laughs."

"By the way, the Captain wants to see you as soon as it's convenient."

"Right," said Cole. "I've got a few things to dump off in my cabin first."

She saluted. "I'm glad you're back, sir."

As he got off the airlift and started walking to his quarters, he passed Lieutenant Sokolov in the narrow corridor.

"Welcome back, Commander," said Sokolov. "The Captain's looking for you."

"Thanks," said Cole. He continued walking to his cabin, waited for the door to identify him and iris, and stepped inside. He put his dress uniform in the closet and placed his medal next to its three siblings in a dresser drawer.

There was a knock at the door. He ordered it to open and Forrice entered.

"I was glad when the word came down that you had survived," said the Molarian. "I wouldn't have given good odds on it the last time I saw you."

"It got a little hairy for a while there," replied Cole. "But what the hell—it goes with the job."

"Before I forget, Mount Fuji wants to see you."

"Jesus! Did he tell every member of the crew?"

"He probably wants to thank you for his medal." Forrice stared at him for a moment. "When you're done with him, I think you'd better go see Lieutenant Mboya."

"Oh?"

"You tried to give her a message, a code, something, on Rapunzel, and she missed it. She knows you were *trying* to tell her to do something, but she couldn't figure out what it was. She was sure she'd gotten you killed until we got the news that you had the whole planetary contingent of Bortellites after you. That's when I knew you'd be okay."

"All right, I'll speak to her and explain it wasn't her fault." He paused. "I tried to tell her what I wanted her to do when we staged that fight, but they pulled us apart before I could get it out. I knew if they thought I was giving her an order they'd never let her leave the planet, so I tried to give her a hint instead, something they couldn't spot. I guess I was too subtle."

"I was listening, too, and I never caught it," said Forrice. "What exactly were you trying to say?"

"I said something about headlines. I hoped she'd figure out I wanted her to go to the press, rather than the Navy. I knew by the next day that she'd missed it."

"I don't blame her for not spotting it," said the Molarian. "You just explained it to me, and I still can't see how it encourages her to go to the press."

"I used an anachronism," explained Cole. "They haven't printed the news on paper in centuries. There is no longer any such thing as a headline."

"Of course there is. It's the catchphrase that leads to a story."

"Okay, I could have used a better hint. But I only had about three seconds to come up with something the Bortellites couldn't understand."

"Well, you certainly did that," said Forrice with his equivalent of a smile. "Anyway, I'm glad you made it back. I hadn't realized how boring duty on the Rim could be until you got here and showed us what it *could* be."

"*I* didn't spot the warship," Cole pointed out. "Lieutenant Mboya did."

"You don't think for a minute we'd have taken any action at all if Mount Fuji or Podok had been in command?"

"Of course not," answered Cole. "But that doesn't mean I actively pursue confrontation with the enemy when I'm outgunned and outnumbered. I'd like to survive this war."

His computer suddenly came to life, and Sharon Blacksmith's image appeared before him.

"Welcome home, Wilson," she said. "You don't look any the worse for wear."

"I was only on the damned planet a couple of days," he replied.

"You'll have to tell me all about it later," she said. "But right now you're wanted in the Captain's cabin. He knows you're onboard."

"I'd hate to try to keep a secret on this ship," said Cole. He stood up. "All right. I'm on my way."

"I'll catch up with you later," said Forrice.

"You can walk me to the airlift."

"Well, I *was* planning to stay behind and steal your medals, but if you insist . . ."

"Why not make me a cash offer?" said Cole. "I'm sure we can come to an agreement."

"You sound like you mean it."

"I didn't join the Navy to accumulate medals. I came to beat the bad guys." He paused. "I still have hopes that there are more of them in the Teroni Federation than the Republic."

"And I always thought you were a realist," said Forrice.

They reached the airlift and parted company, and a moment later Cole was standing before Fujiama's door, waiting for it to scan his retina and skeletal structure. It opened a moment later. He entered and remembered to salute.

Makeo Fujiama was seated behind his desk. When Cole entered, he got to his feet, walked around the desk, and stood in front of Cole, towering almost a full foot above him.

"Before we discuss anything else, Commander Cole, I want to express my gratitude for the medal and citation I have been awarded and for which I suspect you were responsible."

Why tell him that all the medals were a surprise to me? It never hurts to have a superior officer feeling obligated to you.

"You certainly deserve it, sir."

"I am very proud of this medal, and indeed of the *Theodore Roosevelt*'s performance in the recently concluded action."

"As well you should be, sir."

"I wanted to say that on the front end, so that I wouldn't forget it," said Fujiama. "Now suppose you tell me just what the hell you thought you were doing, taking a shuttlecraft against an enemy warship without a direct order from me!"

"I didn't dare risk the *Theodore Roosevelt*, sir, so I took the shuttlecraft, which I assumed was expendable, and manned it with only myself and two volunteers."

"You didn't answer me, Mr. Cole. Why did you take action without informing your superior officer?"

"When you and Commander Podok are off duty and I am in command of the bridge, I have no superior officer," responded Cole.

"Read your Naval Regulations, Mr. Cole!" snapped Fujiama. "You must clear extraordinary actions with the Captain of the vessel."

"I have read them," said Cole. "And they state that when it is impractical, such as a case of hot pursuit or sudden enemy fire, I am to use my best judgment and take what I consider the proper actions."

"What hot pursuit?" demanded Fujiama. "The damned Bortellite ship had already landed on Rapunzel before you ever entered the *Kermit*!"

"If the Bortellites were planning a surprise attack on the citizens of Rapunzel, speed was of the essence."

"If they were planning an attack, they wouldn't have landed a ship that could vaporize the world from orbit but couldn't carry an attack force of four hundred armed soldiers."

"You're absolutely right, sir," said Cole. "I guess that's why you're the Captain and I'm just the Second Officer."

"Spare me your glib, facile answers, Mr. Cole," said Fujiama. "The *Roosevelt*'s an old ship, old and tired. It has no business facing a modern warship. Don't you realize what you might have done?"

"The truth, sir?"

"It would be a pleasant change."

"All right," said Cole. "What I might have done was stay where I was and report the Bortellite ship to Sector Command, which would have relayed the information to headquarters on Deluros VIII, which is more than half the galaxy away and busy directing a shooting war. Then I would have hoped that by the time my report wended its way through channels and the Republic finally decided to take action—which we both know is a highly problematic decision—there would be Men left alive to save on Rapunzel." He paused. "That's what I might have done. What I *did* do was prevent an enemy power from establishing a foothold on a Republic world and keep them from replenishing their rapidly diminishing power supply. I alerted the Republic to the situation and let you take out the warship while it was a sitting duck on the ground—and I did all that without the loss of a single human life. I understand why the Teroni Federation wants me dead. What I don't understand is why my superior officers seem to share that desire."

"Sit down, Mr. Cole," said Fujiama, indicating a chair.

"I'd prefer to stand, sir."

"Sit down, goddammit!" bellowed Fujiama.

Cole sat down.

"I know what you think of me, Mr. Cole, and I can guess what you think of the *Theodore Roosevelt*." He hovered over Cole, glaring down at him. "Let me assure you that there are no cowards aboard this ship. What we have are a bunch of embittered fuck-ups who are serving their penance out here on the Rim. That little contretemps you precipitated on Rapunzel is the closest we've been to the war in four years. None of us signed up to guard a bunch of underpopulated worlds that the enemy couldn't care less about—but as long as Sector Command can't count on us to obey orders, here is where we'll stay. Now do you understand the reason for this interview, Mr. Cole?"

"Yes, sir," said Cole. "I do, and I must admit I hadn't considered the situation in that light. But I took an oath to protect the Republic and harass and harry the enemy, and nothing in that oath allows me to pick my spots."

"Well spoken," said Fujiama. "But part of your oath includes obeying orders and respecting the chain of command, and that is the part you have consistently ignored throughout your career. I don't want it ignored again. I am sick of being *here* when the war is *there*. The Men and aliens on this ship have served their time in the boondocks; they deserve to get back into the fray." He frowned. "The idiocy is that you represent our very best chance of accomplishing that goal. If the press and the people wouldn't let you die on Rapunzel, they're not going to be happy about keeping you out on the Rim when the war is fifty thousand light-years away. So as distasteful as it is, we're going to have to reach an accommodation."

"You don't like me very much, do you?" asked Cole curiously.

"Does that bother you, Mr. Cole?"

"Not really, though of course I'd rather be liked."

"The truth of the matter is that I don't know you well enough to like or dislike you," answered Fujiama. "What I do is fear and envy you. I envy your achievements and your ability to impose your will on extraordinary situations; and I fear what that ability can do to my ship and my future. Is that honest enough for you?"

"Yes, sir, it is," said Cole.

"Is there anything else you wish to say to me?"

"No, sir."

"Now that we understand each other, may I have your promise that you will not put the *Roosevelt*, its shuttlecraft, or any of its personnel at hazard without first informing me?"

"Yes, sir," said Cole. "Now that we understand each other, I will take no such action without first informing you."

"I have a feeling you are playing semantic games with me. I hope you're not, because I am not playing any game when I say that should you break your promise I will not hesitate to relieve you of command and confine you to your quarters for the duration of our tour of duty on the Rim."

"I believe you, sir," said Cole.

"You'd better." Fujiama stared at him for a long moment. "Is our conversation concluded?"

"Yes, sir, it is," said Cole.

Fujiama walked to a cabinet and waved his hand in front of it. The door vanished, and he pulled out a half-empty bottle of Cygnian cognac and two glasses. "Then let's have a drink and try to maintain the illusion of camaraderie."

"Sounds good to me, sir," said Cole, accepting a glass and wondering how long the illusion would last.

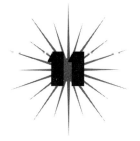

Cole was lying comfortably on his bunk, reading a book on his computer, when the book vanished and Sharon Blacksmith's image appeared.

"You busy?" she asked.

"Do I look busy?"

"Spare me your sardonicism," she said. "New orders just came through. You're going to hear about them anyway, but since I suspect you're responsible for them, I thought I'd let you know now—if you promise to keep your mouth shut and act surprised when they're announced."

"What's up?"

"Orders from the top. The *Teddy R* is being rotated to the Phoenix Cluster, where we and two other ships will patrol the whole damned cluster."

"That's almost as far from the action as the Rim is," said Cole. "How many inhabited worlds in the cluster?"

"A couple of hundred, most of them ours."

"Why do you say I'm responsible for this?"

"You're a hero, remember? The people don't want their hero out on the Rim where nothing's happening, so the Navy is moving us to the Phoenix Cluster"—she grinned—"where even less is happening."

"Is there anything in the cluster worth protecting?"

She shrugged. "Mining worlds, agricultural worlds, three commercial centers. There's supposed to be a hell of a whorehouse on Dalmation II, if that's to your taste."

"I'd ask how you know that," said Cole, "but I'm afraid you might tell me."

She laughed. "Just remember: when Mount Fuji or Podok announces the orders, you're surprised."

"Flabbergasted," he said. "I may swoon."

"You still on blue shift?"

"Yeah. I go to work in about two hours."

"I'm taking a break in the next couple of minutes," said Sharon. "If you're not doing anything, come on down to the mess hall and I'll buy you a cup of coffee."

"Sure, why not?" he replied. "I've read the damned book before."

"Did the butler do it?"

"Frequently. See you in the mess hall."

He broke the connection, went over to his sink and rinsed his face off, and left his cabin.

He was aware of being stared at every time he passed a member of the crew in the corridor, but he had no idea if they were impressed with what he'd accomplished on Rapunzel or resentful of his notoriety. He remembered to return the salutes of each yeoman and ensign who passed him and finally reached the mess hall, where Sharon was waiting for him at a small table.

"You're looking well," she said. "Obviously death-defying adventure agrees with you."

"Give it a rest," he said. Then, activating his side of the table, he ordered coffee. "How's the Peeping Tom business—or is it the Peeping Sharon?"

"Grim," she said, suddenly serious.

"What's up?"

"Same as usual," she said. "You'd better hope no one attacks us in the next two hours, because one of the three gunnery officers on duty is high as a kite, and the other two aren't far behind."

"Where did they get it?" asked Cole. "We haven't touched down in months."

"Where do you suppose? Someone's robbing the infirmary."

"With all the security devices you've got?"

"Someone very creative," she replied. "Or perhaps a lot of someones."

"I'd heard we had a drug problem . . ." he began.

"We've got an *everything* problem," said Sharon. "No one's showed up in the labs for three days. One of the female ensigns would have been raped in the ship's chapel, of all places, if your friend Forrice hadn't happened along. They're not just stealing from the ship, but from each other." She signed deeply. "Putting all our bad apples in one basket may not be the brightest idea the Navy ever had."

"I hadn't realized it was that bad," said Cole. "Oh, Four Eyes and the Captain both mentioned it, but I figured that was just normal bitching."

She shook her head. "It's bad, Wilson."

"Well, as long as I'm stuck here, and my life may depend on them, I suppose it's my job to instill a little discipline if the Captain won't."

"Mount Fuji spends most of his time in his office or cabin and almost never interacts with the crew. I think he's terminally depressed over the loss of his wife and kids." She took a bite of the pastry in front of her. "He was a good man once, and a brave one. In fact," she added, "I've been over the records of every member of the crew, and no one's here for cowardice."

"It doesn't matter," said Cole. "You don't have to be especially brave to fight in a war. If someone starts shooting at you and there's no place to run, you shoot back . . . and in space, there's rarely a place to run. But if discipline is lacking, you go to shoot your pulse cannons and find that they haven't been maintained, you try to maneuver and find no one's programmed the navigational computer for this sector, you start getting short of breath and realize that no one's tended the

hydroponic garden and your emergency oxygen supply is exhausted."
He paused. "Disobeying a stupid order is one thing, and if the Navy
wants to call it a lack of discipline, that's their business; but failing to
maintain your weapons, your equipment, and your ship in time of war
is another, and *that's* the lack of discipline we have to put an end to."

"I agree wholeheartedly," said Sharon. "But things have gotten so
far out of hand that I truly don't know if they *can* be fixed."

"Every problem is capable of solution," said Cole. "What's going
on besides drugs?"

"There's a lot of sex, including some interspecies cohabitation."
Suddenly she smiled. "In fact, I would imagine that carnal intrigue
will raise its lovely head in your vicinity any moment now."

"I beg your pardon?"

"Three of the women on board have a wager on which of them will
go to bed with you first," she said in amused tones. "Do you want their
names?"

"No. I imagine I'll find out soon enough. Is there anything else you
want to tell me?"

"As a matter of fact, there is," said Sharon. "Watch out for Podok."

"Why?"

"She tried to put you on report for disobeying orders and regulations, and instead you got another Medal of Courage. I don't pretend
to understand all the nuances and subtleties of the Polonoi mind, but
my gut feeling is that she resents the hell out of you."

"Thanks for the warning."

Suddenly the Captain's voice and image appeared at stations all
over the ship, including the mess hall.

"This is Captain Fujiama," it said. "The *Theodore Roosevelt* has just
received new orders. At 1700 hours—that's thirty-seven minutes from
now—we are leaving the Rim and relocating to the Phoenix Cluster,

where we will join the *Bonaparte* and the *Maracaibo* in a joint patrol of the cluster's two hundred and forty-one inhabited worlds. Once we're there we have been instructed to maintain radio silence until otherwise notified, so if you have any subspace messages to send, send them now."

The image vanished.

"How long will it take us to get there?" asked Cole.

Sharon shrugged. "That's not my area of expertise. I can find out if it's important."

"No, not really. I was just curious." He paused. "There *is* one thing you can do for me, though."

"Name it."

"Keep me under surveillance around the clock."

"You're that proud of your sexual technique?" she said with a smile.

"I'm being serious. I plan to instill a little discipline on this ship— *my* kind of discipline, if not the Navy's. I figure it'll be resented. If someone sticks a knife between my ribs, I'd like to think he won't go unpunished."

"All right," she said. "Come on back to Security with me, and I'll rig you up so we can monitor you no matter where you are."

"Fine." He finished his coffee. "I'm ready whenever you are."

"Not yet," she said. "*You're* just a hero. *This*"—she indicated the pastry—"is a sinfully rich mixture of chocolate, custard, and two or three ingredients that even the Chief of Security hasn't been able to determine." She took another bite. "I suppose I'll just have to keep eating it until I can identify all the elements."

"How can you eat like this and stay so slender?" asked Cole.

"A little exercise and a lot of worry," she answered. "Especially a lot of worry." She stared at him. "Not as effective as your method of weight loss on Balmoral IV."

"You know about that?"

"It's my job. I know your record as well as you do. What I can't under-stand is how you let yourself be captured. It was such an obvious trap."

"Of course it was. But no one knew where the Teronis were holding Gerhardt Sigardson. I figured the only way to find out was to let them capture me."

"How long did you go without food?"

"A while," he said noncommittally. "But it was essential that we free Sigardson. He knew the disposition of all our forces, and he knew where we planned to strike next. He was a tough customer, but nobody can hold out forever. Sooner or later they'd have broken him."

"The news stories said he was dead when you found him," said Sharon. "I never bought it for an instant."

"He was alive. But they'd been working on him for weeks. He was too feeble to escape with me, and I was too weak to carry him."

"So you killed him?"

He nodded his head. "He knew I had to. Hell, he begged me to." The muscles in Cole's jaw began twitching. "I still feel like shit about it."

"I saw holos of you when they gave you your medals. You looked positively gaunt."

"It's ancient history," he said uncomfortably. "Finish the last ten thousand calories and let's get me rigged so you can monitor me wher-ever I am."

"We probably can anyway," said Sharon.

"Let's make sure."

"All right," she said, finally finishing the pastry. "Let's go."

He followed her to the airlift, and a moment later they entered her office. She ordered the windows on the door to turn opaque.

"Take off your tunic."

He did as she requested.

"Not bad," she said, appraising him with an expert eye. "I might get in on the pool as well."

"If you do, I'll report you to Security."

She laughed, then picked up a small instrument of a type he'd never seen before. "Hold still, now," she said. "This will take a minute."

He felt a sharp stinging sensation in his right shoulder. It subsided after a moment.

"That's the chip everyone will be looking for," she said. "It'll show up on just about any scanner, and it won't hurt a hell of a lot more to take it out than it did to put it in. Now give me your hand."

He extended his left hand, and she sprayed his thumb with a solution that totally deadened it.

"You might want to look away," she said. "You won't feel a thing, but most people will still flinch when they see what's being done."

"How long will this take?"

"Maybe three minutes."

"Let's get going."

He saw her coming at his thumb with some sharp medical instruments, and he took her advice and looked away. He wasn't afraid of the pain, but he agreed that he might flinch, and he didn't want to waste any time.

"Okay, it's all over," she said after she'd finished working on him.

He looked at his hand. It didn't seem any different.

"What did you do?"

"I put a microchip under your thumbnail. It won't register on nine out of ten scanners, and most people will never think to check there, especially once they find the chip in your shoulder."

"What will this chip do?"

"It'll pick up every sound within a fifty-foot radius, and loud sounds from much farther than that. It also sends a homing pulse every five seconds, so we'll always know not only what you hear but where you are." She paused. "There was no way to fit anything visual under your thumbnail, but we do have holo cameras everywhere on the ship, even in the bathrooms."

"You're just a dirty old woman."

"A dirty young woman," she corrected him. "Though I must confess that this job ages you fast—especially aboard the *Teddy R*." She walked to the bank of computers on the back wall and checked one of the machines. "You're transmitting a signal, and everything we've said has been recorded. That means you're done. Put your shirt on so the ladies don't attack you the second they see you, and you can go about your business—which until blue shift doubtless means sprawling on your bunk with a good book or a bad woman."

"You've been looking in on too many private moments," said Cole. "You've got sex on the brain."

"Seriously, by the third day on the job, it's just that much meat on the hoof."

"Thanks for the chips," he said, walking to the door. "I'll catch up with you later."

He went down the corridor, then took the airlift to the gunnery level, where he entered the department. There were three sergeants on duty—a Man, a Polonoi, and a Molarian. None of them looked all that steady on their feet.

The human noticed him and gave him a sloppy salute. The Polonoi seemed to be in a trance, and the Molarian was standing and swaying before a computer.

"I'm pleased to meet you, sir," slurred the human. "That was some show you put on down there on . . . on wherever the hell it was."

"What's your name, Sergeant?" asked Cole.

"Eric Pampas, sir," was the response. "But everyone calls me Wild Bull."

"Why?"

"I used to know," he said with a crooked grin. "But just between you and me, I'm a little wasted."

"Could have fooled me," said Cole sardonically. "How about this one?" he asked, indicating the Polonoi.

"That's Kudop," said Pampas. "I told him and told him that Polonoi can't handle alphanella seeds, but he just had to chew one anyway. He's been like that for hours and hours."

"Have we got a brig?" asked Cole.

"Yes, sir," said Pampas with a grin. "You gonna lock him up?"

"He's not doing much good here," said Cole, "and I'd hate to put him in the infirmary, where he's even closer to a drug supply."

"I'll give you a hand with him, sir," said Pampas. He bent over to lift two of the Polonoi's legs and suddenly staggered. "Wow!" he said, stifling a giggle. "I'm a little higher than I thought."

"What about him?" asked Cole, jerking a finger at the Molarian.

"That's Sergeant Solaniss," said Pampas.

"That's me," chimed in the Molarian, still swaying.

"Do you think if we brought an airsled down here and loaded Kudop onto it, the two of you could take it to the brig?" asked Cole.

"Sure," said the Molarian.

"Hell, what a joke that'll be on him when he wakes up!" said Pampas.

"All right," said Cole. "There'll be an airsled here any moment."

"Don't you have to call for one?"

Cole saw no reason not to explain. "We're being monitored. Someone knows I want a sled."

And within a minute a security staff member had guided an airsled to the department and turned it over to Cole.

"Do you want me to stay here and help out, sir?" she asked, looking at the three gunnery sergeants.

"No, I don't think that will be necessary."

"You're sure, sir?"

"I'm sure."

She saluted, turned, and left.

Cole activated the airsled and set it to hover two feet above the floor. He began directing Pampas and Solaniss as they tried to load Kudop onto the sled, realized they would never manage on their own, and finally gave them a hand. Once the Polonoi was on the sled, he raised the level to four feet and had them guide the sled to the largest of the airlifts.

They descended to the brig. There was no one occupying it. The force field that separated it from the rest of the ship had been deactivated, and they walked right in. Cole ordered the sled to lower to the floor, then told Pampas and Solaniss to put Kudop on his feet. As they were struggling to do so, he walked out into the corridor.

"Activate the force field," he said softly, and instantly there was a faint hum.

It took Pampas and the Molarian another minute to put Kudop in an upright position. Then they walked toward the corridor to join Cole—and bounced right back into the cell.

"What the hell happened?" asked Pampas, blinking his eyes rapidly.

"Someone turned on the force field," answered Cole.

"Why?"

"Probably because I ordered it," said Cole. "I honestly can't think of any other reason."

"What the hell did you do that for?"

"Because we're at war, and none of you were in any condition to prepare or handle your weapons."

"Aw, come on, sir," said Pampas. "We haven't seen a Teroni ship in months."

"I did," said Cole. "Last week."

"Well, if one comes after us, we'll blow it to pieces," slurred Pampas.

"You couldn't hit the wall at ten paces. If we're attacked, my life depends on your being able to function at peak efficiency, and I suspect this ship hasn't been within hailing distance of peak efficiency in years. I happen to cherish my life, and I won't let you be the reason it comes to an end."

"How long do you plan to keep us here?" asked Solaniss.

"As long as it takes."

"As long as *what* takes?"

"You'll figure it out."

He walked down the corridor, their yells and curses following him.

"I assume you captured all that," he said, certain that Sharon was monitoring him. "Put up a sound barrier so they can't be heard. If they're going to shout themselves hoarse, there's no reason why anyone else has to suffer. And place them on half rations. They're so drugged they're not going to be hungry anyway, so why waste the food? Then I want you to run a holo replay, starting from when we carried the Polonoi into the brig and ending when I walked away, and show it throughout the ship every fifteen or twenty minutes for the next day."

As he passed a communications station, Sharon Blacksmith's image suddenly appeared.

"Do you want it sent to Mount Fuji's computer, too?" she asked.

"Why not?" replied Cole. "What's he going to do? Tell me that they should have stayed on duty in that condition?"

"He won't like it. The fact that you did it on your own initiative makes him look bad."

"Then it makes him look bad. Look, what I said to Pampas and the others was the truth. If Rapunzel proves nothing else, it proves you never know when and where you're going to confront the enemy. I'm prepared to die for the Republic if I have to, but I'm not prepared to die because our crew is too drunk or too high to shoot straight."

"Let's just hope our crew doesn't try to save the Teroni Federation the trouble of killing you."

"You think it's a possibility?"

"You toss many more crewmen in the brig and I'd say it's pretty close to even money," she answered truthfully.

"Mr. Cole, report to the bridge—on the double!"

Cole arrived two minutes later and found Podok waiting for him. He didn't recognize the Molarian Officer on Deck. Christine Mboya was seated at the communications complex and seemed unwilling to look up from her work.

"I assume you're the one who wants to see me," said Cole, approaching the Polonoi. "What can I do for you, ma'am?"

"You can begin by saluting and calling me Commander Podok."

He snapped off a salute. "Whatever makes you happy, Commander."

"Commander Podok," she insisted.

"This is silly," said Cole. "How the hell many commanders can I possibly be speaking to?"

"You will address me as Commander Podok or I will put you on report."

"Yes, Commander Podok," he said. "Would it be presumptuous to ask why I have been summoned, Commander Podok?"

"You have incarcerated three gunnery sergeants in the brig," said the Polonoi.

"I know that, Commander Podok," said Cole. "I hope you didn't call me up here just to tell me that."

"Who gave you permission to imprison them?"

"All three were high on stimulants, Commander Podok."

"We only have four gunnery sergeants, Mr. Cole. You have put three of them in the brig, and by doing so you have endangered the safety of the ship."

"The ship would be in a lot more danger if they were maintaining the weapons and ammunition in their current condition," replied Cole.

"Are you prepared to take their place?" asked Podok.

"If we're attacked, then of course I am," answered Cole. "But I think it would be more practical to instill some discipline on the *Teddy R* and stop situations like this from arising in the first place. There are drug dens on Rameses VI that don't have as many addicts as this ship, and there are whorehouses that don't see as much action in a night as the *Teddy R* does."

"Have you any other criticisms to make?"

"When I do, I'll make them directly to the Captain."

"You exceeded your authority by imprisoning them on white shift," said Podok. "I am ordering the three men released. We cannot be without gunnery technicians."

"You're going to be without gunnery experts whether you release them or not. Kudop was chewing alphanella seeds; he's going to be comatose for the rest of the day. The other two aren't much better."

"Are you giving me orders, Mr. Cole?"

"Just advice."

Podok stared at him coldly. "Let me give *you* some advice. If you contradict my orders, it will go hard with you."

"I don't know what I've done to anger you, but I think I should remind you that we're on the same side."

"You endangered the entire ship the very first day you arrived," said Podok. "You single-handedly forced us into combat. The fact that we emerged triumphant does not justify disobeying regulations." She paused and continued to glare at him. "You have been back less than a day and have taken it upon yourself to jail three-quarters of our weapons technicians even as we are about to enter new and potentially hostile territory. Does that answer your question?"

"The Bortellites *are* part of the Teroni Federation," Cole pointed out. "Are you resentful of the fact that we ran them off Rapunzel?"

"I am resentful of the fact that the action was initiated without orders from above and that the chain of command was ignored."

"That's rubbish. *I* didn't order you to attack the Bortellite ship. Fleet Admiral Garcia did."

"Enough of this. You bend the truth the way you bend regulations. I will speak no further with you."

"Then why the hell did you call me to the bridge?"

"To tell you that I am seriously displeased with you and that I am ordering the three crew members released."

"I'll just lock them up again."

"I am ordering you not to."

"Under any circumstances?"

"Under any circumstances."

"Even if they take more drugs and the Polonoi becomes catatonic again?"

"You heard me."

"I certainly did." He raised his voice. "May I assume Security heard it, too?"

Sharon Blacksmith's image appeared. "Heard and captured."

"All right, Commander Podok," said Cole. "Now we're both on record. Are you sure you want to release the prisoners?"

Podok glared at him. He still couldn't read Polonoi facial expressions, but it didn't take much imagination to imagine the loathing. "The prisoners will remain in the brig," she said at last. "You, Mr. Cole, are a dangerous man."

"I'm just an officer trying to do his duty, Commander Podok," replied Cole calmly. "Is there anything else, or am I free to go now?"

"Leave."

He turned to go.

"And salute!"

He turned back, saluted, and walked to the airlift. When he got off and headed off toward his cabin, he found himself surrounded by a dozen crew members, mostly Men, who gave him a rousing cheer. A couple of them reached out and patted him on the back.

He felt confused, but thanked them and made his way to his cabin. He entered, walked to the sink, rinsed his face off, and sat down at the small desk. A moment later Forrice entered.

"Nice going," said the Molarian.

"What the hell are you talking about?"

"You have friends in low places," said Forrice, hooting a laugh. "Sharon Blacksmith piped your meeting with Podok throughout the whole ship."

"Great," he muttered. "As if Podok's not mad enough already."

"Podok's the least of your problems," said the Molarian.

"Oh?"

"The entire crew now knows what you do to people who take drugs while they're on duty. The ones who cheered you at the airlift probably constitute more than half of those whose systems are free of stimulants."

"That's not going to be a problem at all," said Cole. "As far as I can tell, none of the crew are cowards or deserters. Their problem is resentment at being here and boredom now that they *are* here. I think they won't mind a little discipline as long as they can see that it has a purpose; in fact, I think they'll welcome it. I think most of them *want* to be good crew members. It's just that so far no one's insisted on it, and half the regulations that the officers *do* insist on don't make any sense."

"You'd better hope you're right."

"Don't worry about it. If I'm wrong, Security is monitoring me every second."

"That just means they'll know who to charge with your murder," said Forrice.

"Are you always this optimistic?"

"I have to be an optimist," explained Forrice. "I won't have anyone to tease if they kill you."

"I'm properly touched," said Cole. "But just in case they'd rather kill the bad guys, is there anyone else on board who can fill in for our gunnery specialists?"

"I'll find someone," said Forrice. "Now that I'm off blue shift, my duties are somewhat vague."

"So are everyone else's on this vessel. That's one of its problems."

"Well, at least we know the pulse cannon was working a week ago. That's what we used on the Bortellite ship."

"Hitting a ship that's sitting on the ground and doesn't know it's under attack probably isn't the ultimate test of your weaponry," said Cole.

"I agree," said Forrice. "On the other hand, it's better than *not* hitting it."

A light blinked and a bell chimed.

"It's playing your song," said the Molarian.

"It's telling me that white shift ends in ten minutes," said Cole, still sitting. "Time to go to work."

"I don't see you rushing off to the bridge," observed Forrice.

"If I get there early, my guess is that Podok won't let me in. And of course, if I'm late she'll put me on report. So I'll go up and stand just beyond the bridge, and step onto it at precisely 1600 hours."

"Why do you care if she puts you on report?" asked Forrice, puzzled. "You know the Navy isn't going to punish you, not after Rapunzel."

"The Navy is less pleased with me than you think," said Cole dryly. "As for being put on report, if I'm going to punish all the abuses I find on board and toss the worst offenders into the brig, it really won't look very good if I go on report, even if everyone knows it's a trumped-up charge that was filed by a jealous fellow officer."

He got up, waited for the Molarian to spin out into the corridor with his graceful three-legged walk, then strolled over to the airlift and went up to the bridge level. He waited until an automated whistle officially ended white shift and stepped onto the bridge before the last of the sound had dissipated. He stood rigidly at attention and gave Podok a crisp salute as she passed by, while wondering idly if she understood sarcasm when she saw it.

Christine Mboya was no longer at the communications station. She had been replaced by Jacillios, a Molarian female whom Forrice assured him was one of the sexiest creatures alive, an appraisal that was lost on him. The Officer on Deck was Lieutenant Malcolm Briggs, a recent transfer from the *Prosperity*, where he'd struck another officer for reasons that remained vague. His file stated that he was a good officer prior to the incident, third-generation military, filled with energy and confidence, a little headstrong but destined for fine things. Finer than the *Theodore Roosevelt*, anyway.

Cole greeted the two officers pleasantly, returned a lazy salute for Briggs's sharp one, then walked over to the pilot.

"Hi, Wxakgini," he said. "How's it going?"

"The engines are driving us at five times light speed. However, adjusting for the hyperspacial wormhole that we're presently traversing, we're traveling at almost nineteen hundred times the speed of light, sir," replied the Bdxeni from his cocoonlike station.

"That wasn't what I meant, but it'll do," said Cole. "Carry on." *As if you could do anything else with your brain tied in to the engine and the navigational computer.*

He walked over to Jacillios. "Everything under control, Ensign?"

"Yes, sir."

He turned to Briggs. "I don't know who Four Eyes is going to get for the gunnery section, but let's deactivate the major weapons from here until we arrive in the Phoenix Cluster. No sense having some beginner test them when we're going this many multiples of light speed. The most likely result is that we'll shoot ourselves."

"Yes, sir," said Briggs. "I believe we'll reach the cluster in less than two hours, sir. Shall I activate them then?"

"Yeah, do it as soon as we apply the breaking mechanism and emerge from hyperspace." He looked up at Wxakgini. "I assume we're rendezvousing with the *Bonaparte* and the *Maracaibo* once we arrive?"

"Yes, sir," said the pilot. "We are to contact them when we reach the cluster, and then make arrangements to rendezvous. They are due to arrive three and two hours ahead of us. We will emerge from the wormhole in the neighborhood of the McDevitt system, and they are to be waiting nearby, which I take to mean within a light-year."

"Fine. Is there anything else I need to know—Wxakgini, Jacillios, Briggs?"

"There's *is* one thing, sir," said Jacillios. "Security wants to know if the prisoners are to remain on half rations?"

"Only for today," answered Cole. "Their sin is boredom, not treason. And have Security escort each one to the infirmary for a thorough checkup before the next white shift begins. If they've permanently burned out any neural circuits, I want to know before Podok makes another attempt to return them all to duty. I want them to pay special attention to the seed chewer; I've seen what that stuff can do."

"Yes, sir," said Jacillios.

"Speaking of rations, I haven't eaten in about six hours," announced Cole. "I'm off to grab a snack."

He left the bridge and wandered down to the mess hall. Neither Sharon Blacksmith nor Forrice was there, and he didn't know any of the others well enough to sit with them. There was polite applause when he sat down, a little more restrained than when he'd gone to his quarters. He nodded an acknowledgment, then concentrated on the menu until he felt everyone had stopped staring at him.

"Do you mind if I join you, sir?"

He looked up and saw Rachel Marcos standing next to his table.

"Be my guest," he said, indicating the empty chair at the opposite side of the table.

"Thank you, sir," she said. "I just wanted to tell you: I think that was a remarkably brave thing you did today."

"Not really," he said with a smile. "Podok lives by the rulebook. She'd never shoot a fellow officer."

Rachel returned his smile. "I meant putting those three men in the brig. The Captain never had the courage to confront the drug problem."

"Mount Fuji doesn't strike me as a coward."

"I just don't think he cares anymore."

"He cared enough to read me the riot act for taking the *Kermit* to Rapunzel and for manipulating the press."

She shrugged. "Then I guess I was wrong."

"You've been watching him a lot longer than I have," said Cole. "If you think you're right, stick by your guns."

"Argue with you, sir?" she said. "I couldn't."

"Have it your way." He studied her as he ate his soya steak. *Is this hero worship, or are you one of the three ladies Sharon warned me about? I can't ask you, of course, but I think I'll keep the table, and a little distance, between us until I know for sure.*

"I've never been to the Phoenix Cluster before," she said. "I'm really looking forward to it."

"You are?"

She nodded. "I hope we get some shore leave. They say that there's a wonderful theater district on New Jamestown."

"If the cluster's as dull as it's supposed to be, I can't see any reason why we shouldn't get some leave."

"We had some fine theater back on Far London," she continued wistfully.

"Is that where you come from?" asked Cole.

"Yes."

"I hear it's got quite an art museum."

She spent the next half hour extolling the virtues of New London, and then she had to go back on duty. He finished his coffee, tossed his cup and tray in the atomizer, and went down to check on the gunnery department.

Forrice was instructing a team of four—two humans, a Polonoi, and a Mollutei—on the duties involved, and they seemed to be assimilating it. Satisfied, he left and returned to the bridge.

"I hope you had a nice meal, sir," said Briggs.

"I hesitate to call soya products 'nice.' Edible is about the best they can aspire to."

"They say there are some excellent restaurants on Dalmation II," offered Briggs.

"That's not all that's on Dalmation II from what I hear," said Cole.

A guilty smile spread across the young lieutenant's face. "Well, you have to eat, too, sir."

"Good for you," said Cole. "Most healthy young men and women tend to forget that."

"I never said you had to eat first, sir," said Briggs, still smiling.

"Well, it's nice to know you have your priorities straight, Lieutenant."

There was a very mild *bump!* as the ship emerged from its wormhole.

"We have entered the Phoenix Cluster," announced Wxakgini.

"Good," said Cole. "Ensign Jacillios, make contact with the *Bonaparte* and the *Maracaibo* and set up the rendezvous."

The Molarian looked up a moment later. "Something's wrong, sir. I can't raise them."

"It probably just means we beat them here," said Cole.

"No, sir," she said. "I plotted all three of our courses, and we were going to be the last to arrive by almost two hours."

Cole frowned. "Try again."

Jacillios sent out a signal. "No response, sir."

"Ensign, who's the best sensor expert on the ship?"

Before she could answer, Briggs spoke up. "I am, sir."

"What are your qualifications?"

"Qualifications, sir?"

"If I'm going to put every life on the ship in your hands, I want to know that I'm making the right decision."

Briggs just stared at him. "Actually, sir . . ." he began.

"Don't apologize," said Cole. "There's nothing wrong with self-confidence. I just asked the wrong person."

"I don't know the answer, sir," said Jacillios.

"But there's someone on the bridge who does," said Cole. "Someone who's more intimately connected with the ship than anyone else, and more likely to know who will function best to help keep it safe." He walked over to the pilot. "I need your advice, Wxakgini. Who's the best sensor expert aboard the *Teddy R*?"

"Lieutenant Mboya, sir," replied the pilot.

"Thank you." He turned back to Briggs. "Summon her to the bridge, Mr. Briggs."

"She's been rotated to white shift," he said. "She's probably asleep by now."

"Then wake her up."

Christine Mboya arrived a few minutes later, and Cole briefly outlined the situation to her. "Now get on those sensors and see what you can find," he concluded.

She spent about ten minutes scanning, checking, and rechecking. Finally she looked up.

"I can't prove that it was the *Bonaparte*," she said, "but there's a hell of a lot of debris, some small, some big, scattered about twenty lightyears from here—just the kind a ship might leave after it was torpedoed by pulse cannons."

"What about the *Maracaibo*?"

"No trace of it."

"Why do you think this is the debris of one ship rather than the other?"

"Titanium traces," she responded. "The *Maracaibo*'s a newer ship. We stopped using titanium alloys about five years after they built the *Bonaparte*."

"There aren't supposed to be any enemy ships in the cluster," said Cole. "What the hell happened?"

"I don't know," said Christine. Suddenly she tensed. "But it's about to happen again."

"What is it?"

She pointed to a tiny blip on her screen. "A Teroni dreadnought."

"I don't suppose we can match weaponry or defenses with it?" said Cole.

"Not a chance," she replied grimly.

"Pilot, get us the hell out of here!" ordered Cole as the enemy ship continued approaching. The *Teddy R* turned and began taking evasive action, and he turned to Christine Mboya. "What kind of range does their weaponry have?"

"I have no idea what they're carrying, sir," she said. "Just that whatever it is, it was powerful enough to destroy the *Bonaparte*, and possibly the *Maracaibo*, too."

"I don't suppose there are any other Republic ships stationed here?"

"No, sir," said Briggs. "The other three were rotated out two days ago."

"I could try sending an SOS, sir," suggested Jacillios.

"Absolutely not!" said Cole firmly. "If they smell blood, they're going to follow us until they catch us. Patch me through to Four Eyes."

"You mean Commander Forrice, sir?"

"Just do it."

Forrice's image appeared seconds later. "Everyone looks grim," he said, glancing around the bridge. "What's the matter?"

"The *Bonaparte* and the *Maracaibo* were destroyed," said Cole, "and the ship that got them is coming right at us. I want you to stay where you are, and keep your crew there, too. We'll send food to you, and I'll order the medic to stop by in a few hours and give each of you something to keep alert."

"I've spotted it on the screen," said Forrice. "The computer says it's too far away. There's no sense shooting until it gets closer."

"I don't want you shooting at all unless we're disabled," said Cole.

"We can't match firepower with it. Before we get close enough to do it any damage, it'll blow us apart."

"Understood. You'd better let me get back to checking the weapons and making sure they're all activated."

"Right," said Cole, breaking the connection. "How are we doing, Pilot?"

"I have a name," said Wxakgini.

"I know—but by the time I learn to pronounce it the war will be over. Are they following us?"

"They're tracking us," answered Wxakgini, "but they don't seem to be making an effort to close with us."

"All right. Thanks." He turned back to Jacillios. "Are they sending anything at all—warnings, orders, queries, anything?"

"No, sir."

"And they're not closing, they're just tracking us," he said, frowning. "Yet they destroyed the other two ships."

"We *assume* they did," said Christine Mboya. "We don't *know* it."

"The only way to know it is to ask them," said Cole. "I'll settle for assuming."

"But it doesn't make any sense, sir," continued Briggs. "Why would they destroy two ships and then let us escape? Surely they know that once we report it, the Navy will send massive reinforcements."

"Good question," said Cole. "I can think of three reasons, but there might be more."

Briggs frowned. "The only one I can come up with is that they're on their way out of the cluster and they don't care if reinforcements show up tomorrow."

"That doesn't make sense, Lieutenant," said Cole. "We're at war. They destroyed two of our ships. They have a chance to destroy the *Teddy R.* Why let us live, just because they're leaving the cluster?"

"I'm sorry, sir."

"For being wrong?" said Cole. "There's no need to apologize for that."

"No, for speaking before I'd thought. I'll be honest, sir: I was trying to impress you."

"You don't have to apologize for honesty, either, Mr. Briggs," said Cole. "Take a minute, think it through, and try to see what I see." He walked over to the Molarian. "I want to talk to the medic. No, strike that. Patch me through to Security."

The image of a tall, angular being from Pelleanor appeared. It was a dark gray in color, with piercing orange eyes and cheekbones that protruded until they looked like wings. It might have had a gender, but no one except another Pelleanor would ever be able to tell.

"Where's Sharon Blacksmith?" asked Cole.

"Asleep," answered the Pelleanor. "She worked part of red shift and all of white."

"We haven't met," said Cole. "Do you know who I am?"

"Of course," said the plain mechanical tones of the Pelleanor's T-pack. "I have monitored you many times since you came aboard."

"Fine. I want you to designate as large a security crew as you think necessary, and either take the three prisoners to the infirmary or take the doctor to the brig. If he can clean the junk of out any of their systems and get them functioning efficiently within the next two hours, have him do it."

"And if not?"

"Then keep the prisoners in the brig, and have the doctor do whatever's necessary to keep their replacements alert."

"It will be done," said the Pelleanor, breaking the connection.

"Pilot, are they still just tracking us?" asked Cole.

"I've put some ground between us and them," answered Wxakgini, "but I don't know if it was my maneuvering or if they merely allowed me to do so."

"Still no communication, Ensign?"

"None, sir," said Jacillios.

"That figures," said Cole.

"It does, sir?"

He nodded.

"Sir?" said Briggs.

"Yeah, what is it?"

"I've been thinking about the three reasons for their behavior that you alluded to," said the young officer.

"And?"

"One possibility is that the *Bonaparte* or the *Maracaibo* disabled them. Not totally, or they couldn't track us, but enough so that they don't want to engage in a pitched battle, even though they are clearly the bigger, more powerful ship."

"That's one, Mr. Briggs. Got any others?"

"They know the Republic has sent three ships to the Phoenix Cluster. They may be afraid that more are on the way, too many for them to cope with. We could be in the unlikely position of blocking their way out of the cluster."

"We could be," said Cole, though his expression said he didn't believe it for a second.

"For the life of me, sir, I can't think of any other reasons."

"It could be a bluff, for reasons we know nothing about. They could be losing power in their weapons systems; Lord knows each side puts enough saboteurs into the other side's military. Some of their top personnel could be on one of the planets. Or this whole cluster could be a trap, and they might *want* us to escape and bring back a major punishment party that they're positioned to destroy. Or it could be something as unlikely as their religion saying that you can't destroy more than two ships on this day of the week. The problem, of course, is that we have to figure out which is the real reason, and we have to be right the first time."

"How can we tell?" asked Jacillios.

"We need a little more input," said Cole. "I'm sure we'll get it. In the meantime, I think we'd better alert the Captain."

"You didn't alert him when you went to Rapunzel," noted Briggs.

"I took a shuttlecraft with two volunteers, expressly to keep the *Teddy R* and the crew out of danger," answered Cole. "This time the ship's in danger no matter what we do, and that calls for a command decision." He paused. "Ensign Jacillios, you might as well summon the First Officer, too."

"Shall I signal a red alert, sir?" asked the Molarian.

"Hell, no," said Cole. "What if the attack comes in eleven hours, or fifteen, or nineteen? It'd be nice if *some*one was awake and alert. If anyone's sleeping, let 'em sleep. The only one I need to speak to is the Captain."

"Commander!" said Wxakgini urgently.

"What is it?" asked Cole.

"They've turned back."

"Confirmed," chimed in Briggs, staring at his computer. "They've broken off the chase."

"That doesn't make any sense," said Cole. "They've got us on the run. Why would they stop?" He frowned, trying to consider all the possibilities. After a moment he approached Wxakgini. "Pilot, have we charted all the wormholes in the cluster?"

"Just the five major ones, sir," answered Wxakgini.

"Pretend, for the sake of argument, that the Teroni ship is in the exact center of the cluster, rather than out here near the perimeter. Can one of the wormholes take us between 120 and 240 degrees around them?"

"Let me check. It is as much a matter of feel as calculation, at least when I'm tied in to the navigational computer." A pause. "Yes, we can enter a wormhole less than one light-year from here and come out 173 degrees around the Teroni ship."

"Do it."

"Right now?"

"Yes."

"But shouldn't we wait for the Captain?" asked Wxakgini. "He'll be on the bridge shortly."

"I'm in charge until he gets here," said Cole. "I gave you an order."

The Bdxeni made no reply, but an instant later the ship sheared off its path, and shortly thereafter entered the wormhole. Most of the time the crew wasn't even aware of the wormholes they traversed, but once in a while they were physically affected by some element of the wormhole. This was one of those times. A wave of dizziness swept over Cole, and he reached out to steady himself—but his vision started playing tricks on him, and instead of making contact with a bulkhead, he found himself falling to the floor. He saw no reason to get up until they emerged from the wormhole, so he just lay there, keeping his eyes shut and trying to ignore the pain from his bruises.

The ship was back in normal space in less than a minute, and Cole climbed painfully to his feet.

"We have arrived," announced Wxakgini. "If finding ourselves midway between two unnamed class-M stars can be considered an arrival."

"I'm glad the hyperspacial wormholes don't affect *your* race," said Cole.

"They do," replied Wxakgini. "But when I am tied in to the ship's computer, my perceptions are filtered through its logical synapses. Had I been in your position, I would have been just as disoriented as you are."

"For future reference it's comforting to know that you can't get sick or dizzy unless the computer does," said Cole. "Has the Teroni ship spotted us?"

"Not yet."

"Ensign, is the Captain on his way to the bridge?"

"If he wasn't before, I'm sure he'll be now," replied Jacillios.

"Commander?" said Wxakgini.

"Yes?"

"The Teroni ship is approaching us."

"At top speed?"

"No."

"Back off."

"I don't understand," said Wxakgini.

"Move toward the core of the cluster. Don't make any attempt to break out of it."

"Even if they start firing?"

"Ask me then," said Cole, as Fujiama and Podok arrived on the bridge just seconds apart.

"What's going on, Mr. Cole?" demanded Fujiama, staring at one of the viewscreens.

"It would appear that a Teroni ship destroyed the *Bonaparte* and the *Maracaibo*, sir," said Cole. "That same ship is now leisurely pursuing us."

"Leisurely?" repeated Fujiama.

"Yes, sir."

"Explain."

"It was waiting for us near the debris of at least the *Bonaparte*," explained Cole. "We stopped beyond the outside range of its weaponry. Once it spotted us it began approaching us, and since we couldn't match firepower with it, I ordered the pilot to retreat."

"Through the wormhole?" asked Fujiama.

"No, sir," said Cole. "The Teroni ship pursued us for perhaps two light-years and then broke off the chase."

Fujiama frowned. "That doesn't make any sense. We're going to escape, and report what happened, and by tomorrow Admiral Pilcerova will have dispatched a dozen warships to the cluster."

"Admiral Pilcerova is dead, sir," said Jacillios.

"All right—Admiral Rupert, then," said Fujiama irritably. "The point is, if they let us go, they can expect major reprisals."

"If you know it, they know it, too, sir," said Cole.

"What are you getting at, Mr. Cole?" He glanced at another screen. "And why are we surrounded by stars? We aren't we in deep space?"

"I ordered the pilot to circle behind around the Teroni ship, though 'behind' probably isn't the right word," replied Cole. "*That* was the reason we went through the wormhole. One moment, sir." He turned to Wxakgini. "Have they increased their speed?"

"No, sir," said the pilot.

Cole allowed himself the luxury of a small smile. "I didn't think they would."

"Mr. Cole," said Podok, "your first responsibility is the safety of the *Theodore Roosevelt*. You had the opportunity to escape from the cluster and call for reinforcements, and you failed to do so. This constitutes a clear breach of professional conduct."

"The Teroni ship isn't going to be here tomorrow," said Cole. "The reinforcements would arrive too late, and we'd have taken ships away from where they're needed."

"That's a very glib answer to a charge of malfeasance, which I shall enter in my report on the next white shift."

"Why didn't you expect them to come after us full speed and weapons firing, Mr. Cole?" asked Fujiama.

"Sir!" said Podok sharply. "This man has once again disobeyed standing orders. We are in a hostile military situation. Listening to him just wastes valuable time."

Fujiama straightened up to his full height, which was very close to seven feet. "Don't tell me my duty, Commander Podok," he said, articulating each word. "Yours is to put this man on report, and I have no problem with it. Mine is to listen to any input my officers have and to ultimately make a command decision. Mr. Cole, please answer my question."

"There's only one reasonable answer as to why they didn't chase us out past the edge of the cluster and eventually destroy us, sir."

"And that is?"

"They don't know that only three ships were assigned to the Phoenix Cluster," said Cole. "A Republic starship is a valuable trophy, so why wouldn't they chase us until they got within range of their pulse cannons? There can only be one answer: they're guarding something even more valuable. That's why I had the pilot circle around them—to see if they'd chase us in earnest if we weren't heading for deep space, where we might join up with a wing of the Fleet. When they didn't come after us hell for leather, I knew it had to be that they're afraid to get too far from whatever it is they're protecting."

"All I hear is a lot of guesswork," snorted Podok.

"Why do *you* think they're not in hot pursuit?" asked Cole.

"It's no concern of mine," said Podok. "The ship's orders are clear."

Cole looked at Fujiama. "Should I continue, sir?"

"Please do."

"All right. I figure the reason they're here is because the Phoenix Cluster has seen even less military activity than the Rim. Someone very important is having a meeting on a planet in the cluster. The meeting was probably set up when the Republic ships rotated out of here two days ago. The Teronis didn't know that we were bringing in three more ships today."

"Then why did they destroy the first two ships?" demanded Podok, her voice and posture aggressive. "What is it about the *Theodore Roosevelt* that terrifies them?"

"They destroyed the *Bonaparte* because it came out of the wormhole and was a lone ship, rather than part of a military group. Wormholes move, planets move, nebulas rotate; maybe they went after the *Maracaibo* because it got too close to the planet they're protecting." He paused, looking from one to the other to make sure they were following his reconstruction. He was also aware that Lieutenant Briggs was hanging on his every word. "But when we came out of the wormhole that brought us here, we spotted the debris and came to a dead stop, out of range of their weapons. If we get close enough they'll fire, but they're not going to enter a protracted chase, because they don't know that we're the last Republic ship that's going to show up here, and they don't dare leave the planet unprotected. If they don't mind frightening us away, it has to be because they figure to be gone before any reinforcements can arrive."

Fujiama was silent for a long moment. "It makes sense," he said at last.

"Then we must leave the cluster and report it," said Podok. She turned to Cole. "If it turns out that you are correct, I will enter an addendum to my report, though you still clearly disobeyed standing orders by not protecting the ship."

"The ship's as safe here as it would be in deep space," said Cole. "Pilot, has the Teroni ship turned back yet?"

"It is just doing so now, sir," answered Wxakgini.

"Nevertheless, we must leave instantly," persisted Podok. "Even if you are right, they will be free to hunt us down the instant this presumed meeting is over."

"Captain," said Cole, "I put it to you: They're guarding at least one person they think is worth more than a starship, and they'll be gone tomorrow. Do you really want to walk away from an opportunity like this?"

"It would be quite a feather in the *Roosevelt*'s cap," agreed Fujiama wistfully. Then he frowned. "But we've got one functioning gunnery technician, we've only got one medic if we sustain injuries, we've—"

"The *Teddy R* isn't going to fight anyone," said Cole. "We haven't got the firepower."

"Then what the hell are you talking about?" demanded Fujiama.

"We'll get as close to the Teroni ship as we dare and release our shuttlecraft. We won't activate their engines until the Teroni ship has passed them in its pursuit of the *Teddy R*. Then the shuttles fan out and use their sensors to determine which planet is hosting the meeting, drop a well-placed bomb or two, and rendezvous near the wormhole."

"How will you know which planet to bomb?" said Podok. "What if four or five different worlds display life-forms when the shuttles scan them?"

"It'll almost certainly be a planet with no colonies and no native populations," answered Cole. "Even if they think the inhabitants are friendly to the Teroni Federation, why take a chance of an assassination? My guess is they'll find an empty planet, maybe not even an oxygen world, for the meeting. And given where the Teroni ship keeps retreating to, we can probably limit it to three star systems right now, then pinpoint it once we move in."

"Who would command the shuttles?" asked Fujiama.

"I'll take one, and Forrice will take the other."

"We have four shuttles, each named after one of Theodore Roosevelt's children," said Fujiama. "Why use only two?"

"Because if anything happens to the *Teddy R*, you can cram most of the crew onto two shuttles. As Commander Podok points out"—he nodded at the Polonoi—"my first consideration is the safety of the ship."

"How long do you suppose we have before they leave?" asked Fujiama.

Cole shrugged. "It's anyone's guess—but if the *Bonaparte* was three hours ahead of us, we can figure they've been here four hours or more. They'd never have set their people down there if the Bonaparte had shown up before the meeting started."

"Captain," said Podok, "surely you're not going to let Commander Cole and Commander Forrice take the shuttlecraft into what must now clearly be considered enemy territory?"

"No, I'm not," said Fujiama.

"You're not?" exclaimed Cole, honestly surprised.

"I am glad to hear it, sir," said Podok.

"I lost my whole family to this goddamned war," said Fujiama. "I felt that enough Fujiama blood was spilled for the Republic, I've been content to serve out my time doing as little as possible, ignoring the problems I see daily aboard this vessel rather than attempting to correct them." He paused. "I was a good officer once. I know it's difficult to believe, but I was. Through his actions Mr. Cole has reminded me of what I could have become had things turned out differently—and whether he knows it or not, he's convinced me that it's time to get back into this war." He took a deep breath and released it slowly. "Mr. Cole will be in charge of one shuttlecraft, but Commander Forrice will not be in command of the other. Captains don't follow, they lead. I'll be commanding the other shuttle."

"Captain, I must protest!" said Podok.

"That's your privilege," said Fujiama.

"It is more than my privilege," answered the Polonoi. "It is my duty."

"I would never prevent you from doing your duty," said Fujiama. "But neither will I allow you to prevent me from doing mine."

Podok began walking toward the airlift. "I must dictate my report," she said.

"I expect you back here in ten minutes," said Fujiama. "You're going to be in command of the *Theodore Roosevelt* once I depart in the shuttlecraft."

"I will be here," she said without looking back.

Fujiama suddenly realized that Cole had been staring at him with an inscrutable expression on his face. "What are you looking at?" he demanded.

"I was just thinking," said Cole, "that if we survive this mission, I might actually enjoy being an officer aboard the *Teddy R.*"

Cole let Fujiama pick his crew, then selected Forrice, Briggs, and Christine Mboya to come with him. Podok immediately objected, pointing out that if Forrice left the ship, she would be the only remaining senior officer left onboard. Cole found himself agreeing with her.

"Who do you want, then?" asked Fujiama.

"You know, I still haven't ever seen a Tolobite—ours or anyone else's," said Cole.

"You want the symbiote?" asked Podok in disbelieving tones. "Why would you ask for someone about whom you know nothing?"

"If he's sober, that puts him ahead of ninety percent of the crew," said Cole. "And he figures to be sober. I never yet saw a symbiote of any species that could drink or drug without damned near killing its partner. Has he got a name?"

Wxakgini laughed from his position above them. "If you have difficulty pronouncing *my* name, you'll *never* learn the Tolobite's."

"A minor inconvenience," said Cole. "That's my choice. Jacillios, tell him to meet me at the *Kermit* in three minutes."

"To reiterate," said Fujiama to Podok, "you are to approach the enemy ship until it takes notice and begins approaching you. Then you will change course and begin retreating. Mr. Cole and I will detach our shuttlecrafts, but with all systems deactivated. If we run short on air, and we shouldn't, we'll use our oxygen canisters to breathe, so that nothing registers on the Teroni ship's sensors. If it notices us at all, it will probably think we're just dead weight you jettisoned when it started chasing you. Once it's well past us, we will activate the shuttles and race toward the likeliest planets. When we find the one we're looking for, we'll attack before the Teroni ship can get back to protect it."

"How are you going to get back to the ship?" asked Jacillios. "The Teroni ship will be between you and the *Teddy R.*"

"That's easy enough," said Cole. "We've mapped the wormholes. The Teroni Federation has never shown any previous interest in the Phoenix Cluster. It's my guess that they don't know where the wormholes are. We won't try to get past the Teroni ship. We'll head away from it, pick up a wormhole, and meet the *Teddy R* wherever it lets us out."

"You won't have the Bdxeni with you to find the wormholes," said Forrice.

"I'll trust to Lieutenant Mboya's abilities," replied Cole.

"Are you ready, Mr. Cole?" asked Fujiama.

"Yes, sir," said Cole.

"Then let's get going."

Fujiama, Cole, and their small crews made their way down to the shuttlecrafts.

"I'll take the *Quentin*," announced Fujiama.

"I hope you're not superstitious, sir," said Cole.

"No. Why?"

"Because Theodore Roosevelt's son Quentin died when he was shot out of the sky by an enemy plane."

"Then it's time to even the score," said Fujiama.

"Whatever you say," replied Cole. He looked around the deck. "Where the hell is the—?" He stopped and stared, for approaching him was a squat, shining, bipedal being. He'd have had to stretch the word "humanoid" almost past its elastic limits to include this creature. Its skin, smooth and oily, literally glowed. Its upper limbs were thick and tentacular, more like an elephant's trunk than an octopus's legs. It didn't seem to be wearing clothes, but Cole couldn't see any genitalia. There was no neck; the head grew directly out of the shoulders and was incapable of turning or swiveling. The mouth had no teeth and seemed equipped only for sucking fluids. The eyes were very dark and wide-set. No nostrils were evident. The ears were mere slits at the sides of the head. At first Cole thought it was gold in color, but the color fluctuated with every step it took.

Cole looked for the symbiote, but couldn't see one and wondered if he'd been misinformed.

The being emitted a noise that sounded like it was either coughing or choking. It was only when that was followed by the words "reporting for duty, sir" that Cole realized it was its name.

"Where's your partner?" asked Cole.

"My partner, sir?"

"Your symbiote."

"Right here, sir."

"Right *where*?" asked Cole irritably.

"You are looking at both of us, sir."

"Explain."

"I will show you."

And suddenly it wasn't smooth and oily anymore, nor did it glow or vary in hue. Its skin was a pasty gray and looked somehow soft and very vulnerable.

"It's an epidermis?" asked Cole. "That looks like a naturally occurring phenomenon. How does it qualify as symbiosis?"

"What you call an epidermis is a Gorib—a living, thinking entity, sir," said the Tolobite. "My race does not have an internal immune system, so we live in symbiosis with the Goribs. A Gorib filters all germs and viruses out of the air and protects our bodies from infection, and in exchange we supply it with nourishment. We are each telepathically bonded to our symbiote, and we remain together for life. When one dies, both die."

"Interesting," said Cole. "I'm going to need a name for you that I can pronounce."

"I understand, sir."

He stared at the Tolobite, as the smooth, oily second skin began to reappear through the pores of its own gray skin. "How about Slick?"

"Whatever you wish, sir."

"Slick it is." Cole turned to Briggs and Christine. "From this point on, the Tolobite is Slick, whether you're addressing him or discussing him with me."

"Excuse me, sir," said Slick, "but gender-based words such as 'him' do not apply to either myself or my symbiote."

"I'll try to keep that in mind," said Cole. "Now let's get into the shuttle. We're approaching the Teroni ship, and it's only going to be another moment or two before it notices." He turned to Briggs. "Once we're aboard, fill Slick in on what we plan to do. You and he are going to handle the weapons."

"I have only trained on weapons, sir," said Slick as they boarded the shuttle and the hatch closed behind them. "I've never actually fired one in combat."

"Then it will be a useful learning experience," said Cole. "Don't worry; you'll have Lieutenant Briggs alongside you, and we don't expect our target to shoot back." He turned to Christine. "Lieutenant Mboya, once the Teroni ship has passed us and we can activate our systems, I want you to immediately open a communication channel with the *Quentin*. Then the only thing you'll do thereafter is find us some wormholes somewhere beyond our target. I don't care where they lead. If the Teroni ship has mapped them, we're dead meat anyway, and if not, it'll never be able to figure out where we'll reappear."

"Yes, sir," she said.

Suddenly they were floating loose in space.

"I guess the Teronis finally noticed the *Teddy R*," said Cole. "We are not going to be able to track them, not with all our systems dead. I doped out their average speed the last two times they chased us off, and I figure they'll pass us in about eighty seconds. Then we'll give them about four more minutes. We can't count on their following the *Teddy R* any longer than that." He paused. "If Forrice was in charge, he'd zig and zag and tease the hell out of them to keep them interested, but I don't think we can count on Podok to do the same."

"Who do you think they're protecting, sir?" asked Briggs. "An admiral, maybe, or a general?"

"Not an admiral. He'd hold any meetings on his own ship. Maybe a general, maybe a politician. My own guess is a turncoat. Their generals and politicians don't have to come to the Phoenix Cluster to talk to one another. Probably someone is busy selling out the Republic right now—not that we're small enough to sell out in one fell swoop, but it can cause problems for a planet or an army."

"Two and a half minutes, sir," announced Christine.

Cole sat at the command console. "While you're hunting for wormholes and Briggs and Slick are making sure the weapons work, I'm going to have to figure out which planet we're targeting. I can't imagine we're three minutes away from whichever one it is, so it ought to keep us all busy."

They waited in silence, and finally Christine activated the *Kermit*. It shot forward at light speeds, and she opened a channel to the *Quentin* and began charting their position in relation to the known wormholes.

"It looks like three possibilities to me," said Fujiama's voice. "I'll take Crepello IV, you take Bannister II, and whoever gets done first can check Nebout V."

"Sounds good to me," responded Cole. "I don't imagine they came all this way to meet on a chlorine world."

"Let's hope not," said Fujiama. "There must be ten of them in the immediate area; we wouldn't have time to scan more than one or two of them. I don't see how we can have more than three or four minutes at the outside before the Teroni ship returns."

It took Cole less than a minute to determine that there was no life on Bannister II, and he directed his attention to Nebout V.

"Sir," said Christine a few seconds later. "The Teroni ship has broken off the chase and is heading back at top speed."

"Don't worry about the ship," said Cole without looking up. "Worry about the wormhole."

"Crepello IV is clean," announced Fujiama. "Some kind of radiation accident. The whole planet is deserted, and it's too hot for any life-form to survive."

"Okay, then it's got to be Nebout," said Cole. "But so far I'm not getting any life readings."

"Neither am I," said Fujiama. "Could you have been wrong?"

"No," said Cole firmly. "If I was wrong, why the hell is the Teroni ship racing back?" He checked his instruments again. "I think I've got 'em!"

"Which planet?" asked Fujiama.

"None of them—but there's a moon with an oxygen atmosphere circling the gas giant that's nine planets out from Nebout."

"Got it!" said Fujiama excitedly. "And I've found a life reading!"

"Have your computer feed the data to the *Kermit*'s weapons system," said Cole. He turned to Christine. "How are we doing on wormholes? I'll want one out by Nebout IX."

She shook her head. "The closest is near Bannister."

"You're sure?"

"Yes, sir."

"Load its coordinates into the navigation system and then start tracking the Teroni ship."

A ten-second pause. "It's loaded. The Teroni ship should be within range—of their weapons, not ours—in about two minutes."

"How long will it take us to get from the Nebout system to the wormhole?"

She checked her computer. "Seventy-three seconds, sir."

"Lieutenant Briggs, can we reach our target with a pulse torpedo from this distance?"

"Yes, sir," said Briggs. "But the Teroni ship can actually overtake the torpedo before it reaches its target."

"Then we'll have to distract it," said Cole. "Fire the torpedo."

"Fired," announced Briggs.

"And another."

"Fired," confirmed Slick.

"How many do we have left?"

"Only two sir," said Briggs. "This is just a shuttle, not the *Teddy R*."

"Lieutenant Mboya, head for the wormhole. Mr. Briggs, fire a torpedo at the Teroni ship."

"This isn't the *Teddy R*'s weapons system, sir. We'll never hit it."

"We don't care whether we hit it," said Cole. "We just want to distract it."

"Fired," said Briggs.

"They've sensed the torpedo, sir," said Christine. "They're altering course slightly to come after us."

"They know we're going for a wormhole, but they don't know where it is," said Cole. "That may buy us a few seconds."

"I'll buy you a few more," said Fujiama's voice. "Make good use of them, Mr. Cole."

"Sir!" said Christine. "He's not heading for the wormhole! He's going straight at the target."

"For better or worse, you've done your damage. I haven't done mine," said Fujiama. "If they have a choice, they'll come after me before they'll bother with you."

"You're the Captain," said Cole. "It's not worth losing your shuttle to save ours."

"I'm not doing this to save the *Kermit*," responded Fujiama. "I'm doing it to make sure they come after me and not those pulse torpedoes you fired."

"But—"

"No arguments, Mr. Cole. Just get to that wormhole. I've been playing at being an officer and a gentleman for five years; it's time I started acting like one."

"The Teroni ship has changed course again, sir," said Christine. "They're definitely going after the *Quentin*."

"How long before they're within range of him?"

"Maybe thirty seconds."

"Once they nail him, can they reach us, too?"

"It'll be a near thing, but I think we'll make the wormhole by two or three seconds."

"Shouldn't we turn back and try to help the Captain?" asked Slick.

"He's made his choice," said Cole. "The only thing turning back would do is lose two shuttles instead of one. How soon to the wormhole?"

"Forty-five seconds," said Christine.

"Stay on course, and put the *Quentin* on the main screen."

They never saw the Teroni ship; it was still too far away. But one second the *Quentin* was racing for the Nebout IX moon, and the next second there was a blinding flash of light, and then the area was riddled with the debris of the shuttle.

"Damn!" muttered Cole. "I *told* him not to take the *Quentin*."

Six seconds after that, there was a huge explosion on the surface of the moon.

"It worked," said Cole. "They couldn't re-aim their weapons fast enough. The second we enter the wormhole send a message to Podok telling her to get the hell out of the cluster as fast as she can. With no one left to protect, there's no reason for the Teroni ship not to go after the *Teddy R* in earnest."

"Ten seconds to the wormhole," announced Christine. "Eight. Seven. Six. Five. Four. Three. Two."

The shuttle shuddered.

"We're inside!"

"Send that message!" said Cole. "Mr. Briggs, what did they hit?"

"I don't know, sir. We're still traveling at light speeds, and our laser banks are still operative."

"Well, damn it, they hit *something*!"

"I can go outside the ship and see what damage was sustained, sir," said Slick.

"Thanks for offering, but we don't have any space suits for Tolobites," said Cole.

"I don't need one," replied Slick. "My Gorib will protect me."

"Your symbiote?"

"Yes, sir."

"You can go outside in absolute zero, with no oxygen?"

"Not for lengthy periods, but long enough to inspect the ship," answered Slick. "All I need is a lifeline so I don't float away."

"Mr. Briggs, give him everything he needs, seal him in the airlock, and then let him go outside the ship."

"I must point out again, sir: I am not a him," said Slick.

"If you can answer to a name that's not yours, you can let me refer to you by a gender you don't possess," said Cole. "We can argue about all this later. You've got a job to do now."

Briggs sealed the Tolobite in the hatch, waited until he'd attached his line, and then opened the outer hatch door.

"That's a remarkable being, that Tolobite," remarked Cole as Slick made its way around the exterior of the shuttle. "He not only can repair a ship on short notice, but I'll bet he can survive on chlorine and methane worlds for a few hours without any suit or equipment. Why the hell aren't there more of them in the service?"

"He seems comfortable with us," said Briggs. "Maybe it's the Goribs that don't want to serve."

"I suppose that's as good a guess as any," said Cole. "Let's cherish the one we've got. Lieutenant Mboya, how long before we're out of the wormhole?"

"About four minutes, sir."

"If Slick isn't back in the airlock in three minutes, slow down, and if he's not back in three and a half, bring the ship to a stop. That's a pretty interesting symbiote he's got, but I don't know if even a Gorib can handle the transition from hyperspace to normal space."

"I don't know if I *can* stop in hyperspace, sir."

"Let's hope we don't have to find out, but if he's out there in three and a half minutes, try."

It became moot when Slick reentered the hatch two minutes later. Briggs adjusted the temperature, oxygen content, and gravity and then let him in.

"Well?" asked Cole.

"There's been some damage to the tail, sir," reported Slick. "It won't affect us in space, but it will be all but impossible to navigate the *Kermit* in any atmosphere until repairs are made."

"But it won't hinder us from our rendezvous with the *Teddy R?*"

"Not unless we plan to meet them in an atmosphere or stratosphere."

"Thank you, Slick."

"I just received a coded message from the *Teddy R*," announced Christine. "They've figured out where we'll emerge and will be waiting for us. We've made it, sir!"

"*Some* of us have made it," Cole replied. "Now I've got to go back to the *Teddy R* and tell them that their Captain is dead."

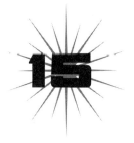

"How's it going?" asked Sharon Blacksmith's image.

Cole lay back on his cot, his head propped up, reading a book on his holoscreen.

"Can't complain." He smiled. "It wouldn't do any good."

"There's still no word from Fleet Command."

"They can't decide whether to decorate me or demote me," said Cole. "And not knowing who or what we killed on that moon doesn't help my case much."

"Want some company?"

"The mess hall?" he asked.

"No. I put on three pounds last month. I'll come to your quarters."

"What about your reputation?"

"On *this* ship?" she laughed. "It'll enhance it." She paused. "I'll be there in a couple of minutes."

"Take your time," replied Cole. "I'm not on duty until blue shift."

She broke the connection and entered his cabin a few minutes later.

"Sorry to intrude," she said. "But I was going stir crazy in that little office of mine."

"No problem," answered Cole, sitting up on the cot and swinging his feet to the floor. "I'm glad to have the company."

"Christine Mboya filled me in on your little adventure," she said, pulling up a chair. "That was quite a noble thing the Captain did."

"You think so?"

"Don't you?" she asked.

"If I'd been on the *Quentin*, I'd have fired most of my payload into the moon, fired what was left at the Teroni ship, and raced off in the opposite direction from the *Kermit*," he said. "I'd have at least forced the Teroni ship to make a choice between us."

"You didn't have anything to prove," said Sharon. "Maybe the Captain felt that he did."

Cole shrugged. "Maybe. But if Forrice had been in charge of the *Quentin* the way I planned it originally, there's a fifty-fifty chance it would have made it back."

"And a fifty-fifty chance the *Kermit* wouldn't have."

"True," he admitted. "But Mount Fuji sacrificed himself. It was a noble thing to do, but I was taught that it's never a good idea to die for your side. The object of the exercise is to make your enemy die for *his* side."

She stared at him for a long moment. "You make too much sense to be on the *Teddy R*, Wilson. I expect you to be transferred any day now."

"Not a chance," replied Cole. "This ship is my punishment. I'm here for the duration. You know," he continued, "you never told me what *you* did to deserve the *Teddy R*."

"I had a discreet affair with an officer aboard my last ship."

"That was all?"

"He wasn't human."

"The mind boggles. Someday when I know you better you must tell me all about it."

"Do you really want to know?"

Cole ran his gaze up and down her body, dwelling here and there on the more alluring curves. "No," he admitted. "I think I'll have more fun imagining."

She chuckled and was about to reply when the image of the Pelleanor from Security suddenly appeared. "I am sorry to disturb you,

Colonel Blacksmith," it said, "but we have just had a Priority One transmission from Fleet Command."

"Patch it through to me here."

"But Commander Cole is with you."

"His security clearance is even higher than mine," said Sharon. "I take full responsibility. Now patch it through."

"Yes, sir."

"Sir?" asked Cole.

"When you don't have a gender, like the Pelleanors, distinctions become difficult," she replied. "Here it comes."

The image of Fleet Admiral Susan Garcia flickered into existence—and froze. Sharon quickly uttered a ten-digit security code and the image came to life.

"Captain Makeo Fujiama will be posthumously honored with the Medal of Courage," said the Admiral. "Commander Podok is promoted to the rank of Captain and is now in command of the *Theodore Roosevelt*. The position of First Officer will remain open, pending an Admiralty hearing on a report submitted by Captain Podok. Commander Wilson Cole will remain as Second Officer, and Commander Forrice will remain as Third Officer. Effective immediately, the *Theodore Roosevelt* will proceed to the Cassius Cluster. The Fourth Fleet is making its big push, and will have to refuel there. The *Roosevelt*'s mission is to do whatever is necessary to make sure that the nuclear fuel stockpiled on Benidos II and New Argentina does not fall into enemy hands."

The image vanished.

"I wonder what reality *she's* been living in?" said Cole. "How does she think we're going to hold off even a single Teroni warship, let along a group of them?"

"Fortunately, that's not your worry, Mr. Second Officer. We've got a new Captain to ponder that."

"And you can bet that Podok will take everything literally and never dream of asking for a clarification," said Cole.

"Well, I've checked the message. There's nothing dangerous hidden in it."

"What might there be?" asked Cole.

"Oh, any number of things. At some point you could have a literally blinding light, or a musical note at the right pitch and volume to permanently deafen the listener—or even some hypnosis-inducing music. We do it when we intercept their messages and send them along to their destinations, and they do it to us."

"And Security is first on the firing line?"

"I'm wearing lenses and ear filters that protect me."

"I'm not."

"If I wasn't sure it was from the Admiral, I wouldn't have opened it here. Our system checks them pretty thoroughly when they come in. Anyway, this one is safe to pass on to Podok. I'll give it to her, and tell her that unless I'm instructed otherwise, I'll make the message available to the crew." She stood up. "It occurs to me that it would probably be better if I didn't contact her from your room."

"Okay. See you later."

She walked out into the corridor. Cole went back to his book for the next half hour, then found himself with another visitor—Gunnery Sergeant Eric Pampas.

"Ah, the Wild Bull himself," said Cole. "How are you feeling today?"

"Ashamed," answered Pampas. "And humiliated."

"Not unreasonable, given the situation."

"I came by to apologize, sir. I'm sure I'm on report, and I deserve to be. But I just want you to know that it won't happen again."

"Why did it happen the first time?" asked Cole.

"I was resentful at being tossed in here with a bunch of deadbeats. And

I was bored. I'm a gunnery expert who hasn't seen an enemy ship in close to a year." Cole remained silent, and Pampas shifted his feet awkwardly. "Anyway, there were days when it was easier to get drugs than food, and everyone else was doing it." Cole continued staring at him, his face an emotionless mask. "That's a shitty excuse, isn't it?" continued Pampas.

"Yes, it is," said Cole.

"I'll tell you the truth, sir. I did it because nobody cared. The Captain didn't care what I did, and back at Fleet Command they didn't care what happened to the *Teddy R*. I mean, look at our weaponry, sir. They can't expect us to go up against a modern, well-equipped Teroni ship with the guns I service. They just didn't give a damn, so the crew stopped giving a damn, too. Then you came aboard, and you *did* give a damn. You risked your life on Rapunzel, and you tossed my whole crew in the brig when no one else cared what we did—and then I heard what you did in the Phoenix Cluster, sir." He paused awkwardly. "I just want you to know that as long as you care, I care, too. I'll take my punishment, whatever it is, but when it's done I want you to know I'll be the best damned gunnery technician you ever saw."

"I don't write reports, Sergeant." Cole paused and studied him. "You'll do."

"Sir?" said Pampas.

"The incident is forgotten," said Cole. "You ever do it again and I'll personally see to it that you spend your next ten years in confinement— but I accept your apology, and I believe you're sincere. As far as I'm concerned, you're back on duty and none of this will go on your record."

"Thank you, sir," said Pampas. "If there's ever anything I can do for you—anything at all . . ."

"Sharon, are you monitoring this?" said Cole, raising his voice.

"Of course," replied Sharon Blacksmith, sending only her voice and not her image, to put Pampas more at ease.

"Okay. Listen to what I tell Sergeant Pampas, but don't make a record of it."

"Understood," said Sharon.

"You're a big man," noted Cole. "And you're in good shape. Even your muscles have muscles. Do you know how to use them?"

"I'm not sure I understand what you're getting at, sir," said Pampas.

"The next time any member of your crew shows up with drugs or any other stimulant, I want you to take it away from him, beat the crap out of him—you won't be monitored and no record will be kept—and deliver the stuff to me. If anyone's dumb enough to ask you to return it, you are to tell him I've got it and he should ask me."

"You're saying I won't get in trouble for beating them up?" asked Pampas.

"I can't report what I can't see or hear," said Cole. "How about you, Sharon?"

"We've been having a lot of trouble with the equipment in the gunnery section," she replied. "Whole hours are going by unobserved and unrecorded."

"Are there any other questions, Sergeant?" asked Cole.

"No, sir," he said. He walked to the door, then turned and saluted. "Damn! I'm glad you're here, sir. It feels like the military again."

He stepped out into the corridor and Cole was alone once more.

"Sharon, try to arrange your schedule so you're on duty the first few minutes that Pampas shows up in the gunnery section each day. If they haven't broken out the drugs within a half hour, they're probably not going to during that shift."

"I can do better than that," she replied. "I can put gunnery on a Priority Watch, so only officers with my security clearance or higher can observe it or monitor the record. That means just you, me, Forrice, and the Captain."

"That'll do," said Cole. "Forrice will go along with it, and the drunks and druggies have to know that it's no use running to the Captain. Sometimes being an unimaginative stickler for the rules can be a positive asset: I wouldn't put it past her to set them down on some deserted planet for being intoxicated on duty."

"You know, in ways she wasn't a bad First Officer. I never saw anyone better at tending to details. I wonder what kind of Captain she'll be?"

"If you're me, the answer is: a hostile one," said Cole, forcing a smile to his face.

"Well, there doesn't seem to be anything in our new orders that might precipitate any arguments. We're out in the boonies again, guarding gas stations or the equivalent."

"You just heard our gunnery expert. Do you really want to be in the thick of the action?"

"When you put it that way, I'm more than happy to protect fuel dumps," she said. "I was momentarily misled into thinking that the *Teddy R* was responsible for our recent triumphs on Rapunzel and Nebout—but of course it wasn't the *Teddy R* at all. It was you."

"I'm just an officer who reacts to what he sees," said Cole. "I realize that on this ship it's been a rarity, but it's really not a very rare or special trait."

"If you convince me of that, I'll probably give up all thoughts of seducing you," said Sharon.

"If I don't convince you of that, you'll probably decide that I won't live long enough to be worth the effort," he replied.

"Nonsense," she said. "Going to bed with heroes is the surest way to avoid long-term commitments." She suddenly looked off to her left. "There's a message coming in from Podok. She wants to see you."

"On the bridge?"

"In her quarters." Sharon grinned. "Watch yourself in the clinches, and remember that the fun parts on a Polonoi are all in the back."

"Based on my limited exposure to them, I can't imagine a Polonoi ever having fun," replied Cole.

He broke the connection, left his cabin, and went down one level, where most of the aliens on the crew had their quarters. He walked to Podok's door, waited for it to scan and identify him, and then entered.

The new captain's cabin was sparely furnished. Nothing looked comfortable. The cot lacked a mattress, the chairs were an alien hardwood, there wasn't a cushion or pillow in the room. The walls were devoid of artwork, but Cole noticed an incomprehensible, nonrepresentational holograph on the ceiling. Whatever it depicted was *moving* back and forth within the frame, but he had no idea what he was looking at.

"You have heard the news, I presume?" said Podok after a moment.

"What news?" he asked innocently. *No sense getting Sharon into trouble by telling you I knew before you did.*

"I have been made Captain of the *Theodore Roosevelt*," said Podok.

"Then congratulations are in order—once we finish mourning for Captain Fujiama, that is."

"I seek no congratulations," said the Polonoi. "I merely inform you of the fact."

"And am I now First Officer?" he asked, a meaningless question designed to further shield Sharon.

"No, Mr. Cole. You remain Second Officer."

"Is it Forrice, then?"

"There will be no First Officer for the time being," answered Podok. "This will doubtless change when the Admiralty Court convenes to discuss my report on the events that transpired in the Phoenix Cluster."

"I'm sure it was fair and accurate, ma'am."

"Call me Captain. 'Ma'am' is a human term, and I am not a human."

"I apologize, Captain," said Cole. "Was there anything else you wished to tell me?"

"Yes," said Podok. "Our new mission will be to protect vitally important fuel depots in the Cassius Cluster. I have already instructed Pilot Wxakgini to take us there, and the ship should enter the Vestorian Wormhole any moment. That will cut our transit time to seven hours." She stared at him. "We shall arrive during blue shift. If at that time you should see any sign of the Teroni fleet, or even a single ship, you are to take no action, but are to report it directly to me. There are no exceptions. Is that perfectly clear, Mr. Cole?"

"It is perfectly clear, Captain."

"I have my orders concerning the fuel depots, and I intend to carry them out to the best of my ability. You turned Captain Fujiama's head and it cost him his life. I tell you here and now: you will not turn mine."

"So what do you think?" asked Forrice as he sat across from Cole in the small officers' lounge.

"About what?"

"Don't be obtuse," said the Molarian. "I'm talking about your not moving up to First Officer."

Cole shrugged. "When you've been a captain twice, the difference between First Officer and Second Officer becomes unimportant."

"But you know Podok's going to have you doing all the First Officer's jobs."

"That's her privilege," said Cole. "She's the Captain. What she says goes."

"Even if she says something dumb?"

"Captains can't say anything dumb," replied Cole with an ironic smile. "That's clearly stated on page three of the Regulations."

"Let's see if you're still smiling a month from now," said Forrice.

"Let's see if we're still alive a month from now," said Cole. "I don't know if it's occurred to anyone else, but the *Teddy R* isn't going to be able to offer much opposition to a fleet of Teroni ships. To tell you the truth, I don't know how we'd do against even one well-equipped ship."

"They must not expect any incursions from the Teroni Federation, or they wouldn't be transferring us to the Cassius Cluster."

"I don't know," said Cole.

"But like you say, we couldn't hold them off."

"I wonder if the Navy wouldn't prefer a dead hero to a live one," said Cole. "Every time I've done something effective it's made the admirals and generals in charge of this war look bad. The press may love it, but I think the brass is getting damned tired of it."

"Well," said the Molarian, "it would explain why they stuck you out on the Rim, and then in the Phoenix Cluster. And if they think the fuel depots aren't known to the Teronis, then that explains our move here—either you serve in total obscurity until everyone forgets you or you die in combat and they have a hero who doesn't embarrass them." He paused. "You'd think our side would *want* heroes."

"To brag about, yes. To work with, no. If I know the press, right now it's looking for high-level officers to crucify for not knowing that the Bortellites were on Rapunzel or that a secret meeting was taking place in the Phoenix Cluster. And if I know the Navy, they've got three full departments of public-relations officers working round the clock to prove to the press that everything that happened was carefully planned in advance. That's why I'm not going to get another medal; the public would demand that I be put in charge of something major, and that's anathema to men and women who haven't had an original thought in years."

"You don't seem especially outraged," noted Forrice.

"Would it do any good?" responded Cole.

"What difference does *that* make?" demanded the Molarian. "There's something wrong when I'm angrier than you over their treatment of you."

"Our side isn't perfect," said Cole, "but we *are* the good guys. It seems more productive to save my anger for the abuses of the bad guys."

Podok entered the lounge just then. She walked over and stood before Forrice. "Commander Forrice, you will be in charge of the bridge during red shift until further notice."

"Yes, Captain," said Forrice, rising to his three feet and saluting.

"Commander Cole, you will remain on blue shift."

"I assumed as much," said Cole.

"May I sit down?"

"You're the Captain."

She turned to Forrice. "I would like to speak to Commander Cole in private. Would you mind stepping outside the lounge for a few minutes?"

"I'd be happy to, Captain," said the Molarian. "I'll stop anyone else from entering until you tell me your meeting is over."

"Thank you," said Podok. She waited until Forrice had left and then turned to Cole.

"I imagine you are very disappointed not to have been made First Officer," she said.

"I can live with it."

"Nonetheless, I want to be totally honest and forthright with you. The reason you have not been promoted is almost certainly my report concerning your conduct on both the Rim and in the Phoenix Cluster."

"I assumed as much," he replied. "They had no other reason to pass me over."

"There will be an Admiralty hearing, and the matter will be resolved," said Podok. "You will either be promoted to First Officer, remain as Second Officer, or be demoted. The matter is out of my hands."

"I am certain that your hands are clean," he said, wondering if she could understand sarcasm.

"All that is behind us. We must still function together on the *Theodore Roosevelt*. Until they promote you or send us a new First Officer, you and I are the two highest-ranking officers aboard the ship."

"I am aware of that, Captain."

"I'll be perfectly candid, Commander. I don't like you. I don't like the fact that you find ways to circumvent regulations, that you obey only those orders you approve of, that you continually put the ship and crew in danger. I cannot argue with the results, at least thus far . . . but if every member of the crew, many of whom all but worship you, were to use their initiative and freely disobey any orders they didn't like, the results would be disastrous. Every military in the history of every civilized race has been constructed as many smoothly functioning cogs in a mighty war machine. Even societies that cherish the individual, such as your own, realize that under certain circumstances, in which category the military falls, every crew member must subordinate his individuality, even his creativity, for the good of the whole."

"I have no disagreement with you in principle," said Cole.

"But not in practice."

"Conditions change, and it would be foolish not to change with them."

"I asked for this meeting not to argue with you, Commander Cole, but to explain my view of the military. My report has been submitted. I wouldn't change it if I could, but it's over. As far as I'm concerned, we are starting with a fresh slate. I am only the third member of my race ever to command a starship, and I would like your support."

"You have it," said Cole. "We have our differences, but I'm an officer in the Republic's Navy, and that means I am loyal to my commanding officer."

"Good," said Podok, rising. "I shall count on it."

She walked out of the small lounge without another word. Cole got up to leave, but found Forrice blocking the doorway.

"Well?" said the Molarian.

"She offered an olive branch," said Cole. "You wouldn't have recognized it as such, but she did the best she could."

"An olive branch?"

"Sorry. As ugly as you are, I should remember you're not human and don't know all the references. She offered to make peace with me, to start over again."

"How long do you think that will last?" said Forrice with a sarcastic hoot.

"Until it stops," said Cole. "I'm off to grab a nap before blue shift."

Forrice stepped aside to let him pass into the corridor. "I'll see you later."

"Fine," said Cole. "Come visit me on the bridge during blue shift. It figures to be pretty dull. If the Navy thought there was a snowball's chance in hell of the Teronis actually finding the fuel depots, there'd be more than just the *Teddy R* here to stop them. They may or may not want the enemy to find *us*, but it figures that the fuel depots are well hidden."

Cole stopped by the mess hall to pick up a cup of coffee to take back to his room with him. The place was deserted except for two human crewmen sitting in a corner and Slick, the Tolobite, who sat alone, eating something that seemed to wriggle as it approached his mouth. Cole decided to stop at his table for a moment.

"I just wanted to thank you again for your efforts the other day," he said. "I've recommended you for a decoration. That's some symbiote you've got yourself."

"He thanks you."

Cole looked surprise. "Can he speak?"

"Only through me," said Slick. "We are linked by a telepathic bond."

"The two of you together form just about the most useful entity on the ship," continued Cole. "You've been sorely misused, or totally unused, to date. That's going to change."

"Thank you, sir," said Slick. "Commander Forrice and Lieutenant Briggs have been schooling me in the gunnery section."

"I suppose you might as well keep it up for a week or two more, until you're comfortable with what you're doing—but turning a crewman who can survive in space without protection, or walk across chlorine or methane planets with no discomfort . . . well, it seems wasteful of your talents."

"I'm glad to find an officer who appreciates my particular talents, sir."

"I do more than appreciate them, Slick," replied Cole. "I *envy* them." He carried his cup to the doorway of the mess hall. "Nice to see you again."

He walked to the airlift, descended to the level where his cabin was located, and approached it, sipping at the coffee to make sure it didn't spill.

"You know," said Sharon's voice in his ear, "you're a senior officer. You could get a yeoman to carry it for you."

"That strikes me as a waste of a yeoman," he said.

"I *knew* I liked you from the first minute you showed up. You want a little company?"

"I'm going to bed," said Cole.

"I know. I've been monitoring you, remember?"

"If I say yes, do you win the pool?"

"I'll let you know after you say yes."

He stopped and took another sip of his coffee.

"I'd love to, but . . ."

"But what?"

He grimaced. "How the hell can I yell at the crew for fraternization?"

"Write a letter of resignation when you enter your room and tear it up later."

"I don't think you *can* resign in wartime."

"I'm tired of making suggestions. Are we going to go to bed together or aren't we?"

"Come on down to the cabin. I'll think of some justification."

"I'm a damned good-looking woman," said Sharon. "This is the first time someone ever needed justification for taking me to bed."

"War makes strange bedfellows."

"You call me strange once more and I'll stay where I am."

"Then I'll fall asleep and you'll have to live with being rejected."

"You don't get off the hook that easily," said Sharon. "I'm on my way."

A male Molarian entered the corridor. Cole decided to break the connection, then realized that he hadn't made it in the first place and had no idea how to stop it. *Well, at least they can't see you*, he thought.

He entered his room, placed his coffee cup on the small desk, took his shoes off, and sat down in front of his computer.

"Activate." It instantly hummed to life. "Any word on Slick's medal yet?"

"There has been no response yet."

"They'd better not be holding it up because I'm on report," said Cole. "He's the one it's for, not me."

He had not asked a question, so there was no reply.

"Any word about who might have been on the moon of Nebout IX?"

"No."

"I'm starting to get annoyed," muttered Cole. "It's like the whole incident never happened. Deactivate."

The computer went dead, and a moment later Sharon Blacksmith entered his cabin.

"Well?" she said.

"Well what?"

"Have you come up with a justification?"

"You had an affair with an alien. They're our allies now, but who knows what the future holds? You're going to have to show me every single thing he did to you, so we can safeguard future officers against such seductions."

"Every single thing?"

"Absolutely."

"I can hardly wait," said Sharon, joining him on the bed.

For the next week life aboard the ship was uneventful. The *Teddy R* continued to patrol the Cassius Cluster without seeing any enemy ships. Podok seemed to be less rigid, though, as Cole pointed out to Forrice, rigidity didn't manifest itself during routine operations.

Cole spent the time continuing to acquaint himself with the ship and its crew. He was visited in his quarters twice more by Sharon Blacksmith, who insisted that any more often would imply an emotional commitment that neither of them could afford to make in this situation. He was content with the arrangement; there was nothing she wasn't willing to try or suggest, and she left him so exhausted that he was certain that if they got together on a daily basis he'd be too tired to carry out his duties.

He began evaluating the crew of the *Teddy R*, not on paper, but in his head. He would trust Forrice with his life, and indeed had done so in the past. Beyond the Molarian, he thought the two most efficient officers were Sharon Blacksmith—he had come to that conclusion before they began sleeping together—and Christine Mboya. He didn't know if Slick was any good at what he was being asked to do, but it didn't matter; that symbiote made him the most valuable member of the crew. Cole found himself wondering five or six times a day what kind of thoughts a sentient epidermis had; he couldn't come up with an answer. He also was developing a soft spot for Wild Bull Pampas; the man had kept his word and insisted on working extra shifts to make up for all the shifts where he'd been stoned. Like many others of the crew, he seemed to crave discipline and purpose, and Cole had called a number of informal meetings to explain exactly what they were doing in the Cassius Cluster and why they had to remain alert.

Podok had been an efficient First Officer, as long as there was a Captain to overrule her. She'd been an excellent Captain since her promotion, but he distrusted her rigidity.

On their ninth day in the cluster, word came through from Fleet Admiral Susan Garcia that the charges against him had been determined to be true, but not serious enough to demote him, and that he would remain as Second Officer. They would be rotating in a new First Officer as soon as conditions allowed.

"Which means when they've got another officer who embarrasses them by being right when they're wrong," concluded Cole as he told Forrice the news in the mess hall. "Of course I put in a strong protest and demanded that you be promoted."

"I think that all but guarantees I won't become First Officer," said the Molarian, uttering a hoot of laughter at his own comment. "It's just as well. As soon as we get a new First Officer, I can get off red shift."

"How the hell much of a hardship can red shift be?" asked Cole. "We're here for the express purpose of preventing the Teroni Federation from appropriating our fuel supplies. Since we haven't spotted a single Teroni ship, what's your objection?"

"We're going to spot one one of these days," said Forrice. "I want to have the gunnery crew properly trained before then. I might add that when he can stop talking about what a great man you are, Sergeant Pampas is proving to be a motivated assistant."

"I'm glad to hear it. I'd also like to know why you think we're going to run into a Teroni ship out here."

"Don't you?"

"Yes. But I'd like to hear your reasons. If they're different from mine and just as valid, I'll have Christine scan the area a little more frequently."

"It's simple enough," said the Molarian. "We know the Bortellites had an energy shortage. If they had to go to Rapunzel for it and risk an armed engagement, that implies the Teronis don't have much, if any, to spare, so they figure to be looking for our fuel depots."

Cole nodded. "Yeah, I used the same facts and came to the same conclusion."

"There's another one, one you'd never think of yourself," added Forrice.

"Enlighten me."

"They know you're our most decorated hero, and they know you're an officer on the *Teddy R*. My guess is that they'll never believe the Navy would order the *Teddy R* out here unless we were protecting someone or something pretty damned valuable—not with Wilson Cole himself onboard."

"Rubbish," protested Cole. "They know I'm in the doghouse."

"They also know you bit them twice while you were on your leash," said the Molarian.

"Enough with the comparisons. You've never seen a dog in your life."

"I've never seen a Domarian, either, but I know they exist," Forrice shot back.

"I've been to Domar once."

"Is it true what they say about the Domarians?"

"Probably. I don't know what they say, but I know what I saw. They're on twenty-foot-long stiltlike legs, and they follow the sun endlessly over the horizon. They never stop, they never sit or lie down, and if one of them falls behind he's killed and eaten by some predator that never leaves the night side. It's more like a funhouse than a planet. Millions of intelligent Domarians—and not a house, a library, or a hospital on the whole damned planet."

"What do they eat?"

"The air."

"What are you talking about?"

"You know how some fish skim through the water with their mouths open just picking up small fish and crustacians?"

"We don't have any fish on my planet, but I'll take your word for it."

"Well, the Domarians have a couple of mouths, large ones, on each side of their jaws, and they pick pollen and microscopic nutrients out of the air. It's weird; I was wearing a helmet the whole time, and it never got dirty, but that air was feeding maybe ten million Domarians."

"I'd like to see it sometime."

"If the Teronis capture it, maybe we'll go there to liberate it."

"What would they want with the damned place?"

"What does any government want with any planet? In the end it boils down to the simple fact that they don't want someone else to have it."

"Makes sense to me," said Forrice.

"That's because you have a sense of humor," said Cole. "I'll be damned if I know why it makes sense to them."

The yellow-alert siren suddenly sounded, and just as suddenly ceased.

"I wonder that the hell *that* was all about," said Cole.

"We might as well go to the bridge and find out," said Forrice.

"Okay—but ask permission before you set foot on it. Podok is very jealous of her prerogatives."

He and Forrice got up from their table and took the airlift to the bridge. Rachel Marcos was standing at attention by her computer, trying unsuccessfully to hold back her tears.

"I request permission to come onto the bridge, Captain," said Cole.

"I also request permission, Captain," said Forrice.

"Permission granted."

Cole was about to step forward when Forrice jabbed him in the ribs with an elbow. "*Salute!*" whispered the Molarian.

Cole saluted, then walked onto the bridge. "We heard the yellow alert for just a few seconds, and then it vanished."

"That is because we are no longer on yellow alert," replied Podok.

"What happened, Captain?" asked Cole.

"Ensign Marcos falsely identified a ship from Lodin XI as being from the Teroni Federation."

"They're very similar, sir," said Rachel.

"Speak only when you are spoken to, Ensign," said Podok. "And address your remarks to me, not to Mr. Cole."

Cole turned to Podok. "These things happen," he said.

"These things are not supposed to happen. I have sent for a replacement. Ensign Marcos will not be allowed on the bridge in the future." She stared at Cole as if she expected him to protest.

"May I make a suggestion, Captain?" he said.

"Go ahead."

"You are absolutely right to remove Ensign Marcos from the bridge," he said. "But her error was one of inexperience. Rather than making her exile permanent, why not let her earn her way back?"

"Explain."

"Run a series of computer simulations," suggested Cole. "When she properly identifies the ship in the simulation as friend, neutral, or foe three hundred times in a row, let her come back to the bridge."

"That is reasonable," admitted Podok. "We will make it five hundred times. And you will not begin for a week, Ensign Marcos, which will give you time to study the configuration of the ships of all known powers."

Rachel turned to Cole. She seemed about to speak.

"Not a word, Ensign," said Cole sharply. "The Captain has made her decision, and you will abide by it."

"But—"

"I told you before to speak only to me," said Podok. "Proceed directly to your quarters. You are confined there for the next three solar days. Your meals will be brought to you, and you will speak to no one. Is that clear?"

"Yes, Captain," said Rachel.

"Then salute and leave."

Rachel saluted, tried to wipe the tears from her face as she lowered her hand, and headed for the airlift.

"Well, since nothing exciting is going on out there," said Cole, "I think I'll leave, too—if that's all right with you, Captain."

"Yes."

"Thank you, Captain," he said, snapping off a salute.

"I'll come with you," said Forrice, also saluting.

He and Forrice walked to the airlift. The Molarian got off at the mess hall, while Cole descended to his cabin, where he found Sharon waiting for him.

"I thought this lock only responded to my voiceprint and retina-gram," he said, stepping inside as the door snapped shut behind hin.

"Security can get into any room," she replied. "What if the Teronis draw and quarter you, or stake you out in the hot sun and turn small starving carnivores loose on you? Someone has to go through your effects, confiscate all classified material, jettison the rest, and clear the room for its next occupant."

"Well, as long as there's a sentimental reason for it, how can I object?"

"I was monitoring the bridge," she said. "You were a little hard on Ensign Marcos, weren't you?"

"My solution will have her back on the bridge in two weeks," replied Cole. "If I hadn't spoken up, Podok would never have let her back. If I seemed harsh, it was for Podok's benefit, not Rachel's."

"She's got a crush on you, you know."

"Podok? God, I hope not!"

"Don't be purposely obtuse. I'm talking about Rachel."

"Not after today, she doesn't."

"Don't bet on it," said Sharon.

He grimaced. "That's just what I need—a twenty-two-year-old ensign with a crush on me."

"Some men would think that was a pretty nice situation."

"Some men like children. I like women."

"I like hearing you talk like that," said Sharon. "It makes me think thirty-four isn't so old."

"Hell, I passed thirty-four without even slowing down," said Cole. "I wouldn't know what to say to a twenty-two-year-old kid."

"I don't think talking is atop her list of priorities."

"It never is," he replied. "The nice part is that eventually they grow up."

"What were *you* doing at twenty-two?" asked Sharon.

"The same thing I'm doing now," he answered. "Trying to sort out the smart orders from the dumb ones. Of course, back then I didn't think twenty-two-year-old girls were too young."

"Well, at least you're honest." She stared at him thoughtfully. "Why did you join the Navy?"

"I don't like walking."

"I'm being serious."

"They offered me a commission. The Army didn't. I figured I could get more accomplished as an officer than a foot soldier." Suddenly he grinned. "I guess I was right. You can't have two ships taken away from you in the infantry. How about you?"

"Me?" she repeated. "I've always been interested in other people's secrets. Now learning them is part of my job." She smiled. "Someday I'll learn all of yours."

"Maybe someday I'll tell them all to you."

"What fun would that be?" She stared at him, trying to interpret his expression. "What's the matter?"

"Nothing," he said. "It's just that that's the first time I've heard the word 'fun' mentioned in, oh, it must be ten or twelve years."

"Yes, I guess it doesn't go hand-in-glove with war," said Sharon. "And speaking of war, just how close were we to that Lodin ship?"

"Rachel would say: not very. Me, I'd say: close enough. If it wasn't within range, it was damned close to it."

"I think that—" Suddenly she frowned and tapped the tiny earphone in her left ear, then looked up. "Got to run."

"What is it?"

"A fight broke out in the science lab, of all places," she said. "It's under control, but I have to get over there."

"The lab? Check the supplies. We've got such a thorough guard on the infirmary that some of the druggies may be trying to mix their own."

"Will do. You want to come along?"

"Nope. I'm being a peace-loving officer this week."

"Catch you later," she said, getting up from the desk chair and walking toward the door, which irised to let her out.

The military's aging me fast, he thought. *I should be flattered that a pretty young girl has a crush on me. Instead I'm annoyed.* He smiled. *Now, that's real maturity.* He called up the book he'd been reading for the past few days and got about two more pages into it when the holoscreen went blank, to be replaced by Sharon's image.

"What is it?" he asked.

"Your friend Pampas found Crewman, or maybe it's Crewthing, Kjnniss, from Jasmine III, stealing the makings for a powerful hallucinogen from the science lab."

"So I was right."

"Let me finish. Sergeant Pampas, doubtless acting upon and misinterpreting your orders, beat Kjnniss to within an inch of his life. Kjnniss is now on its way to the infirmary, where the first thing they'll probably do is hook it up to a bunch of the drugs it would have stolen if it'd had the opportunity."

"I'd have done the same thing," said Cole. "Or at least I'd have tried to. I have a feeling he's about ten times better at it than I am."

"Anyway, I'm putting Pampas under arrest and confining him to his quarters," said Sharon. "I assume you'll be willing to defend him if charges are brought?"

"Yeah. I'll get over to his room sometime before blue shift and hear his side of the story."

"And if and when Kjnniss wakes up, you can get *its* version of the incident."

"Why bother? If it tells the truth, it's guilty—and if it lies, you can add perjury to the report."

"Just the same, it's innocent until proven guilty."

"So check the security disks and he won't be innocent any longer."

"How did a sensible man like you ever rise above the rank of yeoman?"

"I have friends in low places."

He broke the connection and was preparing to visit Pampas when the yellow-alert siren sounded again.

"I wonder what the hell it is this time?" he said in bored tones. "Probably Rachel's replacement identified a meteor storm as the Teroni fleet."

Then Podok's image and voice appeared throughout the ship. "We have a confirmed sighting on a Teroni ship. Be prepared to go to your battle stations should the alert level be raised to red."

"I'd better get back to work, just in case," said Sharon. Her image studied him. "What about you?"

"No red alert, no battle stations," replied Cole. "It's still white shift. This is Podok's crisis, not mine; let her solve it." He paused, then walked to the door. "On the other hand, there's no crisis so bad that truly incompetent command decisions can't make it worse. Maybe I'll go see what's happening."

Cole decided that Podok wouldn't welcome his intrusion in the first few minutes after the sighting of the Teroni ship, and since the yellow alert hadn't repeated or been elevated to red, he stopped to visit Pampas on the way.

"I don't know if you're allowed in here, sir," said Pampas as he entered.

"I know the regulations," replied Cole. "You can't leave, but there's nothing that says you can't have visitors."

"Captain Podok's not going to like that, sir."

"Captain Podok is a stickler for the rules, and I happen to be obeying them to the letter." He paused. "How are you holding up?"

"Pretty good, sir," replied Pampas. "I'm feeling useless, though. Especially the last half hour. What were all those yellow alarms?"

"The first one was a mistake," answered Cole. "The second probably wasn't. Evidently we've sighted a Teroni ship."

"Who made the mistake?" asked Pampas. "Captain Podok, I hope?"

"Captain Podok doesn't make that kind of mistake," answered Cole. "No, it was Rachel Marcos. She's been confined to quarters." Suddenly he smiled. "Hell, damned near everyone I like on this ship has been locked away."

"I don't hold it against you, sir," said Pampas. "It's time we cleaned up this ship, and that starts with the crew."

"I know—but you did put that guy in the infirmary," noted Cole.

"He was putting himself there with all those seeds, sir," replied Pampas. "I just sped him on his way."

Cole chuckled in amusement. "Is there anything you need, anything I can bring you?"

"No, sir. They're feeding me fine, and I've got the ship's whole library at my disposal."

"Another reader? I'm impressed."

"No, sir," said Pampas. "I pull up entertainments, mostly holo-dramas."

"Ah, well, as long as they keep you happy."

"I'd be a lot happier back at my gunnery station, where I could feel I was doing something useful, sir."

"I know," replied Cole sympathetically. "I'll do what I can to get you out of here—and of course if they sound a red alert, I figure that supercedes all minor punishments. The second you hear it, get the hell out of here and go directly to your battle station."

"You mean it?"

"Yes, I mean it," said Cole. "I for one would like to know that our weaponry is functional, and you probably know ten times as much about our cannons and our other stuff as whoever Four Eyes is training right now."

"What about my gunnery mates, sir?" asked Pampas. "How are they doing?"

"Kudop's still in a coma from chewing one seed too many, and since the doctor is a Bedalian whose entire experience with Polonoi has been limited to this ship, I would guess he's going to stay asleep for quite some time."

"And Solaniss?"

"Believe it or not, he's been rotated to Maintenance," answered Cole. "I tried to explain to Podok that we're shorthanded and we need him in

Gunnery, but you know her—if the schedule says he has to rotate to Maintenance, then that's where he's going to go." He paused. "I know there was a fourth gunnery technician, but I haven't met him yet."

"Her," Pampas corrected him.

"Human?"

Pampas shook his head. "An Orovite."

"I don't believe I ever saw one."

"She looks kind of like an ugly Soporian."

"Never saw one of those, either."

"I thought you'd been all over the galaxy, sir," said Pampas.

"Yes, I have," acknowledged Cole. "But usually on the inside of a ship. You'd be surprised how many races you don't meet if you don't touch down."

Pampas chuckled. "Yeah, I see your point, sir."

"Well, I'd better be going," said Cole. "I'll make it my business to look in on you at least once a day. If you need anything, just say so aloud."

"In an empty room?"

"Colonel Blacksmith or one of her subordinates will be monitoring you. They'll also monitor every other square centimeter on the ship, so they may not get back to you immediately—but before too long their equipment will tell them that there was someone talking in your room, even if it was just you saying you wanted a beer, and they'll do what they can for you." Suddenly he raised his voice. "Am I right?"

"Yes, sir," said a male voice that seemed to suddenly materialize high in a corner of the room. "And you don't have to yell."

"They've got a lot of things and people to watch, so don't abuse the privilege," Cole warned Pampas. "But remember it's there if you need it."

"Thank you, sir," said Pampas.

"See you tomorrow," said Cole, walking back out into the corridor.

He considered dropping in on Rachel Marcos, but decided against it. He hated tears, and he was sure she was still crying copiously. He simply didn't want to deal with her supplications or, worse yet, her advances. Instead he stepped out at the mess hall and ordered her the richest dessert on the menu, then found a yeoman who was just lounging around and had him take it to her.

Then it was finally time, he decided, to go up to the bridge. Not that he couldn't observe the Teroni ship just as well from any of two dozen screens scattered around the ship, or on his own computer for that matter—but he was less concerned with the ship than with Podok's reaction to it. The one time he'd seen her in anything resembling a crisis, back in the Phoenix Cluster, her responses had not inspired much confidence in him.

He took the airlift up to the bridge, stood well back for a few moments to make sure everyone was behaving calmly, and then stepped forward.

"Request permission to come aboard the bridge, Captain," he said, remembering to salute when she turned to face him.

"Permission granted."

"Thank you, Captain," he said.

"Why are you here, Mr. Cole?" she asked. "It is still white shift."

"I thought you might enlighten me as to your intentions concerning the Teroni ship, Captain," said Cole. "I really should know if we've hailed it, warned it off, shot at it, or ignored it before blue shift begins."

"That is reasonable," agreed Podok.

"May I first inquire as to the nature of the Teroni ship?" asked Cole.

"It is class Zeta Tau ship, probably built on Tambo IV, and the design places its age at between eight and seventeen years. It carries laser weapons, though this one seems to be retrofitted with at least one pulse cannon was well."

"I assume we've been tracking it?"

"Of course."

"Has it gone anywhere near Benidos II or New Argentina?" asked Cole.

"No," answered Podok. "It seems to be traversing a most irregular route."

"It's looking for them."

"For Benidos II and New Argentina?" said Podok. "They're on every star chart."

"I meant that it's looking for the fuel depots," explained Cole.

"I doubt it. It hasn't come close to them."

"It may not have to," he answered. "It might have the technology to sense the depots from light-years away."

"That is preposterous."

"Perhaps," said Cole. "But once upon a time both your race and mine thought flying just a few feet above the ground was preposterous."

"Do you know for a fact that such technology as you referred to exists?"

"No," he admitted. "And by the same token, I don't know for a fact that it doesn't."

"Then the sole purpose of this exchange seems to be for you to confess your total ignorance of the subject," said Podok.

You may be rigid, he thought while fighting back a smile of admiration, *but you're not stupid, I'll give you that.*

"I apologize, Captain," he said.

"Accepted."

"May I ask again what you intend to do about the Teroni ship?"

"Observe it," said Podok.

"Just observe it?"

"Yes."

"Nothing else?"

"Nothing else," replied Podok.

"May I speak frankly, Captain?"

"I cannot remember you ever speaking other than frankly, Mr. Cole."

"I think you're making a mistake."

"In what way?"

"I think we should blow that ship to pieces while we have the chance."

"My orders do not specify engaging enemy ships in battle," replied Podok. "The *Theodore Roosevelt*'s sole mission in the Cassius Cluster is to make sure the Teroni Federation's Fifth Fleet does not have access to the fuel depots on Benidos II and New Argentina, and that is what we shall do."

"I understand that, Captain," said Cole. "But—"

"If you understand it," she interrupted, "why do you keep disagreeing? Those are our orders. We will obey them."

"That's obviously a scout ship," said Cole. "They're not going to send their fleet, or any substantial part of it, to the Cassius Cluster until they know where the fuel depots are. If you let it locate the depots, you're inviting the very situation we're here to prevent."

"And what if the ship is here for some other purpose?" asked Podok.

"We're still at war," said Cole. "You have every right to attack it."

"I will tell you one more time: My mission orders say nothing about attacking Teroni ships. We are here solely to make sure that they do not appropriate fuel from Benidos II and New Argentina. Is that finally clear to you, Mr. Cole?"

"I understand your orders, Captain," said Cole. "But I think you can safeguard those depots better by destroying this advance scout before it finds them and reports back to the rest of the Fifth Fleet."

"That presupposes that this *is* a scout ship," said Podok. "You have no credible evidence to make that assumption, and even if you are right, I have no intention of disobeying my orders. This conversation is ended, Mr. Cole. Now please remove yourself from the bridge until blue shift."

"Yes, Captain," he said, saluting and heading back to the airlift.

Instead of going back to his room or to the mess hall, he stormed directly down to Security.

"Did you hear her?" he demanded as he walked into Sharon Blacksmith's office.

"Yes, I did," responded Sharon. "You're lucky we don't put people in irons anymore. She doesn't like being contradicted—and you did more than that. You as much as told her she's endangering our mission by following her orders."

"Well, she is, damn it!" snapped Cole. "You saw the readout on that Teroni ship! It's a military ship, any idiot can see that. It's fast, it's not well armed, and it isn't touching down on any planet. What the hell else could it be doing here but looking for the fuel depots?"

"Do you feel better now?" asked Sharon. "Or would you rather hit me now that you're through yelling at me?"

"I'm sorry," said Cole, still visibly agitated. "But Jesus Christ, can't she see what's going to happen if she doesn't take out that scout ship? Sooner or later it's going to locate the fuel depots, and then we're going to be faced with a force we *can't* take out."

"Maybe it won't find them."

"If they sent it here, it has whatever equipment it needs to find them," said Cole. "Even Fujiama would have seen that. Why can't she?"

"You're intuitive. She's literal."

"It doesn't take intuition to see the situation and figure out what's going to happen. A literal mind ought to see it just as clearly. I don't understand her."

"You'd better learn to," said Sharon. "She's the Captain now."

"Yeah," said Cole bitterly, "and she's going to be the Captain when two hundred ships of the Fifth Teroni Fleet show up in two days or two weeks or two months and head straight for the fuel depots. Then what? If you follow her reasoning to its logical conclusion, the only time we can use our weapons is when we're so outnumbered that it won't matter."

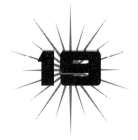

The Teroni ship flitted from one system to another like a bee looking for honey. Twice more during the next three days Cole urged Podok to destroy it, and twice more the Polonoi refused.

"You're going to get yourself in serious trouble," remarked Forrice as he and Cole sat in the mess hall during another white shift. "How many times can you tell her to do something she doesn't want to do?"

"She's going to get the *Teddy R* in serious trouble," replied Cole. "If there was ever any doubt that the Teroni ship was hunting for the fuel depots, it's got to be gone by now. Just what the hell does Podok think she's going to do when the Fifth Teroni Fleet shows up?"

"Ask her."

"I have. Frequently. All she does is say that she's going to obey her orders—but damn it, repeating it over and over like a religious litany doesn't make it possible!"

"I don't know what we can do about it anyway," said Forrice. "Wait till she sees how many of them there are and how many guns they've got and then run like hell, I suppose." Suddenly he frowned. "You don't think she'd consider going up against them in the *Teddy R*, do you?"

"If there's one thing in the whole damned galaxy I don't understand, it's officers," said Cole. "And if there's one officer I especially don't understand, it's her."

"You're an officer yourself," the Molarian pointed out.

"Let me win a couple more medals and you can bet your alien ass they'll bust me down to sergeant or yeoman," said Cole. "I think when we get to the next blue shift, I'll harass the shit out of that little ship and see if I can get it to fire on me. Then even Podok can't complain if I blow it away."

"Have you ever considered that it might blow us away?" asked Forrice.

"Which would you rather face—one scout ship or the whole Fifth Teroni Fleet? Because as sure as we're sitting here, we're going to have to face one or the other."

"The only thing I can think of is to contact Fleet Command, explain the situation, and suggest in the strongest possible terms that they countermand our orders and issue new ones."

"I am not Fleet Command's favorite officer," said Cole. "I could swear that when Admiral Garcia was pinning my Medal of Courage on me she was trying her damnedest to stick the pin into my chest."

"Come on, Wilson," said Forrice. "The damned medal was bonded to your uniform. They haven't used pins in a millennium or more."

"Well, if they did, she'd have driven it into me," muttered Cole. "Anything I tell them will just be written off as the usual insubordination."

"Don't look at *me*," replied the Molarian. "I'm here because I refused an order to execute a wounded prisoner. If I complain, they're going to be sure I'm begging to be allowed to cut and run."

"That's some brass we work for, isn't it?" said Cole.

The holographic menu came to life, then gradually morphed into a written message from Sharon Blacksmith:

If you're going to criticize every officer in the Fleet above the rank of Ensign who isn't named Cole or Forrice, try to keep your voices down.

"You think anyone cares?" asked Cole softly.

The menu displayed a new message:

Do you think you're the only officer with friends in Security?

"Okay, point taken," said Cole.

"You really think she's got spies in Security?" asked Forrice.

"She's the Captain. Anyone who does her bidding aboard her ship can hardly be considered a spy. But to answer your question, yes, I think she's probably got loyalists in almost every department. Wouldn't you, if you were the Captain? I certainly would."

"I don't understand you at all," said Forrice. "Every time I'm convinced you hate her, you say something like that."

"I don't hate her," answered Cole. "I just wish she had a little more common sense, since all of our lives depend on her judgment."

"Don't remind me."

Cole got to his feet. "I'm too restless to just sit here. I've got to walk around."

"Ensign Marcos was released from confinement about an hour ago," said Forrice. "You could pay her a visit and make your friend in Security very jealous."

The menu displayed a new message:

It has come to Security's attention that there is a Teroni spy aboard the ship, posing as a Molarian of command rank. I think we may have to incarcerate him without food or water for the next six hundred years.

"On the other hand," said Forrice without missing a beat, "I'm sure Ensign Marcos would rather cohabit with a handsome vigorous young man rather than an elderly, decrepit senior officer."

The menu changed messages again:

Okay, you can live. But watch your step.

The Molarian hooted a laugh. "I *like* her," he said.

"Come to think of it, so do I," replied Cole. He faced the menu, although he knew that Sharon could hear him no matter where he was.

"But I wish she'd spend less time protecting her sexual turf and more time watching that Teroni ship. Is it getting any closer to New Argentina or the Benidos system?"

Hard to tell. It's not moving in any recognizable pattern.

"Is there any way we can monitor its transmissions?"

We're trying—but it can use an infinite number of frequencies. We haven't pinpointed which one it's using yet—and it could be that it isn't sending any messages at all.

"We ought to blow the goddamned thing to pieces before it does," said Cole.

I believe we've all heard this song before.

"You know, come to think of it, Rachel is looking damned good," said Cole. "Young, round, earnest, trusting. I wonder why I never saw it before."

The menu vanished.

"I think we're free from cynical commentary for a few minutes anyway," said Cole with a smile. "And I'm still feeling restless. I'm going to walk around the ship a bit."

"Good," said Forrice. "Now that you won't be here to make caustic remarks, I'm free to eat a *real* meal."

Cole walked out of the mess hall. He went up to his room, decided he was too wide awake to take a nap, spent a few minutes visiting with Pampas, walked down to the science lab (which was empty, as usual), dropped in at the infirmary to check on Kudop's condition, and finally went to his cabin.

He shaved, took a Dryshower, got dressed again, checked his time-piece to see how long he had before blue shift began, called up a book on his computer, found he couldn't concentrate, and replaced it with a holo of a nightclub performance on Calliope III that featured magicians, singers, and a lot of near-naked chorus girls. It held his attention for almost two minutes before he shut it off.

Suddenly Sharon's image appeared before him.

"You're driving me crazy!" she said. "Can't you just stay in one place and relax?"

"I'm trying."

"You're not trying hard enough. If the Teroni fleet actually shows up during a blue shift, you're going to be too sleepy to react."

"It's the other shifts that get to me," said Cole. "I'll be fine once blue shift begins."

"You're wound up like a spring," she said.

"Haven't you got something better to do than watch me?"

"We're in a dangerous military situation and you'll take over command in an hour. So no, I haven't got anything better to do." She lowered her voice, presumably because there was someone in her outer office. "I suppose I could get away for about twenty minutes and ease your tensions."

"Shoot down that fucking ship," he said. "*That*'ll ease my tensions."

She shrugged. "Well, I offered."

"I'm sorry. I'm not mad at *you*."

"Even so, maybe next time I'll charge you."

"Maybe I'll pay," he said. "Hell, I've got nothing else to spend it on. Besides, someone as pretty as Rachel is probably out of my price range."

"I know heroes like to live dangerously," replied Sharon, "but you're really pushing your luck."

"All right," he laughed. "I feel better. Thanks."

"And I didn't even have to get out of my clothes."

"I think I might as well go to the mess hall and grab some coffee before I go to work."

"Wilson, you've had five cups of coffee already."

"It'll keep me alert."

"It'll keep you running to the bathroom."

"*That*'ll keep me alert, too," he said, getting to his feet.

He spent a boring half hour at the mess hall, played twenty minutes of chess with Mustapha Odom, the seldom-seen engine chief, and finally went up to the bridge.

"Request permission to come onto the bridge, Captain," he said, saluting.

Podok checked the chronometer atop the main viewscreen.

"You're three minutes early, Commander Cole."

"Better than being three minutes late, Captain."

"True," said Podok. "Permission granted."

He walked over to where he could see the main screen at a better angle.

"Looks about the same as it did yesterday," he commented.

"Possibly you were mistaken, and it is not an advance scout at all," suggested Podok.

"It's got to be," responded Cole. "It's been in the cluster for three days now. If it has any purpose other than finding the depots, why hasn't it landed?"

Podok merely stared at him, looking alien and inscrutable.

Christine Mboya arrived and walked to her station, as did Malcolm Briggs. The chronometer struck 1600 hours.

"You're relieved, Captain," said Cole.

Podok saluted and left the bridge.

"You look unhappy, Mr. Briggs," said Cole.

"I was watching the murderball game between Spica II and Far

London, sir," replied Briggs. "It was tied with five minutes to go when I had to leave and report here."

"Nothing much is happening," said Cole. "Put the game on the main screen if you want."

"Thank you, sir," said Briggs. "It'll only be a few minutes, even with time-outs."

He uttered a command to the computer, and suddenly the murder-ball stadium filled the screen. The scene focused on the field, and the activity became more and more frantic. Injured players were carted off the field and replaced by the few remaining healthy ones. Finally the crowd began counting down the seconds, and when they reached zero, they let out an enormous cheer.

"Far London 4, Spica 3," read Briggs. "They must have scored after I left my room. Oh, well, that's the price one pays for making the galaxy safe for overpaid athletes."

Another command and the screen reverted to the Cassius Cluster.

"Something's wrong, sir," said Christine Mboya, frowning.

"What is it?"

"I can't find the Teroni ship."

"How far can it have gotten in four or five minutes?" asked Cole.

She shrugged. "I don't know. I'm still searching for it." Then: "Got it, sir!" She turned to him. "I think we have a problem, sir."

"Explain."

"The Teroni ship, sir—it's in orbit about Benidos II. In the three days it's been in the cluster it hasn't gone into orbit anywhere else."

"That's it!" said Cole decisively. "Pilot, get us to Benidos II, full speed. Mr. Briggs, tell Four Eyes to get his ass down to the gunnery section and supervise the crew. I want to know that our weapons are working."

"What are you going to do, sir?" asked Christine.

"What we should have done three days ago. Mr. Briggs, has Four Eyes responded?"

"Yes, sir," said Briggs. "He says he'll be there within a minute."

"Another problem, sir," said Christine. "A big one."

"What now?"

"I'll put it on the main screen."

He found himself looking at the edge of the Cassius Cluster. For just an instant it looked as it had for days—and then, suddenly, the screen was filled with dozens of ships, then hundreds, all sporting the insignia of the Fifth Teroni Fleet.

"How long will it take them to reach the Benidos system?" he asked.

"Perhaps ten minutes, sir. Eleven at the outside."

"Shit!" said Cole. "There's no sense blowing up the scout ship now. It would just give them another reason to be mad at us."

"Shall I sound the red alert?" asked Christine.

"Yeah, I suppose you'd better. Then pipe your voice throughout the ship and call all hands to battle stations, just in case some of them have never heard a red alert before and don't know how to respond to it. Mr. Briggs, contact Four Eyes again and tell him if his battle station is anywhere except the gunnery section to ignore Lieutenant Mboya's instructions."

"Yes, sir."

"And release Sergeant Pampas from confinement and tell him to get the hell down to the gunnery section."

"But sir, he's not due out for—"

"We haven't got time to argue, Mr. Briggs," said Cole. "If we're going to start shooting, I want at least one technician I trust overseeing the weapons."

"Yes, sir," said Briggs, issuing the orders via his computer.

The red-alert siren bleated three times, fell silent for half a minute, then burst into earsplitting sound again.

"Put me on the ship's speaker system," Cole instructed Christine.

"Image, too?"

"No. Let's let 'em concentrate on what I'm saying."

"Ready, sir," she announced.

"Crew members of the *Theodore Roosevelt*, this is Commander Wilson Cole speaking. The Fifth Teroni Fleet has entered the Cassius Cluster and is on course to reach the Benidos system in about ten minutes. Remain at your battle stations and await further orders."

He gestured to Christine to kill the speakers.

"This is crazy," he said. "What's the point of being at their battle stations? We're not going to open fire on the whole Fifth Fleet. See if you can patch me through to their commander, voice and image."

Christine looked up at him a few seconds later. "No response, sir. I'm using an all-frequency signal, so I know they're receiving it. They just aren't acknowledging it."

"Eight minutes and closing," announced Briggs.

"And we're what, about a minute away?"

"Two minutes, sir."

"Get us over there, Pilot. We might still be able to talk a little reason."

"If not, what do we do next, sir?" asked Christine.

He wanted to say: *We die.* But he knew they were looking to him for leadership. "We improvise."

"We do no such thing," said a voice from the edge of the bridge.

Cole turned and found himself facing Captain Podok.

"What are you doing here?" he asked.

"Like everyone else, I heard the red alert," answered Podok. "In such circumstances my place is here on the bridge. Step aside, Mr. Cole. I will take over command now." She turned to Christine. "Where is the Teroni fleet now, Lieutenant Mboya?"

"They're about six minutes from Benidos, Captain."

"And from the angle of their approach, where is New Argentina—before, beside, or behind the Benidos system?"

"Behind it, Captain," said Christine. "They have to pass Benidos to get to it."

"Get us there quickly," said Podok. "We haven't much time."

"You have a plan, Captain?" asked Cole, surprised.

"I have a clearly defined course of action."

"Would you care to share it with me?"

"You already know it," said Podok.

"I do?"

"Certainly. Gunnery department, lock on to the following coordinates." She rattled off a series of numbers.

"We're locked on, Captain," said Forrice's voice.

"Something's wrong here," said Cole. "You didn't even check the Teronis' position. How can you know their coordinates?"

"Gunnery department, fire ten pulse cannons at maximum strength."

Suddenly Cole realized what Podok's plan was. "Four Eyes, belay that order!" he yelled, but he was too late. An instant later the planet that used to be Benidos II exploded in a flash of blinding white light.

"What the hell have you done!" bellowed Cole.

"My duty," said Podok calmly.

"Your duty? There were three million Benidottes living on that world!"

"The Teroni fleet is capable of killing more than that every minute. I have prevented them from refueling."

"Then they'll get their fucking fuel somewhere else and kill everyone next week instead of tomorrow!"

"I have followed my orders. Mr. Wxakgini, take us to New Argentina."

"So you can blow *it* up, too?" demanded Cole.

"My orders are explicit," said Podok. "Our mission is to prevent the Teroni fleet from using our fuel depots."

"There are five million Men on New Argentina!" rasped Cole. "I'm not going to let you kill them!"

"Mr. Cole, leave the bridge and confine yourself to your quarters until further notice," said Podok. "You have been insubordinate once too often."

"Turn the ship away, Captain," said Cole. "Let them have the goddamned fuel!"

"That is treasonous talk, Mr. Cole. It will be mentioned in my report."

"I'm only going to ask you once more," said Cole. "Turn the ship away!"

"Mr. Wxakgini, full speed ahead," said Podok.

"Don't make me do this, Captain!"

"I have ordered you off the bridge, Mr. Cole. That means *now*!"

"Four Eyes, this is Cole," he said, raising his voice. "Can you hear me?"

"Yes."

"As of this moment, I am relieving the Captain of command. Under no circumstances is any of our weaponry to be fired without my express order."

"Say the first part again," said Forrice.

"You heard me," said Cole. "I am taking over command of the ship."

"You will do no such thing!" said Podok, approaching him ominously.

"I don't want to harm you, Captain," said Cole, backing away, "but I won't let you slaughter five million Republic citizens." He raised his voice again. "Security! Get an armed team up here on the double. Sharon, tell them who to obey!"

"You planned this all along!" shouted Podok. "You and the Molarian and the Security Chief."

"That's not true," said Cole, still backing away. "Even after you destroyed Benidos II I wasn't going to relieve you—but I can't allow you to destroy another Republic world."

"Lieutenant Mboya, Lieutenant Briggs," said Podok, "you are witnesses to this attempt at mutiny. I will expect you to testify at his court-martial."

"It's more than an attempt," said Cole. "I have taken over command. You will be treated with courtesy and respect, but you're not giving any more orders. If we get away from here in one piece, I will deliver you to Fleet Command, turn myself in, and let them sort things out."

Sharon arrived with three armed Security men in tow.

"Colonel Blacksmith, arrest this man!" ordered Podok.

"Colonel Blacksmith," said Cole, "if you arrest me you will almost certainly consign five million Republic citizens to their deaths. Take Captain Podok to her quarters and post a guard there. If she causes problems, move her to the brig."

"If you obey him, you will be equally culpable," warned Podok.

"Captain, we've arrived," said Wxakgini.

"The Captain is no longer in charge," said Cole. "You will address all questions and comments to me."

"Colonel Blacksmith, what do I do?" asked the pilot.

"Obey Mr. Cole," said Sharon. "He has taken command. Captain Podok, will you please step this way?"

"You'll pay dearly for this, Mr. Cole," promised Podok. "And so will your fellow conspirators, Colonel Blacksmith and Commander Forrice."

Yeah, he agreed silently, *we probably will. But at least five million New Argentinians won't. Of course, all that presupposes that we live through the next ten minutes. . . .*

"Christine, damn it, have you opened a channel to them yet?" demanded Cole.

"I'm raising them on close to two million frequencies," she said. "There's no response."

"Can you rig it so they can hear my voice?"

"Yes, but that doesn't mean they'll respond."

"But they'll be able to hear it?" he persisted.

"They've got to," said Christine. "I can't imagine they're not communicating among themselves. This will interfere with that, so I imagine *someone* will listen to it."

"Okay, put me on audio."

She made a quick adjustment. "Go ahead, sir."

"This is Wilson Cole, commanding the Republic ship *Theodore Roosevelt*. This is the ship that is between you and the planet known to us as New Argentina, the planet that holds the fuel you wish to appropriate. I offer you a deal." He paused briefly, ordering his thoughts. "You are free to take whatever fuel you need from the depot—but in exchange, I want your pledge that you will not harm the inhabitants of the planet. If you don't agree to this, I'll destroy New Argentina as I destroyed Benidos II. You have ninety seconds to respond."

He ran a finger across his throat, signaling Christine that he wanted the audio transmission killed.

"You wouldn't really do that, sir?" asked Briggs.

"Of course not," said Cole. "I took over the ship to prevent Podok from doing it. But the Teronis don't know that. All they know is that we just blew up one Republic planet rather than let them get their hands on the fuel, and I've threatened to do it again."

"You think it'll work?" asked Christine, staring intently at her computer as if to urge a response.

"We'll know soon enough," said Cole. He raised his voice. "Four Eyes, get everything ready, just in case."

"It's been ready," said the Molarian's voice, "or have you forgotten what we just did a few minutes ago?"

"I'm going to spend a long time trying to forget it," replied Cole.

"Message!" said Christine excitedly, and the bridge fell silent.

"This is Jacovic, Commander of the Fifth Teroni Fleet. Your terms are acceptable."

"Audio again," said Cole to Christine. Then, "This is Wilson Cole. We will withdraw and allow you to approach the planet." *As if we could stop you*, he added mentally.

He gave the kill sign again.

"Pilot, get us the hell out of here, full speed to the nearest wormhole, and I don't give a damn where the wormhole leads, as long as it gets us out of the Cassius Cluster."

"Yes, sir," said Wxakgini.

"I don't think they'll harm us," said Briggs. "After all, they agreed to our terms."

"Maybe it's escaped your notice, Lieutenant," said Cole, never taking his eyes from the viewscreen where the Teroni ships were approaching New Argentina, "but our terms didn't include safe passage for the *Teddy R*."

"Wormhole coming up in forty-five seconds," announced Wxakgini.

"Does it lead beyond the cluster?" asked Cole.

"It's never been fully charted, but it looks like it'll put us halfway to Antares."

"Am I mistaken," said Sharon, "or did three ships just shear off from their formation and start coming after us?"

"They're not in hot pursuit," said Cole. "I think they're just making sure we don't try to pull any tricks."

"Thirty seconds," announced Wxakgini.

"You want to give them a little farewell present?" asked Forrice's voice.

"No!" snapped Cole. "You let even one of them escape and the whole fucking fleet will come into the wormhole after us!"

"Ten seconds."

"They're not speeding up," said Sharon. "I think we're going to be okay."

And then, suddenly, they were inside the wormhole.

"Well," said Sharon, breathing a sign of relief, "it looks like we survived."

"The hangman will be *so* happy," said Cole. "Or do they shoot mutineers these days?"

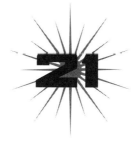

Cole was escorted into the conference room by two armed guards. Forrice, also under guard, was already there, seated at a large oval table. One of Cole's guards indicated that he was expected to sit down as well.

A middle-aged major entered the room, seated himself, and lit up a smokeless cigar. Next he pulled a pair of small computers out of a briefcase and set them on the table.

"There's no sense starting until Colonel Blacksmith arrives," said the Major. "I hope they're treating you well."

"The condemned man has eaten a number of hearty meals," replied Cole dryly.

"I've been on the ship so long it took awhile to adjust to the gravity," added Forrice.

"Yeah, it's a little heavy," acknowledged the Major. "One point zero seven Galactic Standard. Ordinarily we'd be doing this on Deluros VIII, but given the controversy surrounding it, the Navy decided to hold it out here in the Timos system."

Sharon arrived, accompanied by two guards.

"Ah! Colonel Blacksmith," said the Major. "Please be seated." As she sat down, he turned to the guards. "You can leave us alone now. Please wait outside the door."

"We were told to stay with the prisoners," said one of the guards.

"I am their lawyer, and I wish to confer with my clients in private. Check with your superiors, and then please leave us alone."

The guard who had spoken left the room for a moment, then

returned. "I apologize, sir. We were just following our orders." He turned to his companions. "Let's go. We'll wait outside, as he's requested."

After they had left the room, the officer spoke up again. "I suppose introductions are in order. I am Major Jordan Baker, and I will be defending you at your court-martial."

"You drew the short straw?" suggested Cole with an ironic smile.

"I am hoping for a summary verdict of not guilty on opening day," he replied.

"I don't want to prejudice you against your client," said Cole, "but I *did* relieve Captain Podok of command against her wishes."

"And in the process you saved five million lives," said Baker. He patted one of the computers. "We have the entire holographic log, so no one can deny what happened. I think you're going to come out of this in much better shape than Captain Podok."

"That's comforting," said Cole. "May I ask why Colonel Blacksmith and Commander Forrice are on trial at all? It was my decision, no one else's."

"Podok has filed a charge of mutiny against all three of you," answered Baker. "And Colonel Blacksmith *did* support you."

"She wasn't even there!" snapped Cole. "I thought you said you saw the holos."

"I did," replied Baker. "At one point, when you and Captain Podok gave contradictory orders, the pilot asked Colonel Blacksmith which of you to obey, and she told him you were in command."

"I was," said Cole. "It was over by then."

"Oh?" said Baker. "And what if she had told the pilot to obey Captain Podok? Would he still have followed your orders?"

"No," admitted Cole. "No, he wouldn't have."

"That's why she's on trial," said Baker. "The case against Commander Forrice is more nebulous. It's based on the fact that almost immediately after assuming command you contacted him and told him what you had done. He asked you to repeat what you said, you did, and he made no attempt to dissuade you." He paused. "But not attempting to dissuade you is not the same as actively supporting you, as Colonel Blacksmith did."

"If anyone had asked, I would have told them it was high time he took over the ship," said Forrice.

"Then it's just your good fortune that no one asked," said Baker.

"What's going to happen to Podok?" asked Sharon. "After all, she's the one who killed three million Benidottes."

"There will be a Board of Inquiry," answered Baker. "My guess is that they'll say her orders were subject to misinterpretation, so there will be no criminal prosecution. But of course they'll never let her command a ship again. They can't condone that kind of decision making."

"So she kills three million sentient beings and gets off with a reprimand, and we face death sentences for saving five million, is that it?" said Sharon.

"The prosecution is only asking the death sentence for Commander Cole," said Baker. "They want lesser sentences for you and Commander Forrice."

"Would they have been happier if Commander Cole had let Podok destroy New Argentina?"

"The truth? Probably. Then they'd only have one difficult decision to make rather than four."

"Seems like three easy decisions to me," said Sharon. "We saved five million lives."

"You've come directly to Fleet Command and were instantly transferred to Timos III," said Baker. "You've been kept incommunicado."

"So what?"

"So Commander Cole's first official act as Captain of the *Theodore Roosevelt* was to invite the enemy to appropriate the fuel from our depot on New Argentina."

"Thereby saving five million lives."

"You don't know that the Teronis would have destroyed the world. More likely they would have destroyed your ship, taken what they needed with a minimum of force, and left." He paused. "What you don't know is that the Fifth Teroni Fleet then proceeded to destroy military installations on seven Republic worlds. They did not exercise pinpoint accuracy."

"How many dead?" asked Cole.

"Not quite what you saved on New Argentina—but they're still out there, they're still using our fuel, and they're still killing people." Baker stared at him. "They're going to bring that up in court. How do you answer it?"

"We were one ship against two hundred. The choice wasn't between destroying the Teroni fleet or being good neighbors and letting them take the fuel. It was between destroying the fuel and all life on the planet or letting them have it."

"Couldn't you have just destroyed the fuel and left the planet alone?"

Cole shook his head. "It was fissionable fuel. Blow it up and the planet would have been radioactive for the next few centuries."

"Good," said Baker. "Remember that, because they're sure as hell going to bring it up." He turned to Sharon. "Colonel Blacksmith, I don't mean to embarrass you, but I have to ask: Were you having an affair with Commander Cole?"

"If I was, and I am not admitting to anything, there is no recorded proof of it."

"I'm sure there isn't, given that you were Chief of Security. But there is some indiscreet banter on record, which you indulged in with no one else." He stared directly at her. "The prosecution is going to ask you that question when you're under oath. If you hedge or qualify, they will assume you were sleeping with him, and this will color any comments you may make in support of his actions."

"I don't need anyone to support my actions," interjected Cole. "You've got the record of what happened on the bridge. Even after Podok destroyed Benidos I didn't take over. I begged her not to do the same thing to New Argentina. I gave her every opportunity to alter her decision. I warned her what would happen if she tried to blow up New Argentina. Even after I took over, I didn't set her and her supporters on some deserted planet to fend for themselves. I took the *Teddy R* directly to Fleet Command, set Podok free, and turned myself in to the naval authorities. Every single thing I did from the moment she attacked Benidos II I would do again."

Baker looked from each of them to the next. "All right," he said. "Both sides will be taking depositions in the next couple of days, and I would imagine the trial will start within a week. You're one of our great heroes, Commander; the Navy wants this cleaned up *fast*." Suddenly he stopped. "If any of you would rather have a different attorney, the Navy will be more than happy to supply one."

"No, you'll be fine," said Cole. Then, after a pause: "Have you ever participated in a mutiny trial before?"

"Commander Cole, you are the Navy's first mutineer in more than six centuries."

Baker entered Cole's cell.

"How are they treating you?" he asked.

"You didn't come here just to ask me that."

"No, I came to tell you that I was able to get the charges against Commander Forrice dropped." A satisfied smile crossed his face. "I knew they couldn't make it stick. Whatever you said to him, he never responded."

"How about Sharon?"

"Colonel Blacksmith? She'll still stand trial with you. There's no getting away from the fact that she was the first one to acknowledge that you were in charge of the *Theodore Roosevelt*." He paused. "Still, her fate depends entirely upon yours. After all, she can't be guilty of abetting a mutiny if you're not a mutineer."

"So how do things look?"

"There's a lot of extraneous crap, such as you making a deal with the enemy, or what the Teroni fleet did after they got the fuel, but if I can keep the focus on the justification for your actions—the saving of five million lives—I think we can pull out a victory."

"You sounded more confident a couple of days ago."

"A couple of days ago they hadn't announced the prosecuting attorney," answered Baker. "It's Colonel Miguel Hernandez."

"Never heard of him."

"No reason why you should," said Baker. "You've never been court-martialed before. He's the best the Navy's got." He frowned. "I can't figure out why he's here."

"He can't try it long distance."

Baker shook his head. "That's not what I mean. The Navy should *want* you to beat the charge. You did a good thing. You saved a lot of lives. You didn't make your captain walk the plank, or whatever they do these days. You behaved honorably—and you're the most decorated officer in the service. So why the hell did they send a man who hasn't lost a case in, God, it must be fifteen years, to prosecute you?"

"Let's hope it's to make it look good to the press," said Cole.

"Maybe," said Baker. "Still, I find it very disturbing. If I ever saw a case where they should toss in a prosecutor who's still wet behind the ears, this is it."

"There's no sense worrying about it," said Cole. "When do they start taking depositions?"

"They've already deposed Captain Podok, Lieutenant Mboya, and Lieutenant Briggs, and I believe they'd deposing Colonel Blacksmith right now."

"Shouldn't you be there to advise her?" said Cole sharply.

"A member of my staff is with her," answered Baker. "This isn't a civil proceeding, Commander. There's a limit to what we can do when a defendant is being deposed. Anyway, they tell me they'll get to you tomorrow. I'll try to be here for it."

"Don't bother," said Cole. "I've got nothing to hide and nothing to be ashamed of. I plan to answer every question truthfully."

"That's usually the best policy."

"When is Podok's hearing?"

"Three days from now, but the result is a foregone conclusion: a demotion of one rank and a return to active service."

"Not aboard the *Teddy R*, I hope?"

"Probably not."

"And she's really going to get off with just a slap on the wrist?"

"It looks like it, which isn't to say she isn't one bitter ex-captain. She's been having a field day, telling the press that you took over the ship because you refused to take orders from a Polonoi."

"You're kidding!" exclaimed Cole. "She actually said that?"

"She's still saying it. I guess you don't get news holos in here."

"I assume the press is pointing out that it's bullshit."

"Not really. For one thing, the press isn't allowed to get a rebuttal from a prisoner."

"Even so," said Cole, "there have to be dozens of crew members who—"

"You're a mutineer," interrupted Baker. "She's giving them a reason for what you did, one that puts her in a favorable light by putting you in a bad one. Every time a crew member tries to explain that you aren't a bigot, some journalist points out that you're behind bars for deposing a Polonoi."

"Yeah, the press would love that kind of story, wouldn't it?" said Cole. "They love anything that confirms their belief that everyone in the military is a homicidal maniac, a rapist, or a bigot."

"It'll blow over as soon as the trial's done," said Baker. "Who knows? Maybe you'll even get another medal for what you did and you'll be the media's fair-haired boy again." Suddenly he smiled. "As your attorney, I've studied your career pretty thoroughly. I'd say you've used the media for your purposes just about as much as they've used you for theirs."

"My purpose was never personal advancement."

"Do you think they care?"

"No," admitted Cole. "If they did, they wouldn't be so malleable."

"Well," said Baker, "I just wanted to tell you about Commander Forrice. I'd better be getting back to work. I've still got two defenses to prepare."

"Thanks for stopping by," said Cole.

"Is there anything I can do for you, Commander?"

"Can you arrange for me to have visitors?"

"Anyone in particular?"

Cole shook his head. "No, just anyone from the *Teddy R* who might want to stop by. I'd like to see Forrice and congratulate him on the charges being dropped, but I have a feeling that if I expressly ask to see someone, they'll be denied entrance."

"Very likely," agreed Baker. "I'll see what I can arrange."

"Thanks," said Cole. "And if they're not going to allow me any holos, see if you can get me a couple of old-fashioned paper books."

"I'll do what I can," said Baker. He stood before the force field until a guard hit a control panel and created a momentary opening through which he could leave.

Cole spent the next two hours trying to remember stray incidents from his brief time on the *Teddy R* that might help his case, but he finally gave it up. He simply couldn't believe that his actions weren't justified, and he was certain that any reasonable military court would not only agree with him but commend him.

He was just about to lay down on his bare cot and try to take a nap when the force field briefly flickered and Forrice was allowed in.

"I heard the good news," said Cole. "Congratulations."

"It's ridiculous," said the Molarian. "I was too busy to respond, or I'd have told you that you should have taken over the damned ship the day Fujiama died."

"I won't tell them if you won't," said Cole with a grin.

"Have you heard what our beloved ex-captain has been saying about you?"

"Yeah."

"You don't look especially bothered by it."

"What do you expect her to say—that I had excellent reasons for relieving her and that I should be commended for my good judgment?"

"She can get away with what she's doing for a little while," said Forrice, "but sooner or later the press is going to get hold of what really happened on Benidos II, and then they're going to crucify her."

"You're a Molarian," said Cole. "What the hell do you know about crucifixion?"

"I know that all your greatest painters seemed fascinated with it."

"I think they were a little more fascinated with the guy who was *being* crucified in all those pictures."

"Whatever."

"Anyway, I'm glad you're off the hook."

"You'll beat the charges," Forrice said confidently. "I just wish Podok would stop spreading lies to the press."

"The media gets a lot more mileage out of lies and innuendos then it ever does from the truth," said Cole. "Later, after everyone has lost interest, they'll run a correction. Then they can't understand why the person they slandered is still pissed at them."

"You make them sound even more corrupt than the Molarian press."

"It's just the nature of things. Every lawyer starts out seeking justice and winds up seeking victories. Every doctor want to save his patients and ends up wanting to save his investments. And every journalist starts out caring about the truth and ends up caring about circulation."

"I'm sure glad you haven't become cynical and jaded," said Forrice, hooting a laugh.

"I'll leave that to all the inferior races I'm prejudiced against, starting with the Molarians."

Forrice hooted again. "You don't mind if I quote you to the press, do you? They found out where you're being held, and they're holding a vigil outside the building."

"I can use all the goodwill I can get," said Cole. "Buy them a drink, on me."

"I can't afford it," said the Molarian. "There must be a hundred of them."

"A hundred? There's a war going on. Haven't they got something better to do?"

"They smell a story," replied Forrice. "Their hero's suddenly a mutineer and a bigot. Who wants to read about war? This is a juicier story, and if they can just prove you raped Sharon Blacksmith or Rachel Marcos, or better still, a Polonoi, you'll make their year."

"I hate to disappoint them," said Cole, "but I'm going to walk before that tribunal one day next week at noon, and walk out a free man two hours later."

"Maybe instead of a drink I'll give them something to write about. Why should they have to wait for the trial to find out what their new hero was going to do to New Argentina before you stopped her?"

"Why bother?" said Cole. "It won't influence the trial. They already know why I took over."

"It'll make *me* feel better," answered Forrice. "By the way, have you given any thought to whether you'll return to the service?"

"I haven't left it," replied Cole. "Who's in command of the *Teddy R* now?"

"No one," answered the Molarian. "The ship's in port here. They're obviously not going to give it back to Podok, and I hardly think they'll make you captain as a reward for taking it over. I imagine they'll import a new captain."

"How about you?"

"They wouldn't even promote me to First or Second Officer *before* the mutiny, remember?"

"If I were you, I'd be damned bitter about that."

"When I'm through being outraged about you and Sharon, I'll be outraged about me."

"I haven't seen Sharon since our first meeting with Major Baker," said Cole. "Do me a favor and go see her after you leave here. She's bound to be feeling pretty isolated."

"I'll be happy to. And when I get back to the ship, I'll tell some of the others that you could both use some visitors."

"Will any of them be at the trial?"

"From what I hear, just Christine Mboya, Malcolm Briggs, and our pilot of the unpronounceable name. There are no other direct witnesses."

"They've got a holographic recording of the whole damned thing in their possession. I wonder why they need witnesses at all?"

"I have no idea," answered Forrice. "Which is my answer to almost anything the brass does."

"Ah, well, we'll get the trial over with in a few days and then everything will go back to normal."

He should have known better.

The guard entered his cell.

"Commander Cole, come with me please."

"What for?" asked Cole. "The trial doesn't start for two more days?"

"I just know I've been ordered to bring you to the conference room."

Cole got up and walked to the door. "Lead the way," he said.

"I'm sorry, sir, but I'm not permitted to turn my back on a prisoner. You'll have to go first."

"Whatever you say."

"I *do* have something to say, sir."

Cole stopped and turned to him. "What is it?"

"I'm aware of your record, sir, and I know what happened aboard the *Theodore Roosevelt*. I swore an oath to carry out my orders, but I want you to know that I'm ashamed to be carrying out this one. We should be making you an admiral, not trying you for mutiny."

"I thank you for the sentiment, Sergeant . . . ?" said Cole.

"Sergeant Luthor Chadwick, sir. I just wanted to tell you that."

"I appreciate it."

Cole began walking. When he came to a fork in the corridor he stopped. "I've only been to the conference room once, Sergeant. I don't remember which way to go."

"To your left, sir."

"Thanks."

Cole walked a bit farther, finally recognized his surroundings, and speeded up his pace to the conference room, where he found Jordan Baker and Sharon Blacksmith waiting for him. Sharon's guard was stationed outside the room, on one side of the doorway, and Sergeant Chadwick took up a position on the other side. The door snapped shut after he stepped through.

"What's up?" asked Cole. "Have they thrown the case out of court already?"

"Sit down, Commander," said Baker, a troubled look on his face.

Cole took a seat next to Sharon. "Do you know what this is about?" he whispered.

She shook her head.

"Commander, we have a serious problem. What seemed a simple, open-and-shut case that would almost certainly be decided in your favor has somehow metamorphosed into a simple open-and-shut case that is almost certainly going to go against you."

"Nothing's changed," said Cole. "If they've faked some evidence, everyone who was on the bridge that day can testify to what happened."

"Nobody's faking any evidence," said Baker. "This has nothing to do with evidence."

"Then it can't be as serious as you make it sound."

"Would you like to know how serious it is?" said Baker. "I have just received an offer from Miguel Hernandez. If you will agree to plead guilty, he'll request a life sentence rather than the death penalty, and he'll drop all charges against Colonel Blacksmith."

Cole relaxed visibly. "You're interpreting this all wrong, Major. We've got 'em on the run. If he thought he could convict me, he'd never offer a deal."

"He's being generous, Commander. The Navy cannot afford to let you walk out of court a free man."

"What are you talking about?" demanded Cole. "Nothing's changed. You just said as much yourself."

Baker shook his head. "No, Commander. What I said was that the evidence hasn't changed."

"Okay, it's your show," said Cole. "Tell me what the hell's going on."

"It's your friends in the media."

"What do they have to do with anything?"

"Eventually the details of what happened during the mutiny were going to come out," said Baker. "But they came out at the very worst time."

"You *are* going to get to the point sooner or later, aren't you?"

"You recall that Captain Podok had been making headlines for a few days, accusing you of bigotry?" said Baker. "Well, the media latched on to that story, and now they're trumpeting the fact that you didn't mutiny when three million Benidottes were being killed, but that you only took over the ship when it was on the verge of killing five million Men on New Argentina."

"I didn't know what the hell Podok was going to do on Benidos!" snapped Cole. "I tried to countermand her order, but it was too late!"

"You know it, I know it, and anyone who's seen the holo log knows it," said Baker. "But according to the media, the story is not that you saved five million Men on New Argentina, but that the bigoted mutineer who hated his Polonoi captain sat idly by and didn't lift a finger to save three million Benidottes."

"They're actually reporting that garbage as truth?" demanded Sharon.

"They've got half the Republic believing it—and the other half hasn't heard about it yet," replied Baker. "If they still had lynch mobs, there'd be one forming outside this building right now." He paused. "The Navy's under too much pressure to let you walk. It doesn't matter what the evidence says and it doesn't matter what the circumstances were—they *have* to find you guilty. If they don't . . . well, surely you've read about what happens when the public stops supporting a war while the enemy is still shooting."

"Why can't I just tell them the facts of the matter?" asked Cole. "It's still a good story, probably a better one since it's true."

"It might have worked if you'd gone to them before Podok did, before they got hold of what happened to Benidos II and put their own sensationalistic spin on it—but anything you say now would sound like an excuse or a cover-up. Besides, they're way out on a limb on this story. If the truth comes out, that limb will come crashing down and they're going to sound like fools and dupes."

"That's because they *are* fools and dupes!" snapped Sharon.

"As long as their audience doesn't know it, they don't care what you think, Colonel," said Baker.

"I can't believe it!" said Sharon. "I know Wilson Cole's record. He has served with nonhumans his whole career. He has risked his life time and again on their behalf. Hell, you already met his best friend— a Molarian."

"You want a perfect galaxy," said Baker wearily, "and I'm trying to deal with the real one." He turned to Cole. "The Navy knows you did the right thing, Commander. That's why they offered you the deal. Colonel Blacksmith goes free, and at least you don't die."

"What if I say no?" asked Cole.

"Then they'll hold the trial, and they won't be able to resist the media pressure to find you guilty and execute you. It's as simple as that."

"And nobody—not Fleet Admiral Garcia, not General Chiwenka, not the Secretary of the Republic—will say a word in my defense?"

"Not if they still want to be a Fleet Admiral, a General, and a Secretary of the Republic tomorrow morning," answered Baker.

"It makes me wonder why the hell I've been risking life and limb for them," said Cole. "I can't prove it, but I've got a gut feeling that a

Teroni commander named Jacovic is more honorable than the whole fucking hierarchy of the Republic."

"I'd put money on it," said Sharon, making no attempt to hide her outrage.

"Do you want some time to think and discuss the prosecution's offer with Colonel Blacksmith?" asked Baker. "I can leave you two here and come back in an hour."

"No," said Cole. "Tell him I accept."

"Wilson!" shouted Sharon. "You can't do that!"

"If I turn it down, they'll kill me and jail you. If I accept, they'll jail me and turn you loose. It's an easy call."

"Fight it!" she said. "Force them to let the press in. Force the god-damned media to report the *truth*!"

"The media will never be allowed into this court-martial," said Baker. "I guarantee they're not going to be allowed to make the Navy look bad."

"It's not fair!" she insisted.

"Save your breath, Sharon," said Cole. "I've agreed to their terms. You're a free woman. Go back to the ship."

"And you're a disgraced prisoner whose only sin was saving five million lives!" she shot back. "Where's the justice in that?"

"This court-martial isn't about justice anymore," said Cole. "It's about survival. If I survive, then a lot of people at the top won't. If they survive, I won't. And since they're holding all the cards . . ."

"Oh, shut up!" she snapped. "Where's your sense of outrage?"

"You're going to see it pretty soon," he said ominously. "I just accepted a deal that set you free. Now get the hell out of here before they decide they were being too generous. If they lined both of us up before a firing squad, four out of five people would cheer, and the fifth would think we hadn't suffered enough."

She glared at him, but didn't reply.

"Well, actually, Colonel Blacksmith can't return to the *Theodore Roosevelt* immediately," said Baker. "I have to take your answer to Hernandez, have him print up the documents, and bring them to you to sign. *Then* she can leave."

"That's fine, Major. You might as well get the ball rolling right now."

"All right," said Baker, getting to his feet. "I'll tell your guards to take you back to your cells."

"I'd like two favors, Major," said Cole.

"Yes?"

"This is probably the last time I'll ever see Colonel Blacksmith, and I'd like to spend a few minutes with her. Can you tell the guards we're considering the offer? When you return, tell them you brought the papers in case I decided to sign them."

Baker nodded. "Sure, I can do that much for you, Commander. I'm just sorry I wasn't given a chance to win this case. It wouldn't have been hard," he added sadly. "What was the other favor?"

"I'm sure you must have a pen and some paper in your briefcase. Could you leave it with me until you get back? I'd like to write a note to the crew, thanking them for their support, and have Colonel Blacksmith take it to them."

"Happy to," said Baker, handing a pen to Cole. He pulled some paper out of his briefcase and laid it on the table. Then he walked on the door, stepped through to the corridor when it irised to let him out, and spoke in low tones to the two guards. Then the door snapped shut.

"You're a fool," said Sharon.

"I've been called worse," said Cole, pulling a sheet of paper in front of him and beginning to write.

"Who do I deliver this to?" asked Sharon.

"Just post it where the whole crew can see it," he said. "Probably the mess hall."

He spent the next few minutes writing, and when he was done he handed it to her.

"Read it to make sure I wrote legibly enough," he said. "If there's anything you don't understand, just point it out and I'll do my best to make it clear."

Sharon picked up the note and read:

I realized today that I owe the Republic no more loyalty than I owe the Teroni Federation. As such, I feel no obligation to keep any agreement I make with them. I have no intention of meekly accepting a lifetime of incarceration. It'll probably take me two or three years to find a weak spot, but I plan to break out of whatever prison they send me to. Once free I will get out of the Republic as quickly as possible and head to the Inner Frontier. The Republic's going to be too busy fighting a war to waste much time and manpower looking for one escaped prisoner, especially since by then my story might not sound like a series of denials. If anyone hears that I've escaped and has a hankering to do the same, my first port of call will be Binder X. I'll spend twenty days there; anyone who wants to join me is welcome to.

When you get to the ship, go to my cabin and take anything you want from it. Then tell Four Eyes that he can have anything that's left except the medals, which I keep in a small drawer. I want them jettisoned into space once the *Teddy R* takes off again.

I'm sorry I got you into this, but even knowing the results I'd do the same thing again under the same circumstances.

Sharon folded the note and tucked it in her uniform.

"I'll make sure the crew sees this," she said.

"Thanks. I'd like them to know how much I appreciate everything they did for me aboard the *Teddy R*."

"Do you have any messages for Podok?"

"Yeah," said Cole. "Tell her I only hate one Polonoi."

Baker returned a few minutes later, laid the printed agreement in front of Cole, waited for him to sign it, and then picked it up and put it in his briefcase.

"Colonel Blacksmith," he said, "you are now free to return to your ship. There is no mark against your record, no demotion in rank, and the suspension of pay while you were incarcerated has been waived."

She got to her feet, saluted, and left without even a glance at Cole.

"Have they decided where I'm to spend the rest of my life?" he asked when he was alone with Baker.

"Not yet," answered Baker. "Someplace remote, I'm sure. They don't want any outraged citizens taking it upon themselves to kill a discredited hero."

"How thoughtful of them," said Cole dryly.

"I'll probably see you once more before you leave," said Baker. "I just want to say again that I'm sorry things turned out this way."

"I'm probably even sorrier," said Cole.

"Guard!" Baker called out. "We're ready to leave."

Sergeant Chadwick entered the room. "Are you ready, sir?" he said.

"Yes, that's why I summoned you," said Baker.

"I wasn't referring to you, sir. Commander Cole is my responsibility."

"He gave up his commission five minutes ago, Sergeant," said Baker. "Now he's just Mr. Cole."

"Not to me, he isn't, sir," said Chadwick. He turned back to Cole. "Are you ready to return to your quarters, Commander?"

"You mean my cell."

"Yes, Commander."

"Yeah, let's go. It's somehow homier than the conference room."

As they walked along the corridor, Cole looked for weak spots in the building's defenses. He didn't expect to find any, and besides he was sure he'd be transferred in a few days, but he decided that he'd better get in the habit of looking for potential escape routes.

When they reached his cell, Chadwick deactivated the force field to let him pass through.

"I feel terrible about this, sir," he said.

"Yeah, I know," replied Cole. "Everyone feels terrible about it, and no one does anything about it."

"That's not fair, sir. I'm just a Security guard. What could I do?"

"Short of setting me free, not a damned thing," admitted Cole. He entered the cell. "It still feels a little small. I guess I'm going to have to learn to live with claustrophobia."

The force field hummed to life, and Cole lay down on his narrow, uncomfortable cot, dwelling on the realization that he'd spent his entire adult life in the unquestioning service of a military that could do this to him.

The room began to feel more cramped.

Cole felt a hand on his shoulder. He tried to ignore it, but it kept shaking him gently.

"Wake up, sir," said a soft male voice.

Cole opened one eye. "What time is it?"

"It's the middle of the night, sir," said Chadwick. "Please get to your feet, and try not to make any noise."

Cole stood up. "They *must* be anticipating a lynch mob if you're transferring me at this time of day."

"Follow me, sir, and please be as quiet as you can."

Chadwick killed the force field, and Cole followed him out into the corridor that led past the other holding cells, about half of which were empty. When they came to the fork that led to the conference room, Chadwick motioned him to stand still. Then the sergeant looked out cautiously, determined that the right-hand corridor was empty, and led him down it. As they came to a large, well-lit room, Chadwick stopped and whispered to Cole.

"Wait until you hear me talking to them, then walk past as quickly and silently as you can."

I'm in a cell block on a military base, thought Cole, confused. *Just how the hell much danger can I be in?* Nevertheless, he decided his best bet was to obey Chadwick's instructions.

The sergeant entered the room and was greeted by a number of voices.

"Hi, Luthor," said one. "You're working late tonight."

"You bucking for lieutenant, or is this extra duty for oversleeping the other day?" asked another.

"A little of each," said Chadwick easily. He continued bantering with them, and after about a minute Cole quietly walked past the door. He glanced in, saw that it was a staff room, and that Chadwick was at the far end of it, holding forth on some sports figure so that all eyes were trained on him and no one was watching the doorway.

Cole walked about fifteen feet past the room, then stopped and waited. Chadwick emerged in another thirty seconds, walked past Cole without a word, and motioned him to follow. They soon came to an exit and walked through. There was an aircar waiting for them.

"Get in, Commander," said Chadwick.

Cole entered the vehicle, and Chadwick joined him a moment later.

"Where are we going?" asked Cole.

"Not far."

"Off the base?"

"Eventually."

Cole gave up trying to extract information from Chadwick and settled back on his seat. Within a handful of minutes they had reached the military spaceport, and after Chadwick saluted the guards at the gate and presented some coded disks they were passed through.

The aircar glided past a number of ships and finally pulled up to a shuttlecraft that bore the name *Kermit*.

"Get out now, sir," said Chadwick.

Pampas was standing next to the hatch. "Welcome back, sir," he said, saluting.

"What the hell's going on, Sergeant?" said Cole. "I thought you were saving me from a mob?"

"You were half right, sir," said Chadwick. "We're saving you."

"Please board the shuttle, sir," said Pampas urgently. "I don't know how much time we've got."

"Did Colonel Blacksmith inform you of our agreement?" asked Chadwick, who had also gotten out of the aircar.

"Yes, she did," said Pampas. "Please accompany the Commander onto the shuttlecraft."

As soon as they were aboard Pampas ordered the shuttle to take off. Within half a minute a voice came over the radio, demanding that they return to the planet.

"Didn't take them long to notice, did it?" remarked Pampas.

Suddenly the ship's defense mechanisms were activated.

"Well, that was either a warning shot across our bow or they're trying to blow us out of the sky," said Pampas.

"Perhaps we might go a little faster," suggested Chadwick uneasily.

"As soon as we clear the stratosphere," answered Pampas. "If I go to light speeds before then, we'll burn up from the friction." He looked at the computer. "Another shot. I think they're getting really annoyed with us."

"How soon before we're in the stratosphere?" asked Cole.

"About ten seconds, sir," said Pampas.

It was the longest ten seconds of Cole's life, but finally they cleared the layer and went to light speeds.

"Now will one of you tell me exactly what's going on?" said Cole.

"I think it should be obvious, sir," said Pampas. He braked to sub-light speed and pointed to the screen, where the *Teddy R* floated motionless in space. "Welcome home, sir. Your ship awaits you."

"Do you realize how many laws you've just broken?" said Cole.

"Any law that puts you in jail and lets Podok go free needs to be broken, sir," said Chadwick.

"Why are *you* doing this?" asked Cole. "You're not even a member of the crew."

"Wrong, sir," said Pampas. "He's our new Assistant Chief of Security."

"If that was your price, you should have taken money instead," said Cole, as the shuttle docked alongside the mother ship.

Forrice was waiting for them at the hatch.

"Good to have you back, *Captain*," he said, emphasizing the word. "We haven't had much excitement around here the last few days."

"That's due to change any second now," said Cole. "Is the pilot with the weird name still onboard?"

"Yes."

"Tell him to get us out of here *now*!" said Cole.

"Where to?" asked the Molarian.

"Wherever the Republic isn't."

"That sounds like the Inner Frontier to me."

"That'll do."

Forrice passed the word to the bridge.

"I assume everyone who's a party to this understands that once we're there, we can never come back," said Cole.

"Who wants to?" said a familiar voice. "We're on the *Teddy R* because we're troublemakers and malcontents, remember?"

He turned and found himself staring at Sharon Blacksmith. "I suspect this was your idea," he said.

"We took a vote."

"Was it close?"

"It was unanimous," she said. Suddenly she grinned. "Well, it was unanimous after we set all the dissenters down on Willowby IV."

"How many crew members do we have left?"

"Counting officers, thirty-two. But the Bedalian left the ship, so we're going to have to pick up a doctor along the way."

"How about Lieutenant Mboya?"

"Still here."

"And Slick?"

"He's here, too. And before you ask, so is Lieutenant Marcos, who still hyperventillates at the mention of your name. I'll give you a full list once it's clear that we're going to survive long enough for you to read it."

"Bridge!" said Cole, raising his voice. "This is Commander . . ." He stopped. "This is the Captain speaking. Are there any signs of pursuit?"

"Not yet, sir," answered Briggs.

"Let me know if the situation changes."

"Yes, sir."

He turned back to Sharon. "I can't believe that you all abandoned your careers for *me*."

"The way we look at it, the Navy abandoned *us*," she replied. "We may not have a full crew, but every member of it has been willing to leave behind everything they ever knew in order to serve with you. I think that says a little something about them." She stared at him, her eyes bright. "And I think it says even more about their Captain."

They sped past Binder X, past Walpurgis III, past Keepsake and Peponi and New Rhodesia, racing deeper and deeper into the Inner Frontier. Cole finally brought the ship to a halt around Nearco II, an uninhabited water world.

"It's been six full days with no sign of pursuit," he said to Forrice. "I think we're safe."

"We're also rudderless," said the Molarian.

"Rudderless?"

"A military ship with no war to fight," explained Forrice. "I'd call that rudderless."

"I've been thinking about that," admitted Cole. "And I believe I've found us a purpose."

"Which I'm sure you'll tell me in the fullness of time," said Forrice sardonically.

"You'll figure it out," said Cole. "In the meantime, since we're not a military ship any longer, I think the first thing we'd better do is get rid of all the Republic insignia from the exterior of the ship."

"We can't land on a water world to do it," said Forrice. "I'll look for the closest oxygen planet."

"That won't be necessary," replied Cole. "We've got a crew member who's uniquely suited to working in the airless cold of space."

Forrice looked at him suspiciously. "Are you saying that you've already designed a new insignia?"

"Well, new to us, anyway," said Cole. "Tell Slick that wherever he sees the Republic insignia on the exterior of the ship, I want it replaced with a skull and crossbones."

"What does a skull and crossbones signify?"

"I can see your education has been sadly lacking," said Cole. "It's the time-honored emblem of the pirate ship."

Forrice simply stared at him.

"In all likelihood we're going to be out here the rest of our lives," explained Cole. "We've got to make a living. You wanted a rudder; now you've got one."

Suddenly the Molarian filled the bridge with hoots of alien laughter. "I'll say this much: serving with you has been many things good and bad, but it has *never* been dull!"

"That's what you get for living in interesting times," said the new Captain of the *Teddy R*.

APPENDIXES

Appendix One

THE ORIGIN OF THE BIRTHRIGHT UNIVERSE

t happened in the 1970s. Carol and I were watching a truly awful movie at a local theater, and about halfway through it I muttered, "Why am I wasting my time here when I could be doing something really interesting, like, say, writing the entire history of the human race from now until its extinction?" And she whispered back, "So why don't you?" We got up immediately, walked out of the theater, and that night I outlined a novel called *Birthright: The Book of Man*, which would tell the story of the human race from its attainment of faster-than-light flight until its death eighteen thousand years from now.

It was a long book to write. I divided the future into five political eras—Republic, Democracy, Oligarchy, Monarchy, and Anarchy—and wrote twenty-six connected stories ("demonstrations," *Analog* called them, and rightly so), displaying every facet of the human race, both admirable and not so admirable. Since each is set a few centuries from the last, there are no continuing characters (unless you consider Man, with a capital *M*, the main character, in which case you could make an argument—or at least, *I* could—that it's really a character study).

I sold it to Signet, along with another novel, titled *The Soul Eater*. My editor there, Sheila Gilbert, loved the Birthright Universe and asked me if I would be willing to make a few changes to *The Soul Eater* so that it was set in that future. I agreed, and the changes actually took less than a day. She made the same request—in advance, this time—for the four-book Tales of the Galactic Midway series, the four-book Tales of the Velvet Comet series, and *Walpurgis III*. Looking back, I see that only two of the thirteen novels I wrote for Signet were *not* set there.

When I moved to Tor Books, my editor there, Beth Meacham, had a fondness for the Birthright Universe, and most of my books for her—not all, but most—were set in it: *Santiago, Ivory, Paradise, Purgatory, Inferno, A Miracle of Rare Design, A Hunger in the Soul, The Outpost,* and *The Return of Santiago.*

When Ace agreed to buy *Soothsayer, Oracle,* and *Prophet* from me, my editor, Ginjer Buchanan, assumed that of course they'd be set in the Birthright Universe—and of course they were, because as I learned a little more about my eighteen-thousand-year, two-million-world future, I felt a lot more comfortable writing about it.

In fact, I started setting short stories in the Birthright Universe. Two of my Hugo winners—"Seven Views of Olduvai Gorge" and "The 43 Antarean Dynasties"—are set there, and so are perhaps fifteen others.

When Bantam agreed to take the Widowmaker trilogy from me, it was a foregone conclusion that Janna Silverstein, who purchased the books but had moved to another company before they came out, would want them to take place in the Birthright Universe. She did indeed request it, and I did indeed agree.

I recently handed in a book to Meisha Merlin, set—where else?—in the Birthright Universe.

And when it came time to suggest a series of books to Lou Anders for the new Pyr line of science fiction, I don't think I ever considered any ideas or stories that *weren't* set in the Birthright Universe.

I've gotten so much of my career from the Birthright Universe that I wish I could remember the name of that turkey we walked out of all those years ago so I could write the producers and thank them.

Appendix Two

THE LAYOUT OF THE BIRTHRIGHT UNIVERSE

The most heavily populated (by both stars and inhabitants) section of the Birthright Universe is always referred to by its political identity, which evolves from Republic to Democracy to Oligarchy to Monarchy. It encompasses millions of inhabited and habitable worlds. Earth is too small and too far out of the mainstream of galactic commerce to remain Man's capital world, and within a couple of thousand years the capital has been moved lock, stock, and barrel halfway across the galaxy to Deluros VIII, a huge world with about ten times Earth's surface and near-identical atmosphere and gravity. By the middle of the Democracy, perhaps four thousand years from now, the entire planet is covered by one huge sprawling city. By the time of the Oligarchy, even Deluros VIII isn't big enough for our billions of empire-running bureaucrats, and Deluros VI, another large world, is broken up into forty-eight planetoids, each housing a major department of the government (with four planetoids given over entirely to the military).

Earth itself is way out in the boonies, on the Spiral Arm. I don't believe I've set more than parts of a couple of stories on the Arm.

At the outer edge of the galaxy is the Rim, where worlds are spread out and underpopulated. There's so little of value or military interest on the Rim that one ship, such as the *Theodore Roosevelt*, can patrol a couple of hundred worlds by itself. In later eras, the Rim will be dominated by feuding warlords, but it's so far away from the center of things that the governments, for the most part, just ignore it.

Then there are the Inner and Outer Frontiers. The Outer Frontier is that vast but sparsely populated area between the outer edge of the Republic/Democracy/Oligarchy/Monarchy and the Rim. The Inner Frontier is that somewhat smaller (but still huge) area between the inner reaches of the Republic/etc. and the black hole at the core of the galaxy.

It's on the Inner Frontier that I've chosen to set more than half of my novels. Years ago the brilliant writer R. A. Lafferty wrote, "Will there be a mythology of the future, they used to ask, after all has become science? Will high deeds be told in epic, or only in computer code?" I decided that I'd like to spend at least a part of my career trying to create those myths of the future, and it seems to me that myths, with their bigger-than-life characters and colorful settings, work best on frontiers where there aren't too many people around to chronicle them accurately, or too many authority figures around to prevent them from playing out to their inevitable conclusions. So I arbitrarily decided that the Inner Frontier was where *my* myths would take place, and I populated it with people bearing names like Catastrophe Baker, the Widowmaker, the Cyborg de Milo, the ageless Forever Kid, and the like. It not only allows me to tell my heroic (and sometimes antiheroic) myths, but lets me tell more realistic stories occurring at the very same time a few thousand light-years away in the Republic or Democracy or whatever happens to exist at that moment.

Over the years I've fleshed out the galaxy. There are the star clusters—the Albion Cluster, the Quinellus Cluster, a few others, and a pair that are new to this book, the Phoenix and Cassius clusters. There are the individual worlds, some important enough to appear as the title of a book, such as Walpurgis III, some reappearing throughout the time periods and stories, such as Deluros VIII, Antares III, Binder X, Keepsake, Spica II, and some others, and hundreds (maybe thousands by now) of worlds (and races, now that I think about it) mentioned once and never again.

Then there are, if not the bad guys, at least what I think of as the Disloyal Opposition. Some, like the Sett Empire, get into one war with humanity and that's the end of it. Some, like the Canphor Twins (Canphor VI and Canphor VII), have been a thorn in Man's side for the better part of ten millennia. Some, like Lodin XI, vary almost daily in their loyalties depending on the political situation.

I've been building this universe, politically and geographically, for a quarter of a century now, and with each passing book and story it feels a little more real to me. Give me another thirty years and I'll probably believe every word I've written about it.

Appendix Three

CHRONOLOGY OF THE BIRTHRIGHT UNIVERSE

Year	Era	World	Story or Novel
1885	A.D.		"The Hunter" (*Ivory*)
1898	A.D.		"Himself" (*Ivory*)
1982	A.D.		*Sideshow*
1983	A.D.		*The Three-Legged Hootch Dancer*
1985	A.D.		*The Wild Alien Tamer*
1987	A.D.		*The Best Rootin' Tootin' Shootin' Gunslinger in the Whole Damned Galaxy*
2057	A.D.		"The Politician" (*Ivory*)
2908	A.D. = 1 G.E.		
16	G.E.	Republic	"The Curator" (*Ivory*)
264	G.E.	Republic	"The Pioneers" (*Birthright*)
332	G.E.	Republic	"The Cartographers" (*Birthright*)
346	G.E.	Republic	*Walpurgis III*
367	G.E.	Republic	*Eros Ascending*
396	G.E.	Republic	"The Miners" (*Birthright*)
401	G.E.	Republic	*Eros at Zenith*
442	G.E.	Republic	*Eros Descending*
465	G.E.	Republic	*Eros at Nadir*
588	G.E.	Republic	"The Psychologists" (*Birthright*)

616	G.E.	Republic	*A Miracle of Rare Design*
882	G.E.	Republic	"The Potentate" (*Ivory*)
962	G.E.	Republic	"The Merchants" (*Birthright*)
1150	G.E.	Republic	"Cobbling Together a Solution"
1151	G.E.	Republic	"Nowhere in Particular"
1152	G.E.	Republic	"The God Biz"
1394	G.E.	Republic	"Keepsakes"
1701	G.E.	Republic	"The Artist" (*Ivory*)
1813	G.E.	Republic	"Dawn" (*Paradise*)
1826	G.E.	Republic	*Purgatory*
1859	G.E.	Republic	"Noon" (*Paradise*)
1888	G.E.	Republic	"Midafternoon" (*Paradise*)
1902	G.E.	Republic	"Dusk" (*Paradise*)
1921	G.E.	Republic	*Inferno*
1966	G.E.	Republic	*Starship: Mutiny*
1967	G.E.	Republic	*Starship: Pirate*
1968	G.E.	Republic	*Starship: Mercenary*
1969	G.E.	Republic	*Starship: Rebel*
1970	G.E.	Republic	*Starship: Flagship*
2122	G.E.	Democracy	"The 43 Antarean Dynasties"
2154	G.E.	Democracy	"The Diplomats" (*Birthright*)
2275	G.E.	Democracy	"The Olympians" (*Birthright*)
2469	G.E.	Democracy	"The Barristers" (*Birthright*)
2885	G.E.	Democracy	"Robots Don't Cry"
2911	G.E.	Democracy	"The Medics" (*Birthright*)
3004	G.E.	Democracy	"The Policitians" (*Birthright*)
3042	G.E.	Democracy	"The Gambler" (*Ivory*)
3286	G.E.	Democracy	*Santiago*
3322	G.E.	Democracy	*A Hunger in the Soul*

3324	G.E.	Democracy	*The Soul Eater*
3324	G.E.	Democracy	"Nicobar Lane: The Soul Eater's Story"
3407	G.E.	Democracy	*The Return of Santiago*
3427	G.E.	Democracy	*Soothsayer*
3441	G.E.	Democracy	*Oracle*
3447	G.E.	Democracy	*Prophet*
3502	G.E.	Democracy	"Guardian Angel"
3719	G.E.	Democracy	"Hunting the Snark"
4375	G.E.	Democracy	"The Graverobber" (*Ivory*)
4822	G.E.	Oligarchy	"The Administrators" (*Birthright*)
4839	G.E.	Oligarchy	*The Dark Lady*
5101	G.E.	Oligarchy	*The Widowmaker*
5103	G.E.	Oligarchy	*The Widowmaker Reborn*
5106	G.E.	Oligarchy	*The Widowmaker Unleashed*
5108	G.E.	Oligarchy	*A Gathering of Widowmakers*
5461	G.E.	Oligarchy	"The Media" (*Birthright*)
5492	G.E.	Oligarchy	"The Artists" (*Birthright*)
5521	G.E.	Oligarchy	"The Warlord" (*Ivory*)
5655	G.E.	Oligarchy	"The Biochemists" (*Birthright*)
5912	G.E.	Oligarchy	"The Warlords" (*Birthright*)
5993	G.E.	Oligarchy	"The Conspirators" (*Birthright*)
6304	G.E.	Monarchy	*Ivory*
6321	G.E.	Monarchy	"The Rulers" (*Birthright*)
6400	G.E.	Monarchy	"The Symbiotics" (*Birthright*)
6523	G.E.	Monarchy	*The Outpost*
6599	G.E.	Monarchy	"The Philosophers" (*Birthright*)
6746	G.E.	Monarchy	"The Architects" (*Birthright*)
6962	G.E.	Monarchy	"The Collectors" (*Birthright*)

7019	G.E.	Monarchy	"The Rebels" (*Birthright*)
16201	G.E.	Anarchy	"The Archaeologists" (*Birthright*)
16673	G.E.	Anarchy	"The Priests" (*Birthright*)
16888	G.E.	Anarchy	"The Pacifists" (*Birthright*)
17001	G.E.	Anarchy	"The Destroyers" (*Birthright*)
21703	G.E.		"Seven Views of Olduvai Gorge"

Novels not set in this future

Adventures (1922–1926 A.D.)
Exploits (1926–1931 A.D.)
Encounters (1931–1934 A.D.)
Stalking the Unicorn ("Tonight")
The Branch (2047–2051 A.D.)
Second Contact (2065 A.D.)
Bully! (1910–1912 A.D.)
Kirinyaga (2123–2137 A.D.)
Lady with an Alien (1490 A.D.)
Dragon America: Revolution (1779–1780 A.D.)

Appendix Four

AROUND THE
THEODORE ROOSEVELT

The bridge is the nerve center of the warship—but so much is automated, and so much can be accessed from any part of the ship, that the officer in charge of the bridge rarely has to be there in person. All communications come first to the bridge, but can instantly be transmitted to any other location on the ship.

Intraship communications can be strictly audio, but they are more likely to be holographic, with three-dimensional images accompanying the voices.

There's a mess hall, capable of seating up to twenty crew members. Since the ship carries fewer than sixty crew members and works on three shifts, there's no need for a bigger facility. The kitchen is able to prepare food not only for the human crewmen, but for the nonhumans as well.

The gunnery section is in charge of ten pulse cannons (which shoot powerful energy pulses), plus a few laser weapons. Their job is to keep the weapons functioning; the weapons are aimed by computers, not crewmen.

There is an infirmary, smaller than any military crew would like, and divided so that it can accommodate both human and nonhuman patients.

There are two small science labs. Since this is a warship and not an exploratory vessel, they don't see much activity unless it directly pertains to the war or the enemy.

There is an officers' lounge. It is tiny and is where one can often find the officer in command of the bridge when nothing important is happening.

Space is at a premium. There is no gymnasium, no sauna, no game or recreation room, no library. (Well, actually, there *is* a library—but it's in the ship's main computer and is entirely electronic. Any crew member can access any book in the library on his own computer.) There is a very small exercise room.

The crew's quarters are on three levels, two designed for humans, one for nonhumans. The rooms are small, even for the senior officers.

There are no stairs, but there are five airlifts positioned around the ship. The one closest to the infirmary is large enough to accommodate a patient on an airsled.

There is no engine room, or rather, there is no traditional engine room. There is a heavily fortified lead-lined area that houses the engine, but no crew works it. The ship carries one master engineer, and he is needed only on those incredibly rare occasions that something goes wrong with the highly efficient drive mechanism. Since the ship runs on nuclear fuel, it is life-endangering to spend any length of time there, and only the master engineer and the senior officers are even permitted entry to the room.

The ship has a hydroponic garden to help produce oxygen, and it carries supplies of compressed oxygen—but since it can enter atmospheres without burning up, its usual procedure is to stop at friendly oxygen worlds every few weeks to replenish air and water supplies.

The gravity is artificial and regulated to operate at Earth Standard. Each room can vary, based on the occupant's needs and desires, in air content, gravity, and temperature.

Since there is no night or day in space—or, put another way, there is eternal night—the *Teddy R* is on an arbitrary twenty-four-hour day. Unlike everyone's favorite television show, it would be foolhardy to have the Captain, the First Officer, the Second Officer, the Chief Gunnery Officer, and the like all on duty at the same time. What if the ship comes under attack when they're all asleep and some inexperienced lieutenant is the ranking officer on duty? So the Captain is always in charge of one shift, the First Officer of another, and the Second Officer of a third. This is not to imply that the Captain won't be alerted in times of crisis, but it is simply more practical to always have a senior officer in charge of the ship whatever the time of day.

The *Teddy R* is an old ship and would have been decommissioned if the Republic were not at war, but it is in working order, capable of traveling at many multiples of the speed of light, firing formidable weapons with great accuracy, and defending itself against any ship of its class (but not the more powerful, modern battleships and dreadnoughts).

Appendix Five

TEDDY ROOSEVELT— THE MAN BEHIND THE SHIP

President John F. Kennedy was widely quoted for a remark he made when he was sitting down to dinner at the White House with a dozen eminent scientists and artists. "Gentlemen," said JFK, "this is the greatest assemblage of talent to sit at this table since Thomas Jefferson dined alone."

It's a fine, wise, witty remark—but JFK must have thought that Theodore Roosevelt ate every meal at local restaurants for the seven years of his presidency.

Why would I name a ship after Theodore Roosevelt? Because I consider him the most remarkable American in our long history.

Consider: As a boy he suffered from a debilitating case of asthma. Rather than give in to it, he began swimming and exercising every day and built himself up to where he was able to make the Harvard boxing team.

But he'd been making a name for himself before he went to Harvard. An avid naturalist to the day of his death, he was already considered one of America's leading ornithologists and taxidermists while still a teenager. Nor was his interest limited to nature. While at Harvard he wrote what was considered the definitive treatise on naval warfare, *The Naval War of 1812*.

He graduated Phi Beta Kappa and summa cum laude, married Alice Hathaway, went to law school, found it boring, and discovered politics. When Teddy Roosevelt developed a new interest, he never did so in a halfhearted way—so at twenty-four he became the youngest man ever elected to the New York General Assembly, and he became minority leader a year later.

He might have remained in the State Assembly, but on February 14, 1884, not long after his twenty-fifth birthday, his beloved Alice and his mother died in the same house, twelve hours apart. He felt the need to get away, and he went west to become a rancher (and because he was Teddy Roosevelt, one ranch couldn't possibly contain him, so he bought two).

Not content to simply be a rancher, a sportsman, and a politician, he became a lawman as well, and, unarmed, hunted down and captured three armed killers in the Dakota Badlands during the fearsome blizzard that was known as the Winter of the Blue Snow.

He began building Sagamore Hill, the estate he made famous in Oyster Bay, New York, married Edith Carew, and started a second family. (Alice had died giving birth to his daughter, also named Alice. Edith promptly began producing sons—Kermit, Theodore Jr., Archie, and Quentin—as well as another daughter, Ethel.) In his spare time, he wrote a number of well-received books. Then, running short of money, he signed a contract to write a four-volume series, *The Winning of the West*; the first two volumes became immediate best-sellers. He was also an avid correspondent, and it's estimated that he wrote more than 150,000 letters during his lifetime.

He was now past thirty years of age, and he decided it was time to stop loafing and really get to work—so he took the job of police commissioner of the wildly corrupt City of New York, and to the amazement of even his staunchest supporters, he cleaned the place up. He became famous for his "midnight rambles" to make sure his officers were at their posts, and he was the first commissioner to insist that the entire police force take regular target practice.

He made things so uncomfortable for the rich and powerful (and corrupt) of New York that he was "kicked upstairs" and made assistant secretary of the navy in Washington. When the Spanish-American War broke out, he resigned his office, enlisted in the army, was given the rank of colonel, and assembled the most famous and romantic outfit ever to fight for the United States—the fabled Rough Riders, consisting of cowboys, Indians, professional athletes, and anyone else who impressed him. They went to Cuba, where Teddy himself led the charge up San Juan Hill in the face of machine-gun fire, and he came home the most famous man in the country.

Less than three months later he was elected governor of New York, a week after his fortieth birthday. His new duties didn't hinder his other interests, and he kept turning out books and studying wildlife.

Two years later they kicked him upstairs again, finding the one job where his reformer's zeal couldn't bother anyone: he was nominated for the vice presidency of the United States, and was elected soon afterward.

Ten months later President William McKinley was assassinated, and Roosevelt became the youngest-ever president of the United States, where he served for seven years.

What did he do as president?

Not much, by Rooseveltian standards. Enough for five presidents, by anyone else's standards. Consider:

- He created the National Park system.
- He broke the back of the trusts that had run the economy (and the nation) for their own benefit.

- He created the Panama Canal.
- He sent the navy on a trip around the world. When they left, America was a second-rate little country in the eyes of the world. By the time they returned we were a world power.
- He became the first president ever to win the Nobel Peace Prize, when he put an end to the Russian-Japanese war.
- He mediated a dispute between Germany and France over Morocco, preserving Morocco's independence.
- To make sure that the trusts didn't reclaim their power after he was out of office, he created the Departments of Commerce and Labor.

Was there anything he couldn't do? Just one thing. As he explained when his daughter Alice was running wild through the White House, "I can run the country or I can control Alice. I cannot do both." (It was Alice who later said, concerning her father's love for the limelight, "He wanted to be the bride at every wedding and the corpse at every funeral.")

When he left office in 1909, far from relaxing he packed his bags (and his rifles) and went on the first major safari ever put together, spending eleven months gathering specimens for the American and Smithsonian museums. He wrote his experiences up as *African Game Trails*, still considered one of the half-dozen most important books on the subject ever written.

When he returned to America, he concluded that his hand-chosen successor, President William Howard Taft, was doing a lousy job of running the country, so he decided to run for the presidency again in 1912. Though far and away the most popular man in the Republican Party, he was denied the nomination through a number of procedural moves. Most men would have licked their wounds and waited for

1916. Not Teddy. He formed the Progressive Party, known informally as the Bull Moose Party, and ran in 1912. It's thought that he was winning when a would-be assassin shot him in the chest while he was being driven to give a speech in Milwaukee. He refused all medical aid until he had delivered the speech (which ran ninety minutes!), then allowed himself to be taken to a hospital. The bullet would never be removed, and by the time Teddy was back on the campaign trail Woodrow Wilson had built an insurmountable lead. Roosevelt finished second, as President Taft ran a humiliating third, able to win only eight electoral votes.

So *now* did he relax?

You gotta be kidding, right? This is Teddy Roosevelt we're talking about. The Brazilian government asked him to explore a tributary of the Amazon known as the River of Doubt. He hadn't slowed down since he was a baby, he was in his fifties, he was walking around with a bullet in his chest, all logic said he'd earned a quiet retirement—so of course he said yes. "I had to go," he later wrote. "It was my last chance to be a boy again."

This trip didn't go as well as the safari. He came down with fever, he almost lost his leg, and indeed at one time he urged his party to leave him behind to die and to go ahead without him. They didn't, of course, and eventually he was well enough to continue the expedition and finish mapping the river, which was renamed the Rio Teodoro in his honor.

He came home, wrote yet another best-seller—*Through the Brazilian Wilderness*—and wrote another book on African animals, as well as more books on politics, but his health never fully recovered. He campaigned vigorously for our entrance into World War I, and it was generally thought that the presidency was his for the asking in 1920, but he died in his sleep on January 6, 1919, at the age of sixty—having crammed about seventeen lifetimes into those six decades.

And *that*, friends, is a *very* brief biography of the most remarkable of all Americans. I have actually used him in half a dozen science fiction stories, including three award nominees ("Bully!" "Over There," and "Redchapel"), and I certainly plan to use him again.

Name the ship after him? Hell, it's a wonder I didn't name the whole damned Navy after him.

Appendix Six

CHARACTER AND SHIP DESCRIPTIONS

AS INITIALLY PRESENTED TO COVER ILLUSTRATOR JOHN PICACIO

Commander Wilson Cole:

There's not much special or heroic about Cole's appearance. Normal height, normal weight, no scars—not what you'd expect the most dec-orated man in the Fleet to look like (but then, Audie Murphy looked like an innocent, clean-cut kid, still wet behind the ears, rather than the most-honored soldier of World War II). He might be an inch or two below normal, or maybe just a little shorter than people expect their heroes to be. This is a guy who wins his medals with his brain, not his brawn, so as long as he doesn't look like Sylvester Schwarzenegger or Arnold Stallone, whatever you do will be fine.

Makeo Fujiama:

"Mount Fuji" was given the nickname not because he is the Captain, but because he's close to seven feet tall. He's Oriental in look and heritage, but wears the Westernized uniform of the Republic's Navy. He has a strong face that belies his attitude; he's not a shirker or a coward, he's just a used-up man who has lost a wife and three kids to this war and is *tired*—of the war, of command, of living. But he was a good officer once, and from time to time it still shows in his attitude and bearing.

Teddy R:

It's an old ship, war-scarred, tired. If it were around today, we'd say that only the rust was holding it together. The inside hasn't been remodeled, redesigned, re-anythinged in more than half a century. The corridors remind you of a middle-of-the-road hotel that's seen better days. If there's a modern fictional equivalent, try Herman Wouk's *The Caine*.

The first description of the Polonoi:

The Polonoi are humanoid, bipedal, about five feet tall, burly, and muscular (males and females alike). They are covered, top to bottom, with a soft down, which is orange in normal Polonoi.

But the Polonoi in the military are a genetically crafted warrrior class. They have orange and purple stripes, not unlike a miscolored tiger. They are more muscular, able to respond faster physically to any dangerous situation. But what makes this warrior caste really odd is that their sexual organs, their eating and breathing orifices, and all the soft vulnerable spots (the equivalent of our bellies and midsections) have been engineered on the back sides (two words; not "backsides" in the traditional meaning) of them. They are warriors, built to win or die; to turn one's back on an enemy is to present him with all one's vulnerable areas. On the front of the face are large eyes that can see well at night and into the infrared, and a speaking (not breathing, not eating) orifice. Large ears protrude from the sides of the head and are cupped forward; they can hear very little that happens behind them. Their arms and legs are jointed similarly, but not identically, to Men's. Their hands have two opposing stubby thumbs and three more fingers that are so long and pliable that they act almost as tentacles.

If you were to stand a warrior Polonoi next to a Polonoi of any other caste, the casual—indeed, even the expert—observer would have a hard time believing they were even remotely related.

And that's Podok, and all the other Polonoi crew members.

Addendum:

The front of a warrior Polonoi is essentially natural armor, heavy bone beneath the skin. Hit it and you can break your hand. Stab it and you'll break your blade. You *can* shoot it, but the normal handgun, whether it fires projectiles, energy pulses, or lasers, isn't likely to be fatal.

Also: I didn't mention it, because if Podok's not eating in the covor illo it won't matter, but what she, and all military caste Polonoi, have is a long (perhaps 30 inches) prehensile tongue that can extend from their eating orifice. It doesn't see, doesn't smell, and doesn't hear—but has an undefined alien sense that lets it function *as if* it could see, hear, and smell. It can bring food to its mouth, and do a few other things— much as an elephant can do with its trunk—and when not being used the prehensile tongue goes back inside the body.

ABOUT THE AUTHOR

L ocus, *the trade journal of science fiction, keeps a list of the winners of major science fiction awards on its Web page. Mike Resnick is currently fourth in the all-time standings, ahead of Isaac Asimov, Sir Arthur C. Clarke, Ray Bradbury, and Robert A. Heinlein.*

* * * * * *

Mike was born on March 5, 1942. He sold his first article in 1957, his first short story in 1959, and his first book in 1962.

He attended the University of Chicago from 1959 through 1961, won three letters on the fencing team, and met and married Carol. Their daughter, Laura, was born in 1962, and has since become a writer herself, winning two awards for her romance novels and the 1993 Campbell Award for Best New Science Fiction Writer.

Mike and Carol discovered science fiction fandom in 1962, attended their first Worldcon in 1963, and fifty sf books into his career, Mike still considers himself a fan and frequently contributes articles to fanzines. He and Carol appeared in five Worldcon masquerades in the 1970s in costumes that she created, and they won four of them.

Mike labored anonymously but profitably from 1964 through 1976, selling more than two hundred novels, three hundred short stories, and two thousand articles, almost all of them under pseudonyms, most of them in the "adult" field. He edited seven different tabloid newspapers and a pair of men's magazines, as well.

In 1968 Mike and Carol became serious breeders and exhibitors of collies, a pursuit they continued through 1981. (Mike is still an AKC-licensed collie judge.) During that time they bred and/or exhibited twenty-seven champion collies, and they were the country's leading breeders and exhibitors during various years along the way.

This led them to purchase the Briarwood Pet Motel in Cincinnati in 1976. It was the country's second-largest luxury boarding and grooming establishment, and they worked full-time at it for the next few years. By 1980 the kennel was being run by a staff of twenty-one, and Mike was free to return to his first love, science fiction, albeit at a far slower pace than his previous writing. They sold the kennel in 1993.

Mike's first novel in this "second career" was *The Soul Eater*, which was followed shortly by *Birthright: The Book of Man*, *Walpurgis III*, the four-book Tales of the Galactic Midway series, *The Branch*, the four-book Tales of the Velvet Comet series, and *Adventures*, all from Signet. His breakthrough novel was the international best-seller *Santiago*, published by Tor in 1986. Tor has since published *Stalking the Unicorn*, *The Dark Lady*, *Ivory*, *Second Contact*, *Paradise*, *Purgatory*, *Inferno*, the Double *Bwana/Bully!*, and the collection, *Will the Last Person to Leave the Planet Please Shut Off the Sun?* His most recent Tor releases were *A Miracle of Rare Design*, *A Hunger in the Soul*, *The Outpost*, and the *The Return of Santiago*.

Even at his reduced rate, Mike is too prolific for one publisher, and in the 1990s Ace published *Soothsayer*, *Oracle*, and *Prophet*, Questar published *Lucifer Jones*, Bantam brought out the *Locus* best-selling trilogy of *The Widowmaker*, *The Widowmaker Reborn*, and *The Widowmaker Unleashed*, and Del Rey published *Kirinyaga: A Fable of Utopia* and *Lara Croft, Tomb Raider: The Amulet of Power*. His current releases include *A Gathering of Widowmakers* for Meisha Merlin, *Dragon America* for Phobos, and *Lady with an Alien* for Watson-Guptill.

Beginning with *Shaggy B.E.M. Stories* in 1988, Mike has also become an anthology editor (and was nominated for a Best Editor Hugo in 1994 and 1995). His list of anthologies in print and in press totals more than forty, and includes *Alternate Presidents*, *Alternate Kennedys*, *Sherlock Holmes in Orbit*, *By Any Other Fame*, *Dinosaur Fantastic*, and *Christmas Ghosts*, plus the recent *Stars*, coedited with superstar singer Janis Ian.

Mike has always supported the "specialty press," and he has numerous books and collections out in limited editions from such diverse publishers as Phantasia Press, Axolotl Press, Misfit Press, Pulphouse Publishing, Wildside Press, Dark Regions Press, NESFA Press, WSFA Press, Obscura Press, Farthest Star, and others. He recently agreed to become the science fiction editor for BenBella Books.

Mike was never interested in writing short stories early in his career, producing only seven between 1976 and 1986. Then something clicked, and he has written and sold more than 175 stories since 1986, and now spends more time on short fiction than on novels. The writing that has brought him the most acclaim thus far in his career is the Kirinyaga series, which, with sixty-four major and minor awards and nominations to date, is the most honored series of stories in the history of science fiction.

He also began writing short nonfiction as well. He sold a four-part series, "Forgotten Treasures," to *The Magazine of Fantasy and Science Fiction*, is a regular columnist for *Speculations* ("Ask Bwana") and the *SFWA Bulletin* ("The Resnick/Malzberg Dialogues"), and wrote a biweekly column for the late, lamented GalaxyOnline.com.

Carol has always been Mike's uncredited collaborator on his science fiction, but in the past few years they have sold two movie scripts— *Santiago* and *The Widowmaker*, both based on Mike's books—and Carol *is* listed as his collaborator on those.

Readers of Mike's works are aware of his fascination with Africa, and the many uses to which he has put it in his science fiction. Mike and Carol have taken numerous safaris, visiting Kenya (four times), Tanzania, Malawi, Zimbabwe, Egypt, Botswana, and Uganda. Mike edited the Library of African Adventure series for St. Martin's Press, and is currently editing *The Resnick Library of African Adventure* and, with Carol as coeditor, *The Resnick Library of Worldwide Adventure*, for Alexander Books.

Since 1989, Mike has won five Hugo Awards (for "Kirinyaga," "The Manamouki," "Seven Views of Olduvai Gorge," "The 43 Antarean Dynasties," and "Travels with My Cats") and a Nebula Award (for "Seven Views of Olduvai Gorge"), and has been nominated for twenty-seven Hugos, eleven Nebulas, a Clarke (British), and six Seiun-sho (Japanese). He has also won a Seiun-sho, a Prix Tour Eiffel (French), two Prix Ozones (French), ten HOMer Awards, an Alexander Award, a Golden Pagoda Award, a Hayakawa SF Award (Japanese), a Locus Award, two Ignotus Awards (Spanish), a Futura Award (Croatia), an El Melocoton Mechanico (Spanish), two Sfinks Awards (Polish), and a Fantastyka Award (Polish), and has topped the Science Fiction Chronicle Poll six times, the Scifi Weekly Hugo Straw Poll three times, and the Asimov's Readers Poll five times. In 1993 he was awarded the Skylark Award for Lifetime Achievement in Science Fiction, and both in 2001 and in 2004, he was named Fictionwise.com's Author of the Year.

His work has been translated into French, Italian, German, Spanish, Japanese, Korean, Bulgarian, Hungarian, Hebrew, Russian, Latvian, Lithuanian, Polish, Czech, Dutch, Swedish, Romanian, Finnish, Chinese, and Croatian.

He was recently the subject of Fiona Kelleghan's massive *Mike Resnick: An Annotated Bibliography and Guide to His Work*.